LINDA LEITH
PUBLISHING

Cover design: Debbie Geltner
Cover photo: Roumi Photos http://www.roumagnac.net/blog/
Book design and typesetting: WildElement.ca
Author photo: Jocelyn Michel

Printed and bound in Canada by Marquis Book Printing Inc.

**Library and Archives Canada Cataloguing in Publication**

Kirby, Peter, 1953-
    The dead of winter / Peter Kirby.

Issued also in electronic formats.
ISBN 978-0-9879946-2-2

    I. Title.

PS8621.I725D42 2012      C813'.6     C2012-903704-4

Linda Leith Publishing Inc.
www.lindaleith.com

Printed and bound in Canada

# The Dead of Winter

# The Dead of Winter

a novel
by
**PETER KIRBY**

LINDA LEITH
PUBLISHING

TO EMILY AND OWEN

# PART ONE

# ONE
## DECEMBER 15

10 PM

**Mary Gallagher was cold.** She was drifting in and out of sleep on a concrete ledge beside the entrance to a parking garage, the fitful half-sleep that was all she had known for years. She had stuffed newspapers next to her skin under layers of clothing to ward off the cold, and her wool toque was pulled down low over her face. Cocooned in a sleeping bag she got from the Salvation Army three weeks before, and with only her mouth exposed to the damp night, she still shivered.

She sensed the approaching figure before he arrived. The concrete ledge was almost six feet off the ground, and his face was level with hers. He reached up and gently pulled the toque back from her eyes and, so tightly was she wrapped, she couldn't resist even if she had wanted to. She didn't recognize him, but he was dressed in black like a priest, and that gave her a sense of comfort.

"Mary," he said. "Wake up. They asked me to come and get you. We've found a safe place for you. But you must come with me now."

"But, Father, I'm comfortable here. Let me stay. Please. I'm not bothering anyone. I need to sleep."

"I know, Mary, but it's dangerous out here. We have somewhere safe for you, safe and warm."

"Not a shelter. I can't go to the shelters."

"Not a shelter, Mary. It's somewhere where you can be yourself. Come along, Mary. Lower yourself into my arms, and I'll help you into the van." He was already unzipping the sleeping bag.

"But, Father, why can't you let me sleep here?"

"Because we love you, Mary. Come. It'll only take a few minutes, and then you'll be able to sleep comfortably. I have a van, you see it?" He turned and pointed to the van parked at the curb, its engine still running. "Just there, it's not far."

She raised herself up on an elbow and looked towards the white van, snow already sticking to its roof.

"It's warm and comfortable, Mary. And it will only take a few minutes. Come."

She knew it was pointless to argue. She always had to do what people said. It was only on her own that she could decide. She had no fight in her. When the zipper on the sleeping bag was fully open, he flipped the fabric back. She pulled her legs out and swiveled them over the ledge, grimacing with the pain from worn-out joints. He reached for her, and as she leaned forward over his shoulder, he lowered her to the ground. It had been many years since any man had supported her weight.

With one arm around her back to support her, he used the other to lead her by the hand. They walked slowly to the curb, her joints screaming with pain as she shuffled forward, leaning into him for support.

"We'll get you settled in the van, and I'll come back for your stuff. You have a choice Mary. You can sit up front with me, or you can lie down in the back on the mattress. Your choice."

"A mattress sounds good, Father. I haven't seen one in months. If it's OK, I wouldn't mind lying down on the mattress."

"Perfect," he said, as he opened the back door of the van. She peered inside and felt the warm air escaping. It looked inviting. The back of the van was filled with a mattress, pillows, and a couple of heavy-looking blankets. She crawled in on all fours and pulled the pillow under her head.

"I'll just go back and get your stuff."

In a few minutes he returned, opening the back door to drop two overstuffed garbage bags beside her.

"My things, Father. My things."

"All here, Mary. Don't worry. I'm looking after you."

"God bless you, Father."

"You just relax, Mary. But before you doze off, I have a soup for you." He twisted the top off a thermos flask and poured out the soup, handing it to her. She reached out and took the steaming cup. "Careful, it's hot," he said.

He settled himself into the driver's seat and turned to look as she drank the soup, wiping her lips with the back of a filthy hand. A change was coming over her. She was relaxing. She finished the soup and lay back on the pillow. He waited for a while before driving off.

It was still snowing, and it took about half an hour to reach the Old Port. Big leafy flakes of snow were settling everywhere, and the expanse of the port was a white field disturbed only by the tracks of the van, tracks that disappeared in minutes under the snow.

The Old Port had been converted to parkland and open spaces where Montrealers could stroll along the edge of the St. Lawrence River. In the middle of a December night, it was deserted, and he parked the van close to the metal and concrete railing that marked the river's edge. Then he turned in his seat and leaned back to check her neck for a pulse. There wasn't one.

He was surprised at how difficult it was to get her out of the van. She seemed heavier than when he had helped her down from her perch, and her bulky clothing made her difficult to handle.

He had imagined this moment many times, carrying a weightless angel in his arms, and he cursed himself when all he could do was drag her out feet first, letting her shoulders and head take the brunt of the fall to the pavement. Air escaped from her lungs with an animal grunt, and for a second he feared that she wasn't dead. He checked for a pulse again, then dragged her to the railing and stood her up, holding the back of her neck to stop her falling. He wanted the river to take her home. He let go of her neck, and she pitched forward. Then he bent down, took hold of her legs at knee height, raised her feet off the ground, and let her slip over the edge.

He cursed himself again when he heard a thud but no splash and looked down at the dark pile below him. The harbour water was frozen solid, and she lay motionless on the snow-covered ice with a dark trickle of blood spreading out from her head. He knelt down and began mumbling prayers for the dead as she gradually disappeared under the falling snow. In half an hour she was invisible. He went back to the van and drove away.

# TWO
## DECEMBER 24

11.45 PM

**Patsy Cline was singing in the dark** of loss and despair while Vanier sat half-listening, his thoughts wandering off on long tangents and then returning to the song. The ring-tone shook him, and he had to focus to find out where it was coming from. He saw the blinking green light of the cell phone on the floor, rose from the armchair, and picked it up.

"Hello?"

"Sorry to disturb you this time of night, sir, but they're collecting bodies down here."

Vanier reached for the glass of Jameson and listened to the familiar voice. He didn't tell Detective Sergeant Laurent that he had been awake, sort of, or that he was glad to have some contact on Christmas Eve.

"Explain."

"They've found five bodies tonight. That beats all the averages.

Street people by the look of it, all sleeping rough. Two at Atwater, one at McGill, and they just found the last two at Berri. That's where I am now. I think you should come down here. If you can get away, that is, sir."

Crime doesn't take a holiday. It changes costume for the season, and Christmas is the season for domestic violence. Too much pressure to deliver the perfect gift, and not enough money. Too little to say, and too much alcohol encouraging confessions. Never enough love or imagination to deliver the dream. Christmas murders are usually a simple matter; the victim lying in a pool of blood, stabbed, shot, or bludgeoned with whatever comes to hand, the assailant not far away, sitting under the tree crying and sobering up, or in a bar trying not to. They're easy cases, and good ones for a new officer to cut his teeth on. Even the non-domestics were supposed to be easy. Street people die all the time in Montreal's brutal winter, but randomly and alone in the long nights of January and February, and not five a night.

"No, no. It's not a problem, Laurent. I can be there in fifteen minutes. Berri, you said?"

"Yes, sir. When you get to the entrance, one of the uniforms will tell you where I am."


Vanier was happy to get out of his apartment. He had been holed up too long pretending the festive season didn't exist. Patsy Cline, whiskey, and Christmas are a depressing combination.

He drove slowly out of the garage into the Montreal night. Winter had come early, and the second storm of the season had just drifted east after dropping twenty centimetres of snow on the city. A large winter moon hung low in the clear sky. The car was warm, one of the luxuries of parking inside, and the window lowered at the touch of a button, letting in a flood of cold fresh air.

He turned right out of the garage to descend Redpath, a steep street running down to the city from a high ridge on the mountain that dominates the Montreal skyline. The snow-covered pavements were deserted except for the occasional parka-bundled figures leaning forward into the cold as they staggered home from late night réveillons.

At the Berri Métro, the snow had been plowed and piled in high banks on both sides of the street by city crews and contractors earning triple time for working Christmas Eve. They were already beginning the long job of clearing it. Vanier parked opposite the station entrance, but had to walk to the corner to find a spot to cross the snow bank. Uniformed officers who were milling around the station entrance looked up as he approached, their breath making clouds in the frigid air. One went to stop him before another, recognizing Vanier, held him back.

"Bonsoir, Inspecteur, et Joyeux Nöel!" said one of the officers, touching the peak of his cap.

"Joyeux Nöel, les gars," said Vanier, without stopping.

He pulled open the heavy door and made for the escalator. It was shut off, so he took the stairs down to the main concourse. At the bottom, a uniformed officer pointed to the motionless escalator that led down to the westbound Green Line platform, and Vanier took the stairs again; the risers on a stopped escalator are higher than on ordinary stairs. He went down slowly, facing the 500-foot wall of white tile opposite. Like much of the métro system, Berri had been dug rather than tunneled. Engineers blasted a cathedral-sized hole in the rock and built the station in the hole, encasing it in walls of concrete when they had finished. Then the hole was filled in, enclosing a complex of massive internal galleries inside an underground concrete box.

Vanier was breathing hard at the bottom of the stairs.

About two-thirds of the way down the westbound platform,

three uniformed police officers and a métro security officer were gathered around Laurent, looking up at him. At six foot four, with a shaved head and the build of a defensive linebacker, Laurent towered over the group. The three police officers were dressed for the outdoors, holding their fur hats in their hands; Laurent was talking to the security officer. They all turned as Vanier approached down the platform.

"Thanks for coming, sir. What a night. I thought it would be a quiet shift. Instead we get this shit. She's behind the grill," said Laurent, gesturing to a large hole in the wall covered by a steel grill.

Vanier moved over to it. The grill was hinged at the top, and the métro officer pulled from the bottom and lifted it up, exposing a massive ventilation shaft that sucked air from the street into the station. Vanier peered in. The shaft went in flat for eight feet and then rose up like a chimney. On the flat surface, two small feet protruded from a pile of blankets and coats. Cold air from the street wafted down through the shaft carrying the smell of the sleeper, a grimy mix of smoke, damp, greasy food, booze, and human leakage.

Laurent was behind Vanier, looking over his shoulder. "After they found the first body at McGill, word went out to check all the stations, and apparently this is a usual sleeping spot. Easy entry and warm enough to spend the night. This officer found her and tried to wake her," said Laurent, gesturing to the officer. "He climbed inside when she wouldn't move. We're waiting for the Coroner's people before we pull her out."

Vanier turned to the métro officer. "How often do you find bodies in the system?"

"Often enough that we have a policy. If there's no sign of violence, we call in an ambulance, and they get a medic to confirm death. Normally, a thing like this would be natural causes, and the Coroner wouldn't be involved; we'd just hand her off to the funeral home for her last car trip. Only tonight we found three in the system, two here and one at the McGill Métro. Your guys found another two outside at Atwater."

"That's a big number, sir. That's why I thought I should call you," said Laurent.

"You were right," said Vanier, touching the young officer's elbow. "Make sure the crime scene people take it seriously, have them go over the spot thoroughly."

Vanier turned back to stare into the shaft, looking beyond the feet, the bundled body, and several bags at her head. There was no blood, no sign of a struggle. She looked like she was asleep.

"You're sure she's dead?"

"Yes, sir. Checked her myself."

Vanier nodded to the officer that he could lower the grill. "She wasn't in a sleeping bag?"

"No, sir, it looks like blankets rolled around her body."

Vanier looked up at Laurent. "You said there were two here?"

"The other one's down on the Orange Line, northbound. The trains were running until half an hour ago, and then the whole system shut down because of some electrical fault," said Laurent.

"Lead on." The pair walked off in the direction of the Orange Line, another level down.

"Good thing they did have to shut it all down," said Laurent, "or we'd have the Mayor's office breathing down our necks for holding up traffic. The other body's in a utility room at the far end of the platform. Someone gummed up the lock, and since then it only looks like it's locked. Same situation as here, bedded down for the night and never woke up."

A small area of the Orange Line platform was yellow-taped off, and a métro officer was standing guard, leaning against the wall. He straightened up as the two detectives ducked under the yellow tape. The door of the utility room was open, and inside, below the sink, another bundle lay up against the wall. This one had been peeled open to reveal an old, bearded man, his head resting on gloved hands. His face was peaceful despite deep wrinkles, and his eyes were closed as though in sleep.

Vanier held the doorjamb and surveyed the small room. Again, there were no obvious signs of violence, no blood, not even bruising, just the normal wear and tear of a life on the street. It was like looking at a moment captured in a photograph. A yellow bucket on wheels supported a mop leaning upside-down on the wall, an extra-wide broom was propped against the opposite wall under a shelf full of jars of industrial cleaning fluids, and two half-filled garbage bags stood next to the broom. Vanier felt that if he were only to yell loud enough, the sleeping man would wake. But he knew there was nothing to do. The crime scene guys would do more. That was their job. His was to look and to remember, to notice anything strange or out of place. But all he saw was a homeless man finding shelter in a utility closet.

He turned back to Laurent. "So what do we know?"

"Not much. We've had five similar deaths tonight. All older street people sleeping wherever they could find a spot, all bedded down for the night, only they don't wake up. Two women, three men. No signs of violence, and none of them froze to death. The first was found at the McGill Métro, just after ten o'clock, and they were all found in the last two hours. You've got these two here, two more at Atwater, and the McGill guy. The Atwater bodies weren't inside the station, one was at the entrance in Cabot Park, and the other was sleeping on a ledge outside a parking garage. The way this is going, there may be more, sir. Maybe we haven't found them all yet."

Vanier looked up at Laurent, "Well, for the moment, we treat them all as suspicious. Forget natural causes unless the autopsy results tell us something different. In the meantime, let's do what we can to place these people, put names on them. Have someone collect their possessions and bring them to headquarters. Get someone to look at the CC footage. There are cameras all over the métro as well as outside. When did they come in tonight? Did they talk to anyone? I want everything. Also, get photos of each of them, and have someone shop them around the hostels and shelters, the Old Brewery Mission, the Sally Ann, Dans La Rue, the drop-in centres, all the places street people go. Someone knows these people. Someone saw them tonight. Let's find out who they were."

Laurent was busy taking notes, but hardly needed to. In three years with Vanier he had learned the drill. Vanier's mantra was connections and history. Know the victim, find the paths he walked, and you will cross paths with the murderer. He had seen Vanier go through the same drill countless times.

"Chief, you think they were killed?"

"Laurent, I haven't got a clue. But until we know differently, let's assume they didn't just slip away peacefully. Let's get them identified and as much history as possible. These people have families that need to know what happened, even if their families don't give a shit. I want everything we can find on them."

"Oh, and this one," Vanier said, pointing into the cleaning closet at the bearded corpse. "I gave him five dollars last week outside the Sherbrooke Métro. He grinned at me and said, *Merci monsieur, merci.* I want to know who he was. Now, I'm going home. Call me anytime after six tomorrow morning."

He turned to leave and caught a fleeting look in Laurent's eyes and realized his mistake.

"Oh yeah, you're off tomorrow. Find out who's on duty in the morning and leave your notes with him. Enjoy Christmas, and we can talk later. And give my best wishes to your wife and those beautiful children. This is a time for family, Laurent. Enjoy it."

Laurent was taken aback, "Merci, patron, and a Merry Christmas to you too, and to your family."

Vanier turned and walked away, thinking of the flights of stairs that he would have to climb to get out of the station and of Laurent's Christmas wishes. He had told few people that there was no longer any family. Marianne had left two weeks before Christmas last year, and Élise had followed her mother. Alex hadn't lived at home for three years.

Leaving the station, he could see the top of his car over a wall of snow but had to walk to the corner and double back along the road to reach it. The crime scene people might still be at Atwater or McGill, he thought, no harm in trying. He decided to drive by and take a look.

## 1.30 AM

The drive was slow because he had to manoeuvre around the massed armies of snow removal crews along de Maisonneuve. While snowstorms envelop the city, crews fight to keep the roads open by plowing the snow to the sides of the streets. It is only when the snow stops falling that the focus shifts to getting rid of it with tractors, plows, snow-blowers and front-end loaders working day and night to fill eight-wheeler dump trucks. First they clear the main thoroughfares, one side of the street, then the other, then the smaller streets, then the side streets and alleys. The snow is pushed back into the middle of the street to feed giant snow-blowers that are shadowed by long lines of dump trucks fitted with towering wood panels to accommodate extra snow. When a truck is full, it pulls away and is replaced by the next in line. Within days, thousands of tons of snow are lifted off the streets and deposited in dumps all over the island. In the past, the snow was dumped into the St. Lawrence, but snow scraped from the street is toxic with salt, gasoline, chemicals, and garbage, and someone noticed the dead fish in the spring. Now they have to dump the snow in lost corners of the city where it sits in vast landscapes of dirty grey hillocks until early summer when it's all finally melted.

A cruiser was parked at the University Street entrance to the Mc-Gill Métro with its motor running for heat; the snow under the exhaust was black with the crap spewing out. Vanier parked in front of the cruiser and got out. Police officers get very nervous when you approach them from behind. He pulled out his badge and held it in front of him as he walked towards the cruiser. Two officers were dozing in the front seat, and he was disturbing them. They both looked at the badge, and the driver got out of the car. The passenger went back to snoozing. Vanier smelled pizza and wondered if the constable could smell whiskey.

"Yes, Inspector. What can I do for you?"

"Have they finished with the body here, Constable Desjardins?" said Vanier, reading the officer's name badge.

"Yeah. Everyone cleared out about half an hour ago," he said, wiping his sleeve across his mouth to get rid of the food stains. "They brought the stiff to the morgue about an hour ago, but the crime scene people were dragging their asses inside. Christ, you'd think the fucking Premier had died. If you ask me, I think it's the double time they get for the holidays. Anyway, they just left."

"I guess they have their jobs to do."

"Maybe that's it, Inspector. But if we put in this effort for every homeless asshole that turns up stiff, we'd blow the budget in six months. Know what I mean?" He was grinning, inviting Vanier to share his insight. "Nobody cares if we treat them like the shit they are when they're alive, but Christ, all of a sudden they're dead and they've got status. We're all falling over ourselves to find out how they died. But who the fuck cares? You know what I'm saying?"

"So there's no use for me here," said Vanier.

"It's all over, Inspector. And a waste of time if you ask me."

Vanier turned to leave. "Merry Christmas, Constable Desjardins, and the same to your colleague when he wakes up."

"Thank you, Inspector. And the same to yourself."

Vanier walked back to his car. As he drove off, he looked in the mirror and saw the Constable standing in the street looking after him. Vanier wondered what kind of horror it would be to be arrested by Constable Desjardins.

The Atwater Métro station was 12 blocks west, and Vanier circled the Alexis Nihon high-rise that stood over the station complex until he spotted a cruiser and a crime scene van parked by the entrance to the garage. Two officers were stamping their feet next to the cruiser, their breath billowing white in the cold. Vanier got out of the car and walked towards them, badge in hand. They seemed relieved to have some activity.

"Vanier, Major Crimes," he said, shaking cold hands.

He turned to look up at the ledge overlooking the garage entrance where a crime scene technician was on his hands and knees.

The technician looked down and smiled.

"Inspector Vanier, good to see you again. I'm almost finished here. The body was just taken away, and there's not much else. She must have stashed her bags somewhere before settling down for the night. Your people will probably find her stuff in the morning."

"Mr. Neilson, isn't it? Good to see you again. So you found nothing?" asked Vanier.

"Except this." He held up a Second Cup coffee thermos. "Don't even know if it's hers. We'll do the prints, but she was wearing gloves. Maybe she took off her gloves to drink her eggnog; you know, some people never lose their manners."

"Eggnog?"

"Yes, sir, eggnog, with a healthy dose of rum by the smell of it. I was tempted to try it myself." Neilson lowered himself to the ground and walked over to Vanier.

"You'd be amazed how warm it is up there. Every few minutes, the garage vents hot air that seems to just hang there. If I had to sleep outside in the middle of winter, this would be the spot. You don't even have to climb up. You can go up the steps by the building doors and walk along the ledge."

"How did they find her?" asked Vanier.

"One of the tenants was returning home at 8:30 p.m. and noticed her settling in for the night. She called security to have them move her on. Nice, eh? Like *Merry Christmas now fuck off*. The security guard didn't go for it at first, says he was alone and couldn't leave the desk. Anyway, the tenant called back at about 10 p.m. and had a fit when she was told that nothing had been done. She called the building manager at home and the security guard finally went out a little after 11 p.m. He couldn't wake her, so he called 911. So we have a time of death between 8:30 p.m. and 11 p.m."

"Any signs of violence?"

"Nothing. She died in her sleep looking real peaceful."

"There's another body?"

"Yes, Inspector. Just down the street in Cabot Park. I'm going there now. Why don't you follow me? It's in the south entrance to the Métro."

"Let's go."

Vanier turned to the uniforms who were still clapping their hands together and stamping their feet in the cold. "You can close this up. We've finished here."

"That's good news, sir. I hear my bed calling me."

"Enjoy your Christmas, officers," said Vanier.

He got into his car and waited for the crime scene van to pull out. Cabot Park took up a city block in front of the Children's Hospital but, despite its location, it was a lost space, a watering hole for the city's destitute. Every time he passed it, Vanier wondered why some places are shunned by the majority of the citizens and become a gathering point for the outcasts. Were transients simply claiming an unwanted patch of land, or was their presence scaring off everyone else? It was one of the ugliest parks in Montreal. In summer, too many trees choked off light, so that, instead of grass, the ground was hard- packed clay. In fall, mud made it impassable. In winter, the gloom of the bare, black trees darkened even the freshest snowfall. And every day, buses lined up in a circle around the park waiting to start their routes, running their engines, and filling the air with the stink of exhaust fumes.

A squat, ugly building of glass and prison-grey concrete that housed an entrance to the Métro and a control room for bus traffic sat on the northwest corner, an architectural marriage of bunker and telephone booth with less charm than either. When it was freezing, people sheltered inside the bunker waiting for their bus to arrive and uneasily shared space with clutches of drinking and arguing street people.

Neilson parked close to a snow bank on St. Catherine Street, and Vanier pulled in behind him, leaving room for access to the back doors. Flashes of light from the police photographer lit up the bunker as they approached. Neilson was first to the building and pulled open the heavy door for Vanier. It was cold inside. The waiting area was unheated and, even though it was sheltered, the concrete floor and walls radiated damp cold as the wind howled through the doors. But, despite the constant circulation of cold air, the place still stank of alcohol and urine.

The body was tucked under a concrete bench with an empty bottle of wine at its head. Another cocoon wrapped against the elements, hoping to preserve some warmth at the centre. Vanier nodded at the two officers protecting the scene. The photographer was re-packing his equipment, getting ready to leave.

"We'll have head shots of all of the victims ready first thing in the morning," he said to Vanier, lifting the strap of his shoulder bag.

"That's great. Much appreciated," said Vanier.

Neilson knelt down to begin his work, peeling the blankets away.

Another weather-beaten face lined by deep wrinkles. A man, perhaps in his forties, perhaps younger, the street ages people quickly. Vanier looked at the body and wondered how you could retain heat on the concrete floor in the freezing Montreal night. Even with all the layers, the newspapers closest to the skin, covered by a shirt and pants, a sweater and an overcoat, all wrapped in dirty blankets, eventually the cold would seep into the core of the body. How long could you sleep like that, without the cold waking you? Alcohol might buy you some time, but after a few hours the cold would take over, forcing you to wake up or die.

Neilson talked into a hand-held recorder. Vanier looked around but could see nothing unusual, just another victim who went to sleep and never woke up. He turned away. There was nothing he could do.

"Unless you need me, Mr. Neilson, I'll be off. When you've finished, tell these men they can close up the scene."

As he turned to leave, Vanier had a thought. "Mr. Neilson, did you see the body at the McGill Métro?"

"Yes, Inspector. That was my first stop tonight."

"And?"

"There's not much to say. Much the same as this situation, Inspector. A man sleeping rough. No signs of violence, looks like a peaceful end to a hard life. Nothing suspicious, except for the number of them. Could be a bad coincidence. Maybe they all realized it was Christmas Eve and couldn't take it anymore, but that's unlikely. I don't suppose you survive on the streets by being sentimental. Hopefully, the autopsies will tell us something."

"Maybe," said Vanier, almost to himself as he turned to leave.

"Have a good Christmas, Inspector."

"You too, Mr. Neilson. Merry Christmas."

Vanier walked out of the death-cold building into the colder night, got into his car and headed home.

Twenty minutes later he stood at the window in his living room looking down over the city with a fresh glass of Jameson in his hand. Hot air from heating systems rose straight up from rooftop vents to condense into white vapour in the cold, like the smoke from so many campfires. He took in the city below him down to the river and beyond, to the endless blanket of white and grey stretching to the horizon. It would be cold again tomorrow. Yesterday's snow had given way to clear skies that were expected to last for several days and the temperature would fall to a punishing deep freeze. There would be sunlight without heat. Montreal winters are unforgiving, a relentless cold tempered by snowstorms that allow the temperature to rise by a few degrees, then clear skies, and cold again.

He wondered how many people slept outside in weather like this, and what madness drove them to it? And if someone was killing them, why stop at five?

# THREE
## DECEMBER 25

8.25 AM

**The jangling phone woke Vanier** from a fitful sleep on the couch. He reached into his pocket and pulled it out.

"Hello?"

"C'est moi, Papa. Joyeux Nöel."

"Élise, ma belle. How are you? Merry Christmas. God it's great to hear your voice. Where are you?"

"Chez Maman, in beautiful downtown Toronto, as they say." She was whispering in a perfect English accent. He knew that she was talking softly so as not to let her mother know.

"You sound like you're still in bed."

"I am, Papa. I wanted to call you to say Merry Christmas before the day gets started. It's the first thing I did, Papa. I haven't even checked to see if there is a sock from Santa at the end of my bed. Probably not, though. That was your job wasn't it?"

"What? Élise, how can you suggest such a thing?" he said, continuing the fable. "I had absolutely nothing to do with any socks – except for lending you one of mine, because they were the biggest!"

She giggled like the child she no longer was. And then there was silence. He could hear her breathing. He listened, wanting the moment to last, enjoying the unconscious communication of love. Words would break it so he said nothing. Eventually, she stirred.

"I got your present. I love getting parcels in the mail."

"I hope you like it."

"I'm sure I will, Papa. I haven't opened it yet." He knew it was probably in her room, out of the way, not to disturb Marianne with a sign of his presence. Élise would open it when she had time to herself.

"Will you let me know what you think? It's only a small thing."

"I'm sure it's wonderful."

There was a silence. Then, "So, Papa, have you heard from Alex?" The moment was broken, and the tension flooded in.

"Not yet, Élise. I've booked a call for tomorrow. It's hard to get to speak to him, but he told me that you guys email each other."

"Yeah. He emails me all the time, and we talk on Skype. You should get yourself set up on Skype. It's easy, I'll show you how next time I'm in Montreal. Alex would like that, I know he would."

He knew it would be a while before she was next in Montreal. Maybe in the summer, but he couldn't ask. She would take that question as pressure.

"That would be great, Élise. How does he sound to you?"

"It's tough in Kandahar. But he seems to be holding up. It's like he's found his place in the Van Doos. He's assigned to protect the Provincial Reconstruction Team, that's what he calls it. Says he's doing good work too. But it's dangerous. I think of him all the time."

"So do I, Élise, so do I."

"So, when you speak to him tomorrow, wish him Merry Christmas from me. And be easy on him, Papa. I know that you guys fight sometimes but he loves you, Papa, just like me."

"I know, Élise, I know. I am a lucky man."

"So, Papa. Merry Christmas. Je t'aime."

"And I love you too, ma belle. Come back to Montreal soon. Merry Christmas."

"Yeah. I love you too, Papa. Joyeux Nöel."

"Joyeux Nöel, ma belle."

With a click the phone went dead, and Vanier stared at the floor. The single thing that he wanted to do on Christmas Day, and it was done. He looked at the clock. 8.40.

He rose stiffly from the couch and walked to the bathroom, replaying the conversation in his head.

## 11.15 AM

The Métro Security Headquarters consists of a small series of windowless offices deep under the street in the Berri Métro station. Vanier pulled the door open and walked in, already impatient with the diplomatic burden of not stepping on toes. Most people, even policemen, bristle at the sight of métro officers. They don't carry guns, and they make up for that inadequacy with intimidating swat-team uniforms, complete with bulletproof vests and the swagger of schoolyard bullies. But when below ground in their system, even cops have to show them respect.

An officer approached Vanier and introduced himself with an outstretched hand. He was dressed like he was going to lead a Special Forces team to take out a bunch of terrorists.

"Inspector Vanier, it's wonderful to see you again. Inspector Morneau, Métro Security."

Morneau flashed a white-toothed smile that was more formal than friendly, and Vanier racked his brain to remember where the hell he had seen him before.

"Inspector Morneau, good of you to come out on Christmas morning."

"Thank you, Inspector. We're taking this very seriously. We must get it cleaned up as soon as possible."

"It not easy to clean up five bodies, Inspector. It's not like litter."

Morneau didn't notice the rebuke. "Your Detective Sergeant St. Jacques has already been here for some time," he said, gesturing to the back of the office. Vanier followed the gesture and saw Sylvie St. Jacques looking over the shoulder of a computer operator at a bank of TV screens. She was wearing black pants and a thick sweater and had the aura of someone tightly coiled but in control. She smiled up at Vanier as he approached, beckoning with her hand as if to get him to move more quickly.

"Take a look at this, sir," she said. "Victim number four in the station at 8.30 last night."

Vanier looked at the screen she was pointing to. There was a bag lady in a heavy dark coat shuffling down the platform with two large bags in each hand and two smaller ones tied to her belt. She kept her head down as she moved forward to a bench and sat down, arranging the bags around her feet. Then she leaned back against the wall and was still.

"She sits there for half an hour without moving, and nobody so much as looks at her. People wait for trains, get on them and leave or get off and leave. And it's like she isn't there. They all walk around her. Now, fast forward to 9.05."

Vanier watched as the image jumped and then stilled, with 21:05 printed in the bottom left hand corner of the screen.

"Just here, sir. Look."

On the screen, the unmistakable figure of Santa Claus appeared

32

from the platform entrance, complete with a white beard and a bag slung over his shoulder. He looked up and down the platform and then walked directly up to the bag lady, put his bag down beside her, and leaned forward, seeming to whisper to her.

They watched as she raised her head and then her arms as if to welcome Santa. He reached into his sack and pulled out something in the shape of a fire log and handed it to her. She took it and held it for a moment before smiling up at him again. Vanier wondered if she recognized him, or was simply happy to see Santa Claus.

"Now watch this, sir."

In the grainy black and white image, Santa leaned in even closer to the woman, held her chin and kissed the top of her head.

St. Jacques counted, "One, two, three, four, five. Five seconds, sir. He held the kiss for five seconds!"

Breaking the kiss, Santa stroked the old lady's hair and, again, seemed to whisper something to her. Then he picked up his sack and started back along the platform. Before he turned into the platform exit, he stopped and lifted his arm in a farewell wave to the bag lady. Then he was gone.

"We have him going up the escalator and out the door onto St. Catherine Street. Then we have nothing more until 10 p.m.," said St. Jacques.

The operator skipped the tape forward to 22.00, and the image showed the bag lady slowly rise to her feet and put Santa's gift in one of her bags. Then she pulled them all up and began shuffling along the platform, away from the entrance.

"What did he give her?" asked Vanier, trying to understand what he had just seen.

"They found a brand new woolen throw with her, the sort you can find anywhere. Probably useful to keep you warm if you're sleeping rough. Rolled up tight, it could be the gift."

"Anything else from the CC cameras?"

"That's all we have for the moment, but we've lots to review. M. Savard here has been a lot of help." She put her hand on the operator's shoulder and he swiveled around in his chair to face the pair, a huge grin on his face. He was enjoying working with St. Jacques.

"I'll let you get on with it, then. I want every image of Santa that we can get. See if we can get a face shot. And get Santa's timing down; time in, time out."

"What about the Santa suit, sir? Maybe it's a rental."

"Right. Have someone contact the owners of every rental shop in town; there can't be that many. Let's get the names and addresses of everyone who rented a Santa suit. I don't care if it is Christmas morning."

St. Jacques was writing things down. "I'll get onto it but there aren't many people about today. Everyone is off."

"See what you can do. And find out if anyone keeps records of homeless deaths. Take a look at the numbers over the last few months and see if there's anything suspicious. OK?"

"Yes, sir. Oh, and this, sir." She picked up a brown envelope from the table and handed it to Vanier. "These are the photos of the victims."

Vanier reached into the envelope and pulled out five colour photographs. Each was a front-on headshot, like mug shots except the eyes were all closed.

Inspector Morneau had been watching from a discreet distance, listening to the exchange.

"Inspector Morneau. If I go to the McGill Métro, could you have one of your people meet me and show me where the victim was found last night?"

"Certainly, Inspector. I'll send someone. When you arrive, he will be waiting at the ticket booth inside the University Street entrance. He'll be in uniform. Just introduce yourself."

# THE DEAD OF WINTER

## 12.30 PM

Montreal is rooted in hard, volcanic rock by a giant system of tunneled spaces, an underground city that grew like an ant colony. It started with the métro system, opened just before Expo 67, and hasn't stopped spreading. Tunnels are main streets connecting underground neighbourhoods where food courts in shopping centres replace village greens. A 35 square kilometre, neon-lit, climate controlled, private metropolis, a Disney-like masquerade of public space controlled so tightly that real city mayors are jealous. Métro Security and private guards swarm through the spaces keeping order, while security cameras manned in real-time see everything so that reaction is always swift. Doors that open early in the morning to welcome consumers are locked at night like the gates of ancient walled cities. By unwritten and ever-changing rules, access is granted and denied at the whim of high school dropouts with uniforms and failed candidates for the police force. It's a modern world where piped music replaces birdsong and artificial scents replace flowers.

In this world, the homeless must adjust to a constantly changing level of scrutiny. They may be grudgingly tolerated in one area, providing they keep moving through, and forbidden in others. When they walk from a semi public métro tunnel into a commercial space they are picked up on security cameras, and guards appear to make sure that they either don't come in or that they leave quickly.

The McGill Métro station is the heart of the underground city, occupying a four-acre rectangle at the basement level of surrounding buildings. There are only three street entrances to the station, but there are six others through the adjoining shopping centres. The middle of the station concourse is cut open like a trench, and you can watch the trains on the lower level. Two sets of turnstiles guard access to the platforms, one at each end of the concourse.

Vanier tried an office building on University Street but the door was locked, with access only for those with electronic keys. He crossed the street to use one of the street entrances.

It was warm inside, and he undid his coat as he walked towards the ticket booth. A métro security officer was waiting for him. A kid, Haitian by the look of him, with everything hanging from his belt but a gun.

"Inspector Vanier, I presume," he said, reaching out his hand with an ear-to-ear grin that lit up his face.

Vanier took his hand and smiled broadly, reading the name badge, "Constable Duvalier."

"Yes, sir. And before you ask, no relation."

"Well I'm glad to hear that," said Vanier, "Papa and Baby Doc were not the best of people. So, Constable Duvalier, can you show me where the body was found?"

"Of course, Inspector. It was on the eastbound platform, last night. Follow me."

Constable Duvalier waved him through the turnstiles with a sign to the sullen ticket seller locked in his booth.

"He's not happy to be working on Christmas," said Duvalier apologetically, leading Vanier down the stairs. "Time and a half, and an extra day's vacation and he's not happy. What does it take?"

He led Vanier down one flight of stairs to the eastbound platform.

"The body was found down there in the corner," said Duvalier, pointing to the end of the platform. "He was asleep on the floor."

"And nobody told him to leave?"

"That's the thing, Inspector. The rules are clear, no sleeping in the métro. Believe me, it's on the exams to become a métro officer. We all know it. But just because you put on a uniform doesn't mean you hang up your humanity."

Vanier thought about that.

"And all the others, they're in the union. It's not part of their job description."

"And we're all human."

"Christmas Eve, it's minus twenty degrees outside, all the shelters are full, or closed, or they won't take them because they've been drinking. So what do you do? You throw someone out in the street? No. People look the other way. The cleaners push the machines up and down the platform and notice nothing. The train drivers come and go and see nothing. And my colleagues don't happen to look in that direction. The guys on the screens, for some reason, they can't pick it up. What's that? A conspiracy? So he lay there. And he was dead. Who knows how long? Who's to blame?"

"Constable Duvalier, if I was blamed every time I looked the other way I'd be selling newspapers."

"It's not easy. Do it too much and the rules become arbitrary."

Vanier thought about that too.

They walked down the platform to where the body was found. Duvalier stood in a corner at the end of a métro platform and pointed at the floor. The sleeper would have been clearly visible to a driver going in the opposite direction, and to the cameras trained on the platform.

"That's it?" said Vanier, almost to himself.

"That's it," said Duvalier.

They went back upstairs.

"You'll have to exit to the street. All the building entrances are closed."

"Thank you, Constable Duvalier," said Vanier as he turned to climb a shut-down escalator to the street.

## 1.35 PM

On Christmas afternoon, the building housing the Montreal Police Headquarters was almost deserted. Interview Room 6 had been set aside for the personal possessions of the victims, and Vanier was in there because he had nothing better to do. Four separate piles of garbage bags were propped against the wall; the possessions of the fifth victim had still not been found. On a sheet of white paper, someone had given each pile a number. He grabbed two garbage bags that sat under the sheet marked Number 1 and brought them to the edge of the table, next to where he had dropped a yellow note-pad and a pen. He tipped the contents of the first bag onto the table and started taking inventory, listing each piece before putting it back into the bag. Before he had refilled the first bag, he changed his mind and decided to walk to the exhibit room to get cardboard boxes and labels. He grabbed as many of the flat, unfolded boxes as he could manage, putting sheets of sticky labels and a felt pen in his pocket. As an afterthought he grabbed a pair of latex gloves and returned to the room. He pulled on the gloves and got to work, ignoring the fetid smell filling the room.

Sorting through the first pile again, he began listing bulkier items: a sleeping bag and two blankets; a couple of T-shirts, one from St. Petersburg, Florida, the other from the last world tour of the Police; three pairs of formerly white Y-front underwear, three pairs of socks, and three oversized acrylic sweaters. He wrote it all down. Next was a roll of toilet paper and a copy of the *Journal de Montréal* – the insulation of choice for the homeless. The second bag was less bulky. It held a hairbrush and a toothbrush, a half-empty bottle of Bacardi, an empty plastic drinking cup from Starbucks, a zip-lock bag full of cigarette butts, and a half-eaten hamburger from McDonald's. He wondered what kind of homeless person would buy his coffee at Starbucks, and remembered the container found by Neilson last night. He pulled the top off and sniffed. It smelled of rancid milk and alcohol. He set it aside for testing and returned to his inventory. There was a thick plastic bag from the Société des Alcools filled with coins. Vanier counted the coins and wrote down $37.88. There remained two bottles of pills, both Celebrex 200 mg, one empty, the other half-full. Prescribed by Dr. Alain Grenier to George Morissette. The labels on the pill containers also said they were dispensed by the pharmacy at the Old Brewery Mission.

Taking a felt pen from the desk, he wrote on a sticky label: George Morissette. Putting a name on the possessions was progress. He reached back into the bag and pulled out a thick envelope of papers. He emptied the envelope, laid the papers on the table, and sat down.

There was a disintegrating certificate issued by the Ordre de Notaires du Québec certifying that Maître George Édouard Morissette was admitted as a Notary of the Province of Quebec in 1970. Next, there was an old photograph of a pretty woman holding a child of about two on her lap, sitting in a garden, and smiling at the camera. There was a social insurance card, a driver's license that expired in 1980 and gave Maître Morissette's date of birth as March 25, 1949 and a booklet entitled: *Alcoholics Anonymous Montreal Meetings*. Vanier flipped through it, surprised at how many meetings there were, you could go to a different one, three times a day every day and never go to the same place twice in a month. Each listing showed the language: French, English, Italian, Spanish, and there were even bilingual meetings. Finally, Vanier picked up a small book worn with use: *Twenty Four Hours A Day*. Flipping to December 25, he read:

*I pray that I may be truly thankful on this Christmas Day.*
*I pray that I may bring my gifts and lay them on the altar.*

Morissette never got to see December 25. Maybe he would have been thankful if he did. Vanier wasn't sure. He got up and started to assemble the first folded box. Even though the instructions were clear on the box, and he had seen it done countless times, it took effort and cursing until he had a functional Exhibit Box. He filled it, throwing the half-eaten hamburger in the garbage. Assembling another box, he filled it too, and then a third. When he finished, he reached for the sheet of labels. He looked at the name he had written on the first label, George Morissette, and added *Notaire, 25/03/49*, and *Box 1 of 3*, before peeling it off and attaching it to the first box. He prepared another label and attached it to the second box, *Box 2 of 3*, then *Box 3 of 3*. He placed the boxes one on top of the other against the wall and turned to the bags labelled Number 2.

He continued methodically, stopping only after the third pile to go to the staff canteen for a coffee. When he started in the force, the only choice in coffee was milk and sugar. Now the machines interrogated you: Columbian, Costa Rican, Sumatran, or House Blend? And not just regular coffee, perhaps a latte or cappuccino, or even an espresso? Caffeinated or decaffeinated? Vanier pushed the buttons for his usual blend of Columbian regular, milk, no sugar. It tasted a little better than when he had started in the force.

He took the coffee and walked back to the interview room. With only one more pile to go, his mood was lightening. He felt comfortable with this work in the quiet of the deserted building. He was fascinated by the lives of others and how much you could tell about someone by looking at what they hold precious. He was doing something, and time was passing.

The smell from the possessions in the interview room had become stronger, filling the place with a human smell of sweat and dirt. After a struggle, he got one of the windows to open, and cold air entered with a cleansing presence. He kept his face in the rush of outside air flooding into the room while he sipped his coffee and surveyed the work. Eleven boxes were stacked against the wall; he had put a photograph of each victim on their boxes. George Morissette, the Notary from McGill; Joe Yeoman, a Mohawk from the cleaning room in the Berri Métro; and Edith Latendresse kissed by Santa. Mme. Latendresse had four boxes, more clothes but fewer papers, only a social insurance card and some prescription medicine to identify her.

He began emptying the contents of the last two bags onto the table. Victim number 4's bags contained the usual assortment of old clothes, rotting food and little else. There was $8 in change in a sock, a roll of toilet paper and drugs, again prescribed by Dr. Alain Grenier, this time for Pierre Brun: Zeldox and an empty bottle of Oxycodone, a powerful painkiller with street value. Pierre Brun could have eased his pain by taking the pills or selling them. Vanier wondered which he did. And he wondered about Dr. Alain Grenier, who had prescribed drugs for all of the victims.

It was 4.30 p.m. and already dark when he finished by placing the picture of Pierre Brun on top of two boxes piled against the wall. Feeling cold for the first time, he struggled again with the window and closed it.

The temperature outside was still falling, but he had no idea what the weather was supposed to be doing. He hadn't listened to a weather forecast in days. He had all but given up listening to the radio weeks ago, admitting defeat to the omnipresent Christmas spirit. The only exception was the hourly news. Several times a day he tuned to CBC to listen to the news. If there was a death or serious injury of a soldier in Afghanistan, it was always the first story. If nobody had been killed or injured, if there were no ambushes or roadside bombs, he turned it off, relieved until the next time.

He wondered about the people sleeping outside, realizing how little he knew about them. The last few nights had been cold and damp, and he imagined the shelters were full. But there were still people who chose to stay out in the cold. People who refused the warmth of a shelter to hide in a corner somewhere and take the ultimate risk. He grabbed a phone book, turned to the A's and sat down. Minutes later he grabbed his cell phone and pushed number 6 on his speed dial.

"Allô?"

"Anjili, it's me."

Dr. Anjili Segal was one of Montreal's six coroners. She and Vanier had been friends for over ten years until a brief affair at the end of the summer ended quickly when they realized that they were better friends than lovers. As lovers, they brought out the worst in each other. Vanier hoped that they could salvage their friendship, but it was proving difficult; they had crossed so many lines.

Silence, and then, "Calling to wish me Merry Christmas, Luc?"

"Well, yes. Anjili, Merry Christmas. How was your Christmas?"

"Just bloody marvelous, as you Anglos say."

"Anjili, how many times do I have to tell you I am not an Anglo. My name is Luc Vanier, you can't get more Québécois than that."

"Luc you're an Anglo. You spent too much time in Ontario. OK, so we'll settle for Franco-Ontarian. You prefer that?"

"Call me whatever, Anjili. The bodies from the métro."

"Ah, business."

He ignored the rebuke. "I thought maybe you could help me. I've found prescription bottles in the belongings of the victims from Christmas Eve. They all have Dr. Alain Grenier as the prescribing doctor on them, but I've checked. There are 23 people listed as Alain or A. Grenier. I was wondering…"

"The code?"

"Well, yes. The numbers on the label. They link to the doctor, right?"

"That's why you're the detective. Give me the numbers Luc, I'll look them up.

He grabbed a bottle from Pierre Brun's box and read off the numbers. "Wait," she said, and he heard the clunk of the phone on a table. She was back in three minutes. "Dr. Alain Grenier. His office is at 5620 boulevard St. Joseph. That's it, no suite number. The phone number is 514-450-1872. By the way, he was admitted in 1973, which would put him in his sixties. Anything else?"

"I was wondering. I know it's the holidays, but how soon can we get autopsy results?"

"Luc, you never change. Always work, isn't it?"

"Anjili, this is important. There are five people dead."

"I know, Luc."

"I'd like to see something as soon as possible, even something preliminary. We're spinning our wheels here until we get a cause of death."

"We can probably start the autopsies tomorrow morning, I'm not certain but I'll try. It's going to take two days at least to do all five. Listen, I'll call you tomorrow and let you know some specifics."

"Thanks, Anjili. And listen, Happy Christmas."

"Yes, Luc. You too." Vanier knew that tone of voice, tired and unhappy. And he wished he could do something about it.

"I'm sorry to bother you on Christmas Day, but if we have a murderer out there, I want to get him."

"I know you do Luc. I know." She disconnected before him. He dialed Grenier's number, leaving a message with the operator of the answering service for him to call. Vanier clicked off his phone, turned the light off and made his way to the parking lot.


7 PM


Two hours later, Dr. Grenier faced Vanier from behind his desk in his office on St. Joseph Boulevard. He had been at home when he got Vanier's message and called back to suggest they meet at his office where he kept his records. Grenier was tall and thin, with an angular face that struck Vanier as not much given to smiling. He was having trouble making eye-contact. The doctor was wearing a canary yellow cardigan that Vanier decided must have been a Christmas present; it was too bright for him to have chosen it himself.

The office was spartan, a cheap desk with two chairs in front of it, and two grey filing cabinets against the wall. Files were stacked neatly on the right corner of his desk, and others, with notes attached by paperclip, on the left. There was an impressive collection of framed certificates on one wall and a large black crucifix with a suffering Christ on another. Unless you counted the bleeding Christ or the certificates, there was no artwork.

"Thanks for seeing me at short notice, Doctor. The holidays are always hard and I appreciate your time," said Vanier.

"What can I do for you?" asked Grenier.

Vanier opened the envelope and slipped five photographs onto the desk. Grenier spread them out and looked shaken. He didn't look up. "These are the victims from Christmas Eve?"

"Yes, Doctor. Four of them had prescription bottles with your name on them. We're still looking for the possessions of the fifth. Do you recognize them?"

"Of course I do. I was their prescribing physician."

"For all of them?"

"Yes."

Grenier confirmed the names of the first four and identified the fifth, Céline Plante. Then he stood and pulled five files from one of the cabinets. He looked at each and rattled off the dates of birth. Mme. Plante would have been fifty-two on January 3. He looked at Vanier like he was finished.

"I'm trying to piece together as much information about them as possible. Anything will help"

"Well, I'm not sure that I can be of much help. I was only their doctor."

"Why were they seeing you?"

"They were sick, Inspector."

"How sick were they?"

Grenier hesitated. "Very sick. If you were to ask me to name ten of my patients who feature most in my prayers, these five would be on the list."

44

"Why is that?"

"Different reasons. I can go through the files individually and give the Coroner the precise information. However, to put it bluntly, each of them was terminally ill."

"That's why you prayed for them?"

"What do my prayers have to do with anything?"

"Well, if you prayed for them, you were worried about them. And now they're dead."

"Yes, I prayed for them. I pray for many people. I see pain every day, and terrible suffering is the companion of many of my clients. I suppose that's an inevitable part of human existence, but in the bosom of a close family it can, at least, be endured. For the homeless, there is no relief. Without family or friends there's only the pain. That is why I devote so much of my time to my clinic at the Old Brewery Mission. I try, as best I can, to ease their burden, and when medicine isn't enough, I pray for them." His fingers were running slowly over the photographs, touching each one in turn.

"So all five were terminal cases?"

"For one reason or another, yes. But it's more than that. It's hard to understand the level of suffering they were enduring, Inspector. It's not just physical. Street people, the homeless, the destitute, they were all children once, although for most, even their childhood was hell. But, they were all young once with ambitions higher than the streets. And things went wrong and kept going wrong. These five all had their own stories. Pathetic, tragic, inhuman, whatever. Their lives were hell and they knew it. Well, except for Madame Latendresse."

He picked up her photograph and stared at it.

"Except for Madame Latendresse, they were all aware of how bad their situation was. You don't lose your ability to feel just because you're on the street. You can still hurt. And these people hurt terribly. Not just because of their diseases. That's why I prayed for them. That their burdens be eased."

Vanier looked at him. The doctor's eyes were fixed on the photos, and he was talking without giving any information, as if filling the room with sound was enough.

"Was prayer that important to them? You ministered to their health."

"Prayer is important for all of us, even for you. When all else fails, there is always prayer. These people were hopeless cases. There was nothing left to do for them medically except ease their pain. They had entered the jurisdiction – as you policemen are fond of saying – the jurisdiction of St. Jude."

"The patron saint of hopeless causes?"

"I see you remember something of your religious training."

"Were they aware of that?"

"Of what?"

"That there was no hope."

"As aware as they could be."

"So they could have decided to end it all? Suicide?"

Dr. Grenier thought for a moment and looked up at Vanier.

"No. Not suicide. It's true that some street people kill themselves, but it's the younger ones, the drug addicts, people who have fallen too fast. If you can survive two years on the streets, you can survive 30. The streets weed out the suicidal very quickly, and these five were veterans. None of them was suicidal. Madame Latendresse, for example, is, I'm sorry, was – Madame Latendresse was so disconnected from reality that she couldn't contemplate non-existence. She would have carried on in her own world until that world stopped. The others? The others were like the Legionnaires of Cameron."

"What?"

"Not what, Inspector. Who. The Legionnaires of Cameron. Sixty soldiers of the French Foreign Legion  who held off two thousand Mexican infantrymen and cavalrymen for twelve hours. At the end, only six legionnaires remained, and when they ran out of ammunition, instead of surrendering, they fixed bayonets and charged the Mexican army. Surrender was simply not an option. It is the same with these people. Suicide was not an option in their universe. If it had been, they would have done it long ago. These people have been losing all their life but they just didn't know how to give up. They had fallen as far as they did precisely because they couldn't give up and end it all."

"So why would they all die on the same evening?"

Grenier's hands gave a slight tremble. He was making an effort to control himself. "I believe the Coroner will find it was natural causes. Quite a coincidence, I agree. And the scientist in me hesitates to believe in coincidences of that magnitude. But the believer in me knows that it is often difficult to understand God's work."

"Is there anyone else I can speak with to find out more about these people? Who else would have known them?"

Dr. Grenier had a distant look on his face, as though he was operating on two levels, talking to Vanier and thinking; and thinking was taking up more of his mind.

"Well, they were all known in the community, the shelters and the drop-in centres. You might try their social workers; there would be files on them. But social workers have case loads so unmanageable that they can never get to know their clients."

"Anyone else?"

Grenier hesitated again. "If you're looking for someone who might know these people as individuals rather than faces or numbers, you might try Father Drouin. My friend, Henri Drouin. He works out of the Cathedral. He's a good man, a holy man. If he knows these people, he will be able to tell you much more than I."

"How do you know him?"

"Our paths crossed in our missions, and we became friends. He does wonderful work with this community. Sometimes I think that my drugs are a pale substitute for the spiritual comfort he gives to his flock. Because of him, I started attending mass in the Cathedral."

"Could he be involved with these deaths?"

Grenier seemed shocked at the suggestion. "Father Henri? If you knew him, you would know how ridiculous a proposition that is. Take it from me, if that's the direction of your investigation, you are on the wrong track. Father Henri is incapable of hurting anyone. All of these unfortunate people were going to die soon, and they all died on Christmas Eve. That's it. There's nothing more. It's a tragedy, but I don't think there was any human intervention. They were simply called home."

"One last thing, Doctor. Do you own or have access to a Santa Claus costume?"

"What?"

"A Santa Claus costume. Do you have one? Or if you had to, could you get one?"

"Well, I suppose if I needed one, I could always rent one, but no, I don't have a Santa Claus costume. Why do you ask?"

"Just one of the questions that we're working on, that's all. And where were you on Christmas Eve?"

"Me? You think I could have killed these people? Really, Inspector, that's going too far."

"I'm sorry if the question upsets you. But I would like an answer."

"I was at home until about 10 p.m., with my wife. I went to Midnight Mass at the Cathedral. My wife stayed home. She was tired. After Mass, I came home."

"Thank you, Doctor," said Vanier. "One last thing. Could I have a copy of your files on these people?"

"I can't turn them over just like that, it's a question of patient confidentiality. But if the Coroner's office calls, I can have the files copied and delivered tomorrow. I need an official request."

Vanier sat back in his chair, hoping that silence would prompt the doctor to say something, if only to fill the void. Grenier continued staring at the photos for a few moments and then looked up. "Is there anything else?"

"I don't think so. But don't hold back on me, Doctor. If there's anything you think might help me, you should tell me." Vanier stood up and leaned forward with his hands on the desk leaving grease marks on the polished surface. "What are you thinking about that you can't tell me?"

Grenier tried to look Vanier in the eyes but could only manage it for a moment. "There is nothing. I've told you what I know."

"Maybe. But what about what you suspect? Do you have any hunches, Doctor?"

More silence. Grenier was waging an inner battle. "There is nothing more, Inspector."

"If only life were so easy. If only we could choose to avoid the difficult by ignoring it. Doctor, I need help and I get the impression that you're not being entirely candid with me. I think you're holding back."

"That's an outrageous suggestion. If I knew something that might help you I would tell you."

"Doctor, I love my job. And sometimes I get calls from lawyers, from the Chief, from the Mayor's office, asking, *Why are you persecuting this poor man?* I love those calls. If I weren't good at what I do, my ass would have been canned long ago. But I get results. And if I find out that you're holding something back, I'll be persecuting you."

"Are you suggesting…?" he asked, indignant.

"No suggestions. I don't believe in coincidences and neither do you. These people were killed, and I'm going to find the killer. If you know anything and choose not to tell me, that's your problem. But when I find out who did this, I'll figure out if you haven't been entirely cooperative, and I'll come back for you. Accessory? Withholding evidence? Who knows? But I'll be back to haunt you. As for the killer? Pray to St. Jude for him, because his really is a hopeless case. I'll get him."

"You don't even know that they were killed."

"I don't believe in coincidence, Doctor."

Vanier lifted his hands from the desk and stood up.

"One last thing, Doctor. They don't stop. You know that, don't you? Once they start, they don't stop. If you know anything and don't tell me, the next victim is yours. So why don't you go through your Top 10 list and try to predict who that will be. Here is my card, Dr. Grenier. Call me. I don't sleep well, so anytime is good."

Vanier handed him the card. "I can see myself out."

He left Grenier motionless at his desk, looking at Vanier's business card. Grenier hardly noticed him leaving.

## 9.30 PM

The Cathedral, Marie Reine du Monde, squats on a downtown block next to the Queen Elizabeth Hotel, imposing the Catholic Church's presence on Montreal. It's a scale model of St. Peter's in Rome, but along its mantle it's not 13 statues of Jesus and his apostles but the patron saints of Montreal's 13 parishes keeping a close watch on the faithful. Behind the Cathedral, two long three-story buildings house the offices and apartments of the soldiers of the Church.

The snow banks had been cleared outside the Cathedral, and Vanier parked in front. He followed a pathway that had been shoveled from the street up to the main doors, and tried each without success. He followed the cleared snow-track back to the street and walked around the building until he found a shoveled path to a door with a light over it, like a stage door behind a theatre, the only way in after the show was over. He rang the bell. After a few minutes, the door opened a crack, and a frail old priest in a cassock looked at him, his bony, pink hand holding the door, ready to slam it shut it as soon as he could get rid of the visitor.

"Good evening, Father. Merry Christmas."

"Can I help you?"

"I'm Inspector Vanier, Montreal Police. I'd like to see Father Henri Drouin."

"Well, I'm afraid he's not here at the moment. Perhaps you can come back tomorrow?"

"Do you know where he is?"

"No. As I recall, he left after lunch, and I expect to see him when he returns."

"And when might that be?"

"Please, Inspector. This is the priesthood, not the army. He doesn't have to return at any particular time. I expect if you return tomorrow he will probably be here."

"Does he have a cell phone?"

"I'm afraid not. Perhaps I could take a message. He will see it as soon as he returns."

Vanier fished out a card. He wrote his cell phone on the card and handed it to the old priest. "Ask him to call me as soon as he gets back. Any time. Tell him it's important that I speak to him."

"Thank you, Inspector. I will see that he gets the message."

The priest closed the door without waiting for Vanier to turn and leave.

Vanier walked slowly back to his car, wondering where the authority of the police had gone. When he started, a uniform would always get attention and an Inspector would have people jumping to give him whatever he wanted. Now, civilians wanted nothing to do with them. They were tolerated when they were catching criminals, but they were as disconnected from the rest of society as the criminals.

The inside of the Volvo was cold, and Vanier cursed as it took three turns of the ignition for the engine to turn over. His breath was visible and clouding the windscreen as he pulled out of the parking space. He was hungry, and there were only empty cupboards at home; a curry would be just the thing. Pakistanis don't celebrate Christmas, do they?

He turned left onto Sherbrooke and continued west to Notre Dame de Grâce. Lights from the Ganges restaurant reflected on the snow outside. The street was deserted except for two cars parked in front of the restaurant, and he parked behind them. As he walked through the door, he was greeted by a small dark man in a white shirt, hand out and grinning at his arrival. He reached out for the soft hand, as the awesome, comforting smell of an Indian kitchen went to work on his stomach.

"Luc. Wonderful to see you again. Can I wish you a Merry Christmas?" Midhat Mahmud welcomed his first non-Asian guest of the night.

"Midhat, it's great to see you." The restaurant was empty except for members of an extended family from the sub-continent who were close to finishing their meal.

"We are a little quiet tonight, so you can sit wherever you like. Can I get you something from the bar?"

"A pint of Bass, Midhat."

The Bass came with a plate of pappadum, and Vanier drank and began to relax. He munched on the pappadum and inhaled the aromas. Sitar music played in the background, and Christmas was a thousand miles away. The waiter came, and Vanier ordered batata wada to start, followed by lamb dopiaza, mixed vegetable bhaji, rice and nan.

Midhat returned from the kitchen, pulled up a chair, and sat down opposite his friend. They had met years ago when Vanier, still in uniform, had stopped in for a meal after a long shift. As Midhat was presenting the bill, Vanier asked him what he thought of the execution of Prime Minister Bhutto in Pakistan. It had happened years earlier, but Vanier had been fascinated by what amounted to a judicial murder. His question struck a chord, and Midhat, who had recently graduated from Concordia and had been thrown into running a family business serving strange food to an even stranger population, sat down and unloaded. Born in Pakistan and educated in the West, he had a lot to say and was happy to have a Quebecer to say it to. Vanier had tried to explain that he wasn't a native Quebecer, but it didn't matter, the restaurateur was happy to have any connection to the society he and his family were living in.

On that first night, Vanier learned about the corruption of Pakistani politics, the revolving doors of civil and military governments, and a people cursed to be ruled by criminals whose main ambition was to suck everything of value from the poor country. Vanier kept coming back to Ganges, and kept learning.

After a few years, they began to call each other by their first names. Then Vanier's son Alex was born, and Midhat and his new wife Jamilah showed up unannounced at the Vanier house with a hand-made vase from Pakistan for the baby. Vanier reciprocated a few years later, bringing a selection of OshKosh baby clothes to the new parents of Samir in their first floor walk-up in Park Extension.

"So how are the children, my friend?" asked Vanier.

"Wonderful. A real blessing. Samir is working with some of the best doctors in blood diseases. I can't believe it but in three years he will be a fully qualified doctor and a specialist. And it's not too soon. He'll be able to take care of the aches of his poor father. And Aliza, bless her. In her second year in law, and what a mouth on her! She would argue with you over the colour of the sky. She is brilliant, and what a sense of justice she has. Just think Luc, if I am ever run over by a bus, I'll have my son to look after me and my beautiful daughter to sue the son of a bitch who drove the bus – and the City for letting the son of a bitch drive the bus!"

They both laughed.

"And yours, Luc? How are Alex and the beautiful Élise?"

Midhat was one of the few people Vanier had told about Marianne's leaving, and he did it only after Midhat asked one time too many why Vanier was eating so often in the restaurant.

"Alex tells me that he is doing important work in your part of the world. He seems to think that he is making a difference," said Vanier.

"Making a difference? If only you could know, Luc. He is changing the world and making it better. I wish you Canadians knew how important it is. You should be bloody proud, Luc, a son like that."

"I am, Midhat. But you know how it is with fathers and sons. We can't say what we want to say. We think a nod is a paragraph and a sentence is a book, and, in the end, all that's important is left unspoken."

"We keep a lot inside, Luc, that's true. Too much, maybe. But you tell Alex when he comes back here to get his skinny Canadian ass down to Ganges, and we will fatten him up, all on the house. I don't think they serve good Indian food in the military."

"They probably don't serve any Indian food in the army. I'll bring him down myself."

"And Élise? Tell me, how is Élise?"

"I spoke to her this morning. It seems like a long time ago. She called to wish me Merry Christmas. She's with her mother in Toronto. Still studying. She goes to university next year. Journalism. Maybe one day we'll be looking at her on television. I can just see it now. Alex fighting in some foreign war, and Élise reporting on it, and me down on my knees in front of the television praying for both of them."

They laughed again.

"Already, they are adults."

"It happened too quickly, Midhat. Twenty years in a heartbeat. One moment, you're building sandcastles in Kennebunk, and the next you're waiting for a phone call from Kandahar."

The food arrived, bubbling in stainless steel bowls on a hot plate with two candles. Vanier had ordered for one, but Midhat gestured for an extra plate, sitting with his friend through the meal, and helping himself to the comforting food of a homeland he hardly knew.

When they had both eaten their fill, they sat in silence listening to a plaintive sitar solo. A waiter took away the plates and came back with a brown bag with the leftovers. Vanier left a fat tip, because he knew that when he got home he would be amazed at how much food he had been given to take home. Enough for two meals during the week, even things he couldn't remember ordering.

A honking noise broke through the sitar music and brought them back to Montreal. Tow trucks were cruising up and down the street, blaring their horns as a warning that any cars on the street were about to be towed to allow the plows to remove the snow. Vanier rose slowly, lifted the bag from the table, and reached for Midhat's outstretched hand.

"You take care of yourself, Luc."

"You too, Midhat, you too. Give my love to Jamilah and the children."

"To be sure."

Vanier walked out into the night, accelerating with each step, as he pondered the possibility of his car being towed. It was still safe. He opened the back door of the car and put the brown bag carefully on the floor, snug between the seats. Settling into the driver's seat, he turned on the radio. Bing Crosby singing "White Christmas." He turned off the radio and drove home in silence.

# FOUR
## DECEMBER 26

## 5 AM

**Vanier was nervous,** preparing himself to talk to a boy who was a man. Not a man, a soldier – a different kind of man. Vanier knew soldiers. On his mother's side they were all farmers, tied to the same patch of land for generations. But his father and his father's father had been soldiers. His father had dragged the family to every military base in Canada. Often to leave them waiting while he served overseas. More often to leave them waiting while he drank with his soldier buddies. Then one day he left them for good with an inconvenient bullet that entered his brain through the roof of his mouth and left a red splash pattern on the living room wall for Vanier's mother to clean off. Vanier had watched while she did it.

All Alex knew of his grandfather were the photos and medals, a hero his father never talked about or explained.

The phone rang at 5 minutes after 5 a.m.

"Alex?"

"Hey. Merry Christmas, Dad. How're you doing?" Vanier tried to picture his smile.

"It's me should be asking that. I'm fine. Stuck in the snow and the cold as usual. Hey, Merry Christmas, Alex."

"It's got to be better than here. Fucking desert gets to you pretty quick. So what's new with you?"

"You know how it is Alex, crime's a growth business. Close one file, open another. There's always something going on. For everyone we put away, there are two more getting out. And there are always the kids following in the father's footsteps. I guess we're fighting our own war over here."

"Yeah? They got IEDs in Montreal?"

"Well no, it's not a war, Alex. Not like what you're doing. Sorry. I just meant…"

"Yeah, I know."

"I suppose we're both fighting evil, eh?"

"I suppose. But I got bigger guns!"

"They won't be issuing C7A2s here for a while. But I bet it would get me respect in Hochelaga."

"We ain't getting respect here. They're laughing at us. Fucking government is corrupt, and we're getting shot at to keep them in business. The Afghan soldiers would sell you out in a second if they could make a deal. The place stinks."

"Alex, I saw your guys on TV the other night. It looks pretty rough over there. I worry."

"Ah come on, Dad, don't start that again. I'm here. I'm serving in this shithole, but it doesn't do me any good to know you're worrying about me. I'm not a kid."

"OK, Alex, but I'm your father. That's what fathers do, they worry."

"Yeah, but that puts pressure on me, you know."

"Look, I'm sorry. It's just that what we see here is the worst.

On TV, it's always the bad stuff."

"There's a lot of bad shit to film. It's fucking dangerous, but I'm sur-rounded by great guys, and we all look out for each other. So the jour-nalists want blood and guts and blown-up troop carriers. Maybe that's a good thing, let people know what the fuck is going on, you know?"

"I suppose. But you don't see much good news."

"Good news? There isn't any. And if you read crap in the papers about how we're changing lives, don't believe it. It's a gang of fuck-ing thieves running the country, and another gang of murdering bastards trying to take over – and neither side gives a fuck about the average Afghan."

"So you think we should leave?"

"No. Just let us do the job. We're fighting people who don't give a fuck about the Geneva Convention, and we have to do it like Boy Scouts. It burns me up."

"Don't worry, Alex. Your tour is up in four months and you can come home."

"Yeah. I guess. Anyway. Change the subject."

Vanier changed the subject. "I spoke to Élise yesterday, she sends her love."

"I know. She sent me an email. She said that you might be think-ing of joining the human race and getting Skype."

"Ha. Well, no promises, but you never know. I'll give it serious thought. Élise said she'd help me."

"Do it. You'll be amazed how easy it is once you get started."

"So, tell me, what do you do for relaxation?"

"Well, last night we had a concert with Blue Rodeo and a bunch of comedians. And we had a Christmas supper, turkey, roast po-tatoes. The food was good. We even had the Minister of Defence spooning out the gravy."

"And how was he in the kitchen?"

"He was shit in the kitchen. Just over here to get his photo taken."

"That's what the politicians are for, Alex, spooning out the shit!"

"Yeah, that's funny. It's true. But my time's up. I gotta go. There are guys lined up behind me, Merry Christmas, Dad. Take care."

"Love you, Alex. Take care."

The phone clicked dead. Vanier picked up the cold coffee and focused on the conversation, trying to recognize what was really said; the statements, the inflections, the pauses. It was a police technique to squeeze meaning from everything. Often what was unsaid was the most important. He knew that he couldn't understand what it meant to serve in Afghanistan. But he knew enough to be scared. He was scared for Alex. And scared of what he recognized in his son. When Vanier was honest with himself, and it didn't happen often, he saw in Alex the same attitude that he saw in the violent scumbags that he spent his life trying to shut down. And when he tried to dismiss those thoughts, he'd think of his father, and know his fears were justified.

It was still dark outside. The sun wouldn't rise until after seven. Vanier looked down on the white and grey city. He turned back from the window and put the half cup of coffee into the microwave and pushed one minute. It was steaming when he took it out. He thought about cooling it with a shot of whiskey and decided against it.

## 8.30 AM

Vanier pulled into the parking lot of Police Headquarters and saw Chief Inspector Bédard's car parked in its reserved spot nearest the door. It was a bad sign. There was nothing going on except the homeless deaths, and Vanier hated to think that the Chief Inspector was taking a special interest in the case.

Even in the quick walk to the door Vanier felt the cold. It was at least minus twenty Celsius, and he didn't think it was going to get any warmer. The last storm was long gone, and the temperature had tumbled under the cloudless sky. The only consolation was the sunlight.

In the first floor Squad Room, Sylvie St. Jacques was pinning photos and coloured arrows to a map of downtown Montreal mounted on corkboard, putting together the visual layout of what had happened. Sergeants Janvier and Roberge were staring at computer screens, and D.S. Laurent was reading a newspaper. When he saw Vanier, he held up the *Journal de Montréal*, his bald head disappearing behind it. The headline read: "Santa Slays the Homeless."

"And a good morning to you too," said Vanier.

"The Chief asked to see you as soon as you got in," Laurent said.

"Shit."

It was the last thing Vanier needed after a few hours sleep on the couch. He took the newspaper from Laurent and opened it to the main story, scanning it quickly. It was accurate, with too many details, even down to Santa as a suspect.

"They got everything pretty much right, didn't they?" said Vanier. "But they don't know anything we don't know. I suppose that's a good thing. How do they know about Santa?"

"My guess is someone in the Métro Security told them," said Laurent. "The only ones that knew about the Santa character are us and the Métro guys. It had to be one of them."

"And where did they get the murder angle? Suspicious, yes, but murder?"

"Suspicious doesn't sell papers, sir. Mass murderer on the loose gets people out of their beds to buy the rags."

"I suppose you're right," said Vanier, imagining what the Chief would make of it. The Chief had probably already taken calls from the Mayor.

Vanier glanced at the other newspapers lying on the desk. They each had the story on the front page. *The Gazette*: "Christmas

Spirit Dies With Five Homeless Deaths;" *The Globe and Mail*: "Mass Murderer in Montreal?;" *La Presse*: "Homeless Deaths Ruled Suspicious;" and the *National Post*: "Métro Deaths: Montreal's Homeless at Risk." Only *Le Devoir*, Montreal's intellectual daily, reputed to have a paid circulation in the high three figures, was understated: "System Failing the Homeless." Only the *Journal de Montréal* had the Santa angle.

Vanier turned to leave, "I'm off to see the Chief."

As he passed St. Jacques, she turned to him. "I'll be finished with this in a few minutes."

"You're doing a great job," Vanier said, glancing at the map as he walked out.

## 9 AM

Chief Inspector Bédard's door was open, the secretary who usually guarded his lair off for the holidays. The Chief was sitting behind his desk in full dress uniform reading the papers. When you started as a cop, you got a uniform, and if you climbed the ladder high enough, you finished with a better uniform, but there were two differences between recruits and the polished brass. The obvious one was the amount of equipment you carried on your belt; recruits had more stuff hanging from their belts than New Guinea headhunters. Vanier sometimes thought that when he retired he could make a fortune designing stuff that could be attached to the belts of recruits. The Chief had nothing, not even a gun. The other difference was the amount of bullshit you could generate and consume before you felt sick. Recruits had a low tolerance for bullshit, but if you wanted to rise up the ladder, you had to develop a taste for it.

Vanier walked in and stood in front of the Chief's desk, waiting for him to look up, examining the fat that bulged under his uniform. He was like a giant, over-ripe pear with his neck bulging three chins out of a white shirt collar. Bédard looked up warily.

"Good morning, Luc, sit down."

Vanier dropped into the wooden chair in front of the desk, and the two men stared at each other in a test of who would speak first. There was no contest. Vanier was still a working cop, and Bédard broke.

"The press, Luc. How does *Journal de Montréal* know more about this investigation than I do? Am I supposed to read the damn newspapers to know what is going on in my own squad? Does that make sense?"

Again the stare, eye to eye, Bédard trying to remember the old days interrogating suspects. Vanier stared back.

"No, sir. But they have more staff than we do. We've been working with close to zero."

"It's Christmas, Luc. I know how you feel. But all you have are five suspicious deaths. I can't cancel leave on the basis of a suspicion. It's going to take time to find out how they died. Even so, I need to show some progress. Results, Luc, I need some results. And I need to know what's going on.

"Does that mean that I get more officers?"

"No. Not unless you tell me that you have something real to go on. Are these five deaths a coincidence, or do we have a maniac on the loose?"

"We don't know yet. It could be nothing, sir."

"I know that. But the papers don't think it's nothing. Have you seen the TV? It's the first story on every newscast. Before long, the entire city will be yelling for answers. The Mayor called me at home last night. Did you ever try to bullshit the Mayor?"

"No, sir. I've never spoken to the Mayor. But I suspect that he recognizes bullshit."

"He's an expert. He can recognize it a mile away. And I don't want to be giving him too much."

"Sir, we're doing what we can. Any available officers you can throw our way would be appreciated. That way, you can tell the Mayor that you're dedicating resources to the case."

"I know what I can tell the goddamn Mayor, Luc. And I *am* dedicating resources to the case, Luc. You have a bloody team. What leads are you following?"

"Sir, we've got a good start on the identities, and we're following up with the families and people who knew them. We're canvassing the shelters and other spots to see what we can find out. We're also following up on Santa suit rentals. Even without a cause of death, that's a lot of work, sir. The more people we have, the quicker we can get through all the details. With more manpower we can cover leads faster."

"Look, I'll see what I can do about extra officers. In the meantime do what you can. And Luc, you have my numbers, call me. When the Mayor calls I have to answer the phone even if I'm taking a shit. I want to be able to give him something more than he can read in this rag," he said, gesturing at the *Journal de Montréal*. "I can't have him knowing more than I do just because his staff spoke to the bloody journalists. Treat this as a mass murder until we know it's not. Pull out all stops, Luc. I need results. Do you understand?"

"Yes, sir. So, does that mean that I'm off budget? Even if I don't get extra people, can we authorize overtime?"

"Luc, you know that we're close to year-end, and I'm not going to piss away a good year because we panicked before we knew anything for sure. If you can tell me there's a mass murderer loose, things will change. For the moment, do what you can with the resources you have."

"What we have is a skeleton staff. Everyone is off singing carols."

"People need family time at Christmas. Luc, do what you can. Give me something."

"Yes, sir," said Vanier. Figuring the meeting had ended, he got up from the chair.

"And think about this, Luc. How do these journalists know so much about this situation? Some of them were on top of this from the start. There are details here," he said, lifting the paper for emphasis. "Stuff that only someone connected to the investigation would know: the Santa character, the unknown cause of death, the absence of a suspect. How do they know so much? Find out who it is, Luc. I don't want anyone from my squad talking to the press."

"Neither do I, sir, but I don't think that it's one of our people. It's probably someone in the Métro Security."

"Luc, if there is a madman loose I want you to catch him. I don't want this played out in the media. And keep me informed of every move that you make."

"Yes, sir." Vanier turned and grabbed the door handle to leave.

"And, Luc, why didn't you call me?"

"I did, sir," Vanier lied, turning back to face him. "I called yesterday on your cell number. I couldn't get through."

"Well, OK. Sorry. I may have had my cell phone off for a few hours. You know how it is, Christmas and all. Anyway, from now on keep me informed."

"Absolutely, sir. In fact, after my meeting with the team, I'll call to debrief you."

Bédard was on the phone before Vanier closed the door.

## 9.45 AM

D.S. St. Jacques had transformed one wall of the Squad Room, pinning photos of the five victims *in situ* on the map of downtown Montreal, with arrows leading from them to the places they were discovered. Next to each photo she had pinned a bullet-point list of what was known of each of the victims. Most of that came from Vanier's notes on their possessions. Off to the side were several of the clearest prints of Santa, but nothing approaching a clear face shot. He was tall, probably six two or three, not overweight. His costume made it difficult to tell, but he looked fit.

Vanier took a seat. "So what do we know?"

St. Jacques looked over to Laurent and saw that he wasn't going to take the lead.

"Well, sir, we have five unexplained deaths on Christmas Eve. From your work yesterday with the possessions, we have four unverified identifications: George Morissette, found at McGill, Joe Yeoman and Edith Latendresse, both found at Berri, and Pierre Brun in Cabot Park. We need to confirm the identifications and get a positive I.D. on the fifth. We've started tracking down the next of kin, and we also need to find the possessions of the fifth victim."

"The identities are verified," said Vanier. "Dr. Grenier confirmed them from the photos. We have names and ages. The fifth victim is Céline Plante, 52 years old, well, almost 52. An alcoholic who has been on the streets for most of her life. And Dr. Grenier says they were all terminally ill. What else?"

St. Jacques looked at Vanier. "That's all I know," he said. "The bastard wouldn't give me specifics."

St. Jacques continued. "The Coroner's office reports that they can do two or three autopsies today and the rest tomorrow."

"Ask them to request the medical records from Grenier. He refused to turn them over without an official request."

"Will do," said St. Jacques. "There's not much else. We're waiting to learn more from the Coroner."

"We have a person of interest, Father Henri Drouin. He's not a suspect, but I want to talk to him in a bad way. He's a priest who works in the Cathedral, and Dr. Grenier says he was the spiritual advisor to the victims and knew them all. I went looking for him last night, and he's disappeared. We need to find him as quickly as possible. Any luck on the Santa suits?"

"Not much, sir. There were almost 400 Santa suits rented out over the holidays. Four different companies – two downtown, one in NDG, and the other in Laval. We've talked to the owners of all the stores, and they're all ready to show their records."

"OK. Have a couple of officers pick them up and bring them to their stores. No, forget Laval for the moment. Let's concentrate on the Island. Not all Santa suits are the same, so bring photos of our Santa and get the names and addresses of everyone who rented a similar suit. See if they recognize anything special. And tell them that when the rentals come back, they should check for dirt and moisture and hold onto anything that looks that looks like it was worn outside. You can't go wandering around in the middle of winter in a Santa costume without getting wet."

"Yes, sir," said St. Jacques. "Oh, and the Coroner's office is having someone dig out what they can on any similar deaths in the last year. They said that it might take some time but I'll keep after them. Nobody seems to keep records on the numbers. I called the city, the hospitals, the shelters. Nobody counts them but people were guessing anywhere from twenty to forty people, depending on what you include: drug overdoses, beatings or just plain natural causes."

"Any calls?"

"Since I came on shift, we've had 23," said Janvier. I'm taking them with D.S. Roberge."

"Anything interesting?"

"Nothing on the victims. The usual crap on Santa: looks like my cousin Pierre, that sort of thing. We're taking the details but it's going to take time to check them all out. But look at the photos. You can't see the guy's face, and he's dressed in a costume."

"So how did the papers get the photos? Can someone talk to Morneau and see if he has any ideas?"

"Yes, sir. I'll do it," said Janvier.

"So, St. Jacques, you keep following up with the Santa suits.

Janvier and Roberge, keep on the phones and let me know if anything strange turns up. See if you can track down next of kin. And can we all try to figure out who's feeding the press? Laurent, you and I are going to find Father Drouin."

Vanier's phone rang. He fished it out of his pocket and didn't recognize the number.

"Vanier," he said.

"Inspector Vanier, this is Sergeant Julie Laflamme. Just calling to tell you that I've had a call from Chief Inspector Bédard. He wants me to handle the media on the homeless cases. I am on my way to Montreal now, and I wanted to ask you not to make any public statements until we have had a chance to talk. Is that OK, sir?"

"Perfect, Sergeant Laflamme. When are you proposing to get here?"

"I should be there in two hours. I was skiing in Tremblant. I'm trying to set up a press conference for 3 p.m. They're clamouring for information, but let's keep things quiet until then, Inspector. It's important that we manage the communications on this one, sir."

"Sergeant Laflamme, the media seem to be doing pretty well without any help from me. But you have my word on it. I'll hang up on any journalist who calls me. See you soon." Vanier clicked disconnect.

Turning to Laurent, Vanier asked, "Who were you with on Christmas Eve? I didn't see anyone."

"D.S. Fletcher, sir. He worked Christmas Eve, but he's off today."

"So where was he when I was there?"

"He was interviewing staff, I think. It'll be in his notes. He's been following up, though. I spoke to him twice this morning."

"Can't he let it go? It's Christmas, for Christ's sake."

"He's keen on the case. He wants to be up to speed when he gets back."

The phone on Laurent's desk rang. He picked it up and listened.

"OK. Thanks."

He replaced the receiver and looked up at Vanier.

"Father Drouin is downstairs. He showed up at the front desk and said that you had been looking for him."

"Have them put him in Interview Room 2. I'll talk to him. You watch from outside. Make sure that we get it all on tape. I want a transcript. Let's go."

They took the elevator down to the basement. The building was quiet. Headquarters was on minimal staff, with officers taking a short break from the madness, trying to build family as kids laughed and friends told stories. Vanier wondered why Fletcher couldn't let go. Why was he calling for updates?

## 10.30 AM

Interview Room 2 was designed to elicit the kind of communication that occurs between doomed miners trapped hundreds of feet below ground, intimate, and of no consequence to the outside world. It was a stark, windowless box, empty except for a table and two chairs, with a two-way mirror built into one wall. The mirror encouraged introspection. Father Henri Drouin sat on one of the flimsy plastic chairs, his shoulders sagging and his eyes staring at the floor. Vanier walked in carrying a yellow note-pad and a brown envelope, nodding at Drouin without saying anything. Drouin half rose from his seat and returned to his sitting position. Vanier reached out his hand, and Drouin stood again to shake it, looking like he hadn't laughed in twenty years, like he was carrying an invisible weight.

"I'm Detective Inspector Vanier, Major Crime Squad. I was looking for you last night at the Cathedral. The priest who answered the door said that you disappeared after lunch and nobody knew where you were."

"It's a problem that I have, Inspector. Every Christmas it's the same thing. The priestly equivalent of post-partum depression, I suppose."

Vanier thought that was an attempt at humour, but checked himself. Drouin was serious. "Are you depressed?"

Drouin sat up. "Advent is such a wonderful time in the Church, building up inexorably to that glorious moment when our Saviour is born. The churches gradually fill with the faithful until Christmas morning, when it's standing room only for the flock adoring their Creator. And then, the next moment, it's empty again. They're only there for the show. When I look at the packed church at Christmas, I can't help thinking how empty it will be after the last service, and how it will stay empty for most of the year."

"The three Bs, I suppose," said Vanier.

"What?"

"Baptism, bondage and burial. Most people only want the church to be there for the baptism, the wedding and to see them off in style at the end."

"Something like that, Inspector. It's the church as theatre, and Christmas is a perennial favourite. It's always a shock, and I've never learned to deal with it. I get angry. Then I get sad and question myself. Then I question the faithful. Then I question the church itself. With experience, I have found that the best thing to do is to just get away."

"So where did you go yesterday?"

"I went to my family, to my sister and her husband in Dorval. That was a mistake. They have their children and their Christmas is for the children, you know, presents first, video games and toys, then a feast and as little thought about Our Lord as they can manage. I'm an embarrassment to her."

"I'm sure that's not true," said Vanier.

"Oh, she loves me, in her own way, but she thinks that I've wasted my life."

"And what do you think?"

The priest looked up at Vanier, but didn't answer.

"So how long did you stay?"

"They had guests, and I saw I was holding them back. My presence seemed to remind them of what Christmas was supposed to be. I was making everyone uncomfortable. So I stayed for an hour, perhaps an hour and a half, and then I left. I drove back to town and parked at the Cathedral."

"So what time did you get back to the Cathedral?"

"Around 5.30, maybe six o'clock, I suppose. But I didn't want to go in. I decided to go for a walk. Around Old Montreal mostly, it was beautiful, very quiet and peaceful. There was hardly any traffic. Walking through the old streets I felt that I was back in a Quebec of the past. In a Quebec that still believed in Christ. It was comforting." The priest drifted off, remembering his walk, Vanier waited for him to come back.

"So what did you want to see me about, Inspector?"

"I am investigating the deaths of five homeless people on Christmas Eve. Your name came up as someone who might know the victims."

"I've seen the newspapers. You think they were killed, Inspector?"

"I didn't say that. Right now, I don't think anything. I just want to find out who these people were. We've got their names, but we don't know anything about them. I thought you could give us some information about who they were."

Vanier sat back into the chair like someone with nowhere to go, but desperately in need of a rest. He stared at the wall, giving Drouin room to talk.

Drouin waited.

Vanier barely stirred. "I'm tired. Maybe it's the season," he said, almost to himself. "This time of the year is difficult for many people, isn't it, Father?"

Drouin was lost in thought and didn't respond immediately. Finally he said, "It should be a time of rejoicing."

"I haven't been rejoicing. You know what I have been doing?

70

I've been pulling corpses out of holes. At this time of year, who wants to do that? But you know what keeps me going? These people were daughters and sons, maybe sisters or brothers. Maybe they even had children, grown children. Grown children celebrating Christmas in their own families while their mother or father slept on the street. Did anyone spend a few seconds this Christmas wondering where any of these people were? Christmas is a time for families isn't it, Father Drouin? No matter how dysfunctional. And yet they all died alone. I suppose that's what hit me the most. Five deaths in one night, and they all died alone. That shouldn't happen at Christmas."

Vanier sat up and pulled the pack of photographs out of the envelope. He laid each of them out on the table in front of Drouin.

"Do you recognize any of these people?"

Drouin leaned over and examined each photo carefully. "Yes, Inspector. I know all of them." He began pointing to each photograph. "Céline, Joe Yeoman, Madame Latendresse, Pierre Brun, and George Morissette. They were all what we call clients. I ministered to them. It's hard to believe they are all dead in one night."

"You don't seem shocked."

"I am beyond shock, Inspector. When I saw the reports in the newspapers I knew that I would probably know some of them. I don't know what's happening. I have to believe that God is at work. But He knows so many ways to test us poor humans."

Vanier pulled a pen out of his pocket and began writing as Drouin talked, scribbling bits and pieces of information of the lives of the unknown. Even though the interview was being taped, he felt compelled to take notes, to write things down. Scribbling scraps of information in an effort to create individuals where before there had been only empty space, to make people out of corpses.

Laurent watched through the two-way mirror as Drouin released every scrap of information he had on the five. Vanier slouched in his chair but he was listening intently, for similarities and for differences, to hear what connected them, other than their common status at the bottom of the pile. Drouin talked of people who used drugs and alcohol to feel nothing, and of the more effective disconnection of mental illness. He talked of diets of hostel meals and rotten food scavenged from dumpsters at the back of restaurants, clothes picked from piles of cast-offs with nothing ever fitting or doing the job of keeping you warm or your feet dry. And he talked of the terror of street life in the winter, when the choice was between a quiet, dark corner where you might never wake up or a single bed in a warehouse of coughing, ranting, fighting, and crying outcasts like yourself. Each of the victims was a walking encyclopedia of medical disorders: scabs and sores that never healed on the outside, and fevers, diseases, and delusions that ate away the inside.

Drouin's streets were full of thieves, con men, liars, murderers, and bullies, people who were by turn predators and victims, depending on circumstances and opportunity. Alcoholics who craved nothing but a deadening slumber. Young girls taking their first hit in a desperate search for happiness. And end-of-the-road junkies secretly hoping the next trip would be their last. Men, women and children selling their bodies because that was all they had left to sell. Children running from abuse. The depressed, the schizophrenics, the paranoid, the delusional who don't know what planet they're on, and the just plain unlucky souls life has decided to torture. A population of modern-day Jobs, invisible to all, including Vanier.

He learned about the individuals.

Pierre Brun, who appeared every winter and disappeared again in the late spring, nobody knew where. Some said to a farm in the country, others that he walked to the Maritimes and back. He never said. He just disappeared every June to reappear in October. Nobody remembers seeing Brun in Montreal in the summer.

The completely and irredeemably mad Madame Latendresse, who had more interaction with the voices in her head in one hour than she had in a week with any human. If you got her to speak, she was disappointed to have been dragged away from her imaginary friends and impatient to return to them.

Céline Plante, an alcoholic prostitute who knew nothing but life on the street from the time she was 12 years old. When Vanier suggested that, given her state, she might have been a former prostitute, Drouin disagreed; there was always a market, no matter how rotten the fruit. From time to time she would show up at the various missions and shelters, and most times she would be refused because she was drunk. She worried about her diminishing client base but couldn't imagine any way out.

George Morissette, a notary whose wife and only child died 30 years ago in a fire in their cottage up north. That was at the end of the summer he had skipped cleaning the chimney to save $50. He had spent thirty years dying with them. It took him twenty years to descend from notary to bum, but he had managed it with the help of the bottle and a broken spirit. It took ten years to descend from bum to corpse.

Finally, there was Joe Yeoman, a Mohawk whose life was a progression in and out of prison; who used anything, drugs, alcohol, sex, or violence, to numb whatever pain he felt.

"Father Drouin, can you think of a link between these five people? A person, maybe, or even a place? Did they know one another?"

"Inspector, the homeless live in a small world. They know everyone in their brutal village. Their world is so small that what connects them is trivial compared to what keeps them separate. All paths cross. From what I read in the papers, these people were found where they were sleeping for the night. It may be hard for you to imagine, Inspector, but if you have a place to sleep for the night, you have a sanctuary. These people were found dead in their sanctuaries. For people like this, a place where you can be alone and safe is a prize, and there are only a limited number of such places in any city.

What the human spirit needs, even the homeless, is privacy. When you go home at night and close your door, I assume you can be alone, even when you live with someone you love. Imagine never being able to do that. Imagine never having a private moment. That's why for some lucky ones, there is a secret place where they can stay warm and unmolested for a whole night, perhaps longer. When a street person finds such a place, it must be protected. It must be approached with caution, for fear that others will discover it. Imagine, Inspector, if you haven't slept warmly or with any privacy for months, what it would mean to find one space where you could lie down and sleep undisturbed for an entire night. It would be a dream. These people seemed to have found their private space. Where they were found may have been their sanctuary.

"If these people were murdered, it wasn't random, it was by someone that knew where they slept, and I can't think of anyone they would have trusted with that knowledge."

"That's an interesting point, Father. If I wanted to learn more about who these people were and who knew them, what should I do?"

"You could start with the shelters. They're the great centres of traffic for the displaced. Some are exclusively for men and others take only women; some take both, but in different facilities. And it's not just for the overnight stays, it's for the lunches or dinners. These five would have used several different shelters. If you use one shelter too much, you get pressured to begin a program, and none of these would have started a program. After the shelters, there are the drop-in centres, usually in church basements. In the drop-in centres, street people can escape the cold by paying the modest price of exposing themselves to volunteers who want to save their souls. Then there are the meeting points, the low traffic corners of the city that street people have made their own. You would be amazed how many such spots there are, Inspector."

"These people would have a fairly regular existence?

"Of course, they are human beings like you and me, Inspector. We all have routines and follow them. The homeless have routines, too. You just have to be able to see them. Haven't you ever seen the same person every day at a particular spot? With each of these five, if I wanted to find them on a particular day, it wouldn't be too hard. They all had more or less regular routines; areas of the city where they hung around, shelters they frequented, parks or lost corners of the city where they rested during the day."

"And who are the people that connect these five?"

"Well, to start with, me, I suppose. I ministered to them all. But there are many others, Inspector. The people who work at the shelters and the drop-in centres, the social workers, the doctors, the nurses. That may seem like a lot, but think about all of the people you have contact with every day. With these people, it's possible to name everyone who might have had some real contact with them. I doubt you could say that about you or even me."

Vanier resisted the urge to tell him that he knew what it was like to go an entire weekend without talking to anyone other than clerks at the supermarket and the liquor store.

"How did you minister to them, Father Drouin?" asked Vanier.

"I talked to them. No, more importantly, I listened to them. I got to know them. And I'll tell you something, Inspector, I loved each one of them. If these people were murdered, you must find the person who did that. These people were children of God, not garbage. Society would like to ignore them. But remember, Jesus said, *Whatsoever you do to the least of my brothers, you do unto me.*"

Vanier tried to look beyond all the priests he had known, and tried to understand the man in front of him.

"So what were you doing on Christmas Eve, Father?"

"I've told you. Christmas is a very difficult time for me. I battle resentment. I resent all those people who show up in church only at Christmas, all those seasonal Christians. God's house is full one or two days a year and empty all of the others. I can't understand that. I want to tell these people if you don't believe, don't come, don't waste your time and mine. And yet I have to welcome them. And I have to work very hard at being welcoming."

"So where were you on Christmas Eve?"

"I was free until Midnight Mass when I was needed for the big show with all the costumes. I skipped supper. I went for a walk at about 4.30 and didn't come back to the Cathedral until about an hour before Mass. About 10.30, I suppose."

"Where did you go?"

"I walked, Inspector. There was a snowstorm. It was like being in one of those glass souvenir balls that you shake to make the snowflakes float all around. It was beautiful. The city was silent and I felt God's presence. Perhaps that's an occupational hazard, but it was peaceful in the storm. I felt like I was walking with God. I walked for hours."

"You walked for six hours?"

"I suppose so. Is that odd?"

"Did you meet anyone, talk to anyone?"

"No. I avoided contact. If I saw someone approaching, I crossed the street. Sometimes I would turn into a side street and walk the other way to avoid contact. I craved solitude. Well, not solitude exactly. I just didn't want to share the experience. As I said, I felt like I was walking with God and I didn't want to share that with anyone."

"And what time did you get back?"

"I told you. I got back to the Cathedral at 10.30.

"Who was the first person you saw when you got back?"

"Monsignor Forlini, when I presented myself for duty. That would have been about 11."

"So, just so that I can get this clear, between 4.30 p.m. and 11 p.m. on Christmas Eve, there is nobody who can confirm where you were?"

"That's correct, Inspector. I suppose you could say I was missing in action during that period."

"Father Drouin, do you own a Santa suit?"

Drouin looked at Vanier as though he had asked if he wore a yarmulke.

"That's what's wrong with Christmas. Christmas is about Jesus Christ, not Santa Claus. Christmas is the celebration of the birth of humanity's Savior. And Santa Claus is the last thing that Christians should be thinking about. So, to answer your question, Inspector, no, I don't have a Santa Claus costume."

"I need to ask these questions, Father," said Vanier.

"I understand, Inspector. If someone killed these poor people, you must find him."

"I intend to," said Vanier. "I will probably have more questions for you. But that's it for now."

"Anything I can do to help, just ask me. You know where I am."

"I do, Father."

Through the two-way mirror, Laurent watched both men rise from the table. Vanier led Drouin out and walked him down to the main entrance, and waited in the cold while he went to his car. The priest didn't look back.

Vanier returned and joined Laurent in the viewing room.

"What do you think, sir?" asked Laurent.

"I don't know. I'm struggling to get over my prejudices against the Church, trying to see him simply as a man with a mission to love his fellow man. I have no problem understanding people who dedicate their lives to others. But I don't get the inner joy from him. People who do this type of work, the ones I've seen exude goodwill, they're happy. Drouin is angry, not joyful. Maybe he was shocked by the deaths. Who knows? But he was missing when Santa was giving out his gifts."

"So he's a suspect?"

"Damn right. So let's see what we can find out about him. Get some history, but do it delicately. I don't want the Archbishop calling the Chief. And nail down the time of the last image of Santa in the Métro. Would he have had time to get back to the Cathedral for 10.30? While you're at it, check out the alibi. Can we get confirmation that he was seen at 11?"

"I'll get onto it."

## 12.45 PM

There was a line of people waiting in the numbing cold to be let into the Holy Land Shelter for lunch. A few were recognizable as down-and-out street people, but others would not have been out of place on the bus, or in the checkout line at the supermarket. Some were only boys trying their best to look like men; others looked old before their time. Most of those in line ignored Vanier and Laurent as they walked past, but some instinctively reached out a hand with an ingratiating smile, unable to miss an opportunity to ask for change.

Laurent held the door for Vanier and followed him into the warmth. Their path was blocked by an unsmiling man standing like a nightclub bouncer in a suit cut tight to emphasize muscle that you can only build with regular work with weights.

"Don't I know you?" Vanier asked, searching his memory for a name.

"I've met a lot of cops. After a while they all look the same. Know what I mean?"

"We're looking for M. Nolet."

"Through those doors, to your right."

The detectives started to move towards the door, and then Vanier stopped. "Audet. Marcel Audet, isn't it? You were put away, what was it, seven years ago?"

"Yeah. And? I've done my time."

"Got lucky, didn't you? The poor bastard didn't die from the beating, just became a vegetable. So it was assault, not murder. Now you're back out on the street."

"Like I said, I've done my time."

"And the other guy's probably still hooked up to some machine somewhere, wishing you'd come back and finish him off."

"That's all behind me. I'm clean. I've found a purpose in life."

"I bet you have," said Vanier.

"What do you know? When you deal with filth every day, you become filth," he said, turning away from Vanier.

Audet walked to the front doors and opened them, letting the patrons stream in. He had them well trained. There was no pushing or shoving. They were on their best behaviour, like schoolchildren passing the headmaster. Vanier watched the parade of desperate men shuffling towards a meal. He didn't believe in change. Once a villain, always a villain. He turned to follow the directions to Nolet's office, and his path was blocked again, this time by a short balding man with a broad smile.

"I am Nolet. You were looking for me?"

Vanier was puzzled until he noticed the closed circuit cameras. *Christ, they'll have them in churches next.*

"You have closed circuit TV in a homeless shelter?" asked Vanier.

"We have a difficult clientele. Certain security measures are in the best interests of everyone. How can I help you?"

"We'd like to talk to you about the five people found dead on Christmas Eve. Is there somewhere we can talk?"

"Yes, of course," said Nolet, looking quickly to Audet as though he was asking permission. Audet turned away from them. "Let's go to my office."

The desk and chairs were the throwaway type. A threadbare orange carpet covered the floor, and papers covered the desk. In contrast to the cheapness of the rest of the office, a bank of six television monitors flickered with images from different parts of the shelter. Nolet seemed to feel the need to explain.

"Times have changed, gentlemen. We live in a tough world and we have to take steps to protect our guests. Fights and thefts are common. So we had a security system installed."

Vanier stared at the screens. They covered the spot where people lined up to enter the shelter, the doorway, the dining room, what looked like a recreation room, and the two massive dormitories.

"Very impressive, M. Nolet. What are you scared of?"

"I am not scared, Inspector. I've worked here fifteen years, and I understand the clientele. They don't scare me. To tell you the truth, I hardly use the cameras but M. Audet finds them useful. And I must admit that there are fewer incidents since he joined us. He seems to have a knack for keeping things under control."

"And when was that, M. Nolet."

"What?"

"When did M. Audet join you?"

"Maybe four months ago. The new Board decided that we needed a stronger hand to beef up security."

"So it wasn't your choice?"

"I didn't disagree. I knew his background and I was happy to give him a chance to turn his life around."

Laurent was distracted, looking at the television monitors.

"M. Audet has had quite an influence on this place since he's been here. He manages the shelter on a day-to-day basis. He's Operations Manager, that's the title the Board gave him. That frees me up to do more important work, like raising funds, buying supplies and the like, making sure we don't go bankrupt. He has a firm hand, but you need that around here."

Nolet moved behind the desk and motioned them to sit in the two chairs in front. He gathered the papers on the desk and moved them to the side, folding his hands in the cleared space. Vanier pulled the photographs out of the envelope and placed them face up on the desk.

"We think we have their names but would like you to confirm any that you know."

Nolet picked up each photograph and named each one.

"What do you know about them?"

"They were all hardcore street people, desperate cases – and we know desperate in this business. These are the kind of people who brought me into this work. Back in those days, I thought I could change things, you know, really help people. But, I've known Joe Yeoman for close to twenty years, and nothing's changed. The others, ten, fifteen years each. It doesn't matter. You know what I've learned over twenty years? We can't change them. Sometimes we can make them comfortable, but their fate is what it is. Or was, I suppose. And worse than that, they kill the idealism that was in you. They don't change, but you do. You get hard, immune. It's a tough life, Inspector."

"You don't seem surprised that they're dead."

"Surprised? No. With these, and too many others, it's just a matter of time. You get to recognize it, Inspector, when people are on their way out."

"I can understand that, M. Nolet, but all five on Christmas Eve?"

"Coincidences don't happen. Is that it? You sound like an educated man, Inspector, and I get educated people in here all the time, from the universities or the government. Like they just figured out the solution to the problem. They tell me about the importance of measurement, of empirical data: probabilities, cause and effect, action and consequence, and all that shit. Last week someone told me that if you can't measure it, you can't manage it, like that was supposed to help me. Well, I know a little bit about statistics. I understand the odds. And let me tell you, statistics don't predict real life. Real life happens. Shit happens. So all five of them died on Christmas Eve. You know what's surprising? That they weren't all dead years ago. They defied the odds for years. And, you know what the tragedy is? It's the lives that they led for the last twenty years.

You didn't come to me last month and ask why these people were on the streets. That's the goddamn crime."

"M. Nolet, if these people were killed on Christmas Eve, I want to find out who did it."

"You're right, I'm sorry. If they were killed, that's just one more affront they shouldn't have had to endure. It's just I don't believe they were killed."

"Why not?"

"Because nobody cared enough about them to kill them."

"Maybe somebody did."

"It will be a first. What do you need to know?"

"Well, when was the last time you saw them?"

"That's difficult, Inspector. Of course, if they stayed the night, there would be a record. But we don't keep records of people who simply come in for a meal. And these were not regular sleepers. We have rules here, and lots of people can't deal with the rules. Doors close at eight o'clock, a shower and a shave and in bed by nine. No smoking, no booze, and no drugs. We're not running a hotel here. That's why so many still stay out, even in winter."

"Could you check your records and let me know if any of them stayed overnight in the last month?"

"Of course, Inspector."

"And the monitors," Vanier pointed to the bank of screens. "Do you keep the tapes?"

"Well, I'm not an expert, but I'm told that everything is held on a disc for forty-eight hours, and then it disappears. So that won't help you. Everything before Christmas will be gone."

"Did they have any friends?"

"Friends? Inspector, these people don't have friends. They might have a regular spot where they go and whoever is there is their friend for the moment. If they don't show up, they're not missed. This is a sad community of loners. Look," he said, pointing at one of the monitors, "that's the dining room. What do you see?"

They looked up to see men sitting around tables and servers passing out food.

"Who's talking to who?"

When asked to look for one, the officers saw a pattern. The servers touched shoulders and elbows and whispered into ears while depositing plates. Some diners reacted with a smile, others didn't. But between the diners, there was silence. It wasn't so much a communal meal but a hundred men eating alone.

"Our people are trained to say a word or two to everyone. Food for the soul you might say. But look at how our clients act with each other."

"It's like there's no one there," said Laurent.

"Right. If you're living on the street, you're alone."

Laurent was staring intently at one monitor. Then he got up and moved to the wall behind the door just as Audet came bursting in. Nolet rose sheepishly to his feet like a child caught sitting in his father's chair.

"I was just..." Nolet said to Audet.

Audet ignored him, turning to Vanier. "You still here?"

Vanier grinned at Audet.

"Very useful, these monitors, M. Audet," said Laurent.

Audet spun around to face Laurent.

"So, why would you be assaulting one of your own clients?" asked Laurent.

"What the fuck are you talking about?"

"On screen three. About ten minutes ago. I saw you punch an old man in the stomach. He fell to his knees. What was that about, M. Audet?"

"Listen, my job is to keep order. It's for everyone's good. If someone gets out of hand, well, I have to calm them down. That's all. I didn't do any damage to him. I just calmed him down."

"He didn't look excited, M. Audet. He was eating his dinner.

Looked like you called him over, said a few words in his ear, and then punched him in the stomach. It looked like an unprovoked assault to me, M. Audet."

"Well, why don't you go see him? See if he wants to press charges." Audet pushed passed Nolet and sat down behind the desk. It might have been Nolet's office, but Audet was in charge.

"Now, if you're finished wasting my time, I've got work to do."

Vanier rose, "Thank you, gentlemen."

In the parking lot, Vanier turned to look back at the shelter before getting into his car and saw Audet staring at them from the office window.

"Curious," said Vanier, as he turned the ignition.

"What's that, sir?" asked Laurent, buckling himself into the passenger seat.

"Marcel Audet, working in a homeless shelter. A man more at home kicking the life out of a bum than helping him into his pajamas. What's he up to? "

"Conversion is out of the question?"

"Conversion? Doesn't happen with people like that. When he punched that guy, he was showing his authority, you know, like a schoolyard bully, one punch just to show who's boss. He's not changed. Only question is, what's he up to?"

Vanier was lost in thought as they drove west along St. Antoine, parallel with the Ville Marie expressway, the unofficial border between rich and poor. North of the expressway were the offices and high-rises of downtown; south were the working-class neighbourhoods of the Point and St-Henri, whose proximity to downtown was making them vulnerable.

In most cities, the poor clung as close to downtown as they could, while the middle classes and the jobs moved to satellite towns along circling freeways that sucked the heart out of a city. But Montreal is an island, and the drift out of downtown wasn't an easy option. Everyone wanted to live on the island to avoid nightmare commutes across the bridges. So, instead of retreating to the leafy suburbs and leaving the poor to reign over a hollow shell of an empty city, the rich have been fighting the poor in a street-by-street campaign for territory. Gentrification almost always wins, pushing the working poor out, or limiting them to the least accessible enclaves. The Ville Marie expressway used to be a natural barrier, a concrete river that repelled the condominium developers, but now the concrete river had been forded. Condominium projects in abandoned factories next to the canal served as beachheads from which developers launched drawn-out campaigns to take block after block of the surrounding neighbourhood. Working class communities that had thrived for generations in the shadow of downtown were being destroyed as condo developments raised rents and made the poor unwelcome in their own streets. Families scattered to find affordable places to live, always further away, and, inevitably, with less of a community than they had known before.

"Tell you what, Laurent. When you get a chance, get me a list of everyone who's involved with Holy Land Shelter, employees, management. Don't forget the Board of Directors. These places usually have a Board stacked with upstanding members of the community. Nolet said that Audet was brought in by the new Board. What's going on? See who's involved. As much as you can find out."

Laurent was lost. "You think there may be a connection to the homeless deaths?"

"No. But it's curious all the same. I'd love to know what Marcel Audet is doing serving the homeless. He's a parasite. When he thinks of other people, it's only to figure out how he can profit from them. He's a thug, with just enough brains to be dangerous."

## 3 PM

The Press Room was steaming hot from television lights and loud with the chatter of journalists. Wires littered the floor, threatening to topple the distracted. Sergeant Julie Laflamme was at the podium trying to impose calm in a tailored uniform that emphasized authority and curves in that order. Vanier stood behind her with his hands in his pockets, scanning the room and nodding with a half smile to reporters he recognized.

"Ladies and gentlemen, if we can get started," said Laflamme for the third time.

The noise level diminished slightly, and cameramen began to focus.

"I am Detective Sergeant Laflamme of the Communications Division. I propose to read a prepared statement first, and then I will take some questions." She waited for five beats to allow a gap in the recordings, a gift to the news editors, and then she started.

"Between 8 p.m. and 11 p.m. on Christmas Eve, the bodies of five people were discovered in various parts of downtown Montreal, three men and two women. The victims were found at various locations. One, a male, in Cabot Park; a female in the entrance to a parking garage on Atwater; two victims, one male and one female, were found at different spots in the Berri-UQÀM complex; and another male was found inside the McGill Métro station. Until we have notified their next of kin, we are not releasing the identity of any of the victims.

"We wish to stress at this point that we are treating these deaths as suspicious, but this is not officially a murder inquiry. We are keeping an open mind on every possibility. We are continuing to collect information and follow up on certain lines of inquiry. The investigation is being led by Detective Inspector Vanier of the Major Crimes Squad." She waved her hand to indicate Vanier, who smiled for half a second.

"The Coroner is in the process of conducting autopsies on the victims to determine the causes of death. We expect to have one or two preliminary reports tomorrow.

"In the meantime, we ask that all requests for information be made through my office, and we promise to respond quickly. The Montreal Police Service is taking these incidents very seriously, and is sparing no resources in its efforts. Now, any questions?"

"Inspector Vanier. Were there any signs of violence on the bodies?"

"Let me answer that," Laflamme responded, and Vanier looked bemused. "The investigation is still at a very preliminary stage, and we cannot discuss details concerning the deceased or of the various scenes at this point."

"Inspector Vanier, were you at the crime scenes?"

If Laflamme was under pressure she didn't show it.

"It is premature to refer to the places where the individuals were discovered as crime scenes. As we said earlier, we have no evidence yet to confirm or to discount a crime. We are treating the deaths only as suspicious. But we can confirm that Inspector Vanier has been working on this investigation from the beginning."

"There have been suggestions that someone dressed as Santa Claus was seen with some of the victims. Can you confirm?"

"We are reviewing hours of closed circuit television footage to identify who, if anyone, may have had contact with the victims during the hours prior to their death. It does appear that a person dressed in a Santa Claus costume may have had contact with at least one of the deceased, but it would be premature to confirm any more than that."

"Wouldn't Santa have been very busy on Christmas Eve?"

The room erupted in laughter, and Laflamme put on her patient schoolmistress-dealing-with-hijinks face.

"Next."

"Is there any connection between the victims? Did they know one another?"

"We believe that all of the victims were what you might call street people. They were homeless. While that might be a connection, we have not yet established if they knew each other."

"Have there been any other suspicious deaths of homeless people in the last months?"

"We are looking into that. We have asked the Coroner's office to provide us with a report of all the homeless deaths in the last three years. We want to know if there is anything unusual in the past that might have been missed. Last question."

. "Has the squad cancelled leave to deal with the investigation?"

"As I said, Inspector Vanier and his team have been working on this throughout the holidays. We do not expect the holiday period to interfere with our work. Thank you." Laflamme picked up her notes and began to walk away from the podium, followed by Vanier.

"Inspector Vanier." Laflamme looked back to see Vanier level with the microphone at the podium as the question was shouted. "How do you like your new handler?" Laughter again.

Vanier leaned into the microphone. This time his smile lasted longer. "No comment."

## 6.15 PM

Vanier gunned the Volvo through light snow onto Highway 40 heading west. Laurent had told him that a major storm was on its way, thirty centimetres before dawn. It was already dark. The highway was deserted, and he pushed the button to let Tom Waits sing of *Warm Beer and Cold Women,* the wipers keeping time, snow flakes hitting the windshield hypnotically, and a box wrapped in Christmas paper on the seat beside him.

He followed the highway to Hudson, the horse-rearing capital of Quebec, fishtailed through the slippery exit, and, after fifteen minutes of slow driving, pulled into the empty visitor parking lot of the Lafarge Retirement Home.

He rang the bell, and Sister Véronique appeared in the opened doorway with a smile on her old face as though she was relieved to see someone from the living, and not another delivery of someone who would not be leaving.

"M. Vanier, how good to see you again. Come in, come in. What a night it is."

He walked past her as she poked her head out to look at the storm. Closing the door with an exaggerated shiver she turned, extending both hands to Vanier.

"And a holy and happy Christmas to you, M. Vanier." She smelled of lemon, pine, and wax.

"The same to you, Sister. I hope you're keeping well."

"I am, thank God. And who wouldn't at this time of the year? Isn't this a joyous time?"

"It is, Sister."

"Every mother should have a son like you who would come out to see her on a night like this. She's in the lounge. Let me take your coat and we can go in."

She hung his coat in a closet.

Vanier eyed the expanse of deep red carpet and the shining wood beyond and bent down to remove his wet boots, leaving them to drip into the carpet while he followed her silently in stockinged feet.

As they entered the lounge, a sea of heads rose expectantly. *No such luck, ladies, it's only Luc Vanier, visiting his mother on the day after Christmas.* Some looked away when they realized that it wasn't son Marc or daughter Mary, or one of the grandchildren. Others still tried for eye contact. She was sitting alone in a straight-backed chair at the far end of the lounge. She hadn't raised her head when he entered.

He pulled up an armchair and sat in front of her, staring into the blank eyes. Then he leaned over and planted a kiss on her cheek.

"Happy Christmas, Mum."

He dropped the Christmas package lightly into her lap. It could have been a grenade or a flower for all the reaction it got. He had had it wrapped in Place Ville Marie by volunteers collecting money for the Children's Hospital. Since Marianne had left, he had every important present, and there weren't many, wrapped by women who could wrap presents better than he could. It made no difference. The hands lay unmoving underneath the package. He reached over and turned each hand upwards so that they held the gift.

"So things are going great, Mum, really great. Élise is growing up so fast, it's incredible. She's becoming a real lady. She couldn't come today. She has a thing at the church but she told me to give you a big hug from her. And to wish you a Merry Christmas. That's what she said, merry, not just happy."

Vanier stood up and leaned over to hug his mother. "That's from Élise, Mum," he whispered into her ear. She stared, unblinking.

"Marianne couldn't come either. She sends her apologies. Had to be with Élise at the church too," he lied, "and Alex sends his love."

Vanier looked around. The room was quiet, as though the residents were waiting for the party to begin, like toys waiting for a child. Or maybe they were having the party when he arrived and stopped, unwilling to let him into their secret. Three women were looking at him, smiling.

"So we had a great Christmas, Mum. I wish you had been there. We had the whole thing. The turkey was the best in years, crisp golden brown skin and moist inside. The whole house smelled of roast turkey. Potatoes, mashed, sweet, and roast. You remember Mum, how much I love roast potatoes, don't you? Especially the way you used to make them. And the stuffing Mum, nobody makes stuffing like yours, with the sage and onions, but Marianne's came in a close second. She uses your recipe. We had Brussels sprouts, peas, green beans, and those carrots that you like in thin sticks. And then we had one of those old-fashioned Christmas puddings with holly on the top. I poured some brandy on it and set it on fire. What a feast. We had friends over to help us eat it all, and there's still enough left over for a week."

He reached across and took her hand. "Mum, I wish you could have been there. You should have seen us. What a time."

He took the package from her hand. "Aren't you going to open your present, Mum? Let me help."

Vanier took the present and began to unwrap it. He opened the box and looked inside like it was a surprise. Reaching in, he took out a fur scarf and held it up. "What do you think, Mum? It's made of fox, I think. It's like one you used to have years ago, the one you were wearing in that photograph of you and Dad in Winnipeg. When was that? Could have been 1953, before my time. Let me help you put it on."

He gently placed it around her neck, took her hand, and drew her fingers down its soft length a few times. He placed her hand back in her lap and sat down. He looked into her eyes and convinced himself that they had changed, softened a little.

"So, I'm still busy Mum. Always something new, always chasing after the bad guys. This time, we have a really bad sort. But we'll get him, Mum. We'll get him soon."

Vanier sat there looking into her eyes. Eventually, he became aware of eyes on him and stood up to kiss his mother on the cheek.

"I have to go now Mum. I'll be back soon, don't worry."

He bent again and kissed her on her head, holding the kiss. Standing up, he looked around at several faces that had been watching, and mustered a broad grin. "And a very Merry Christmas to all of you."

Most smiled back.

Vanier left, turning once at the door to the lounge to look back at his mother sitting motionless in her chair. *Bye, Mum.*

The drive back was difficult. The storm was in full force, and vis-ibility was close to zero. He played Coleman Hawkins, and, as always with the Hawk, felt better, like a load was slowly lifting. Tom Waits to walk with you on the way down, the Hawk to bring you back up.

# FIVE
## DECEMBER 27

## 7 AM

**The early morning sun reflected red and gold** off downtown buildings, promising a cold day under a cloudless sky. Sunlight was flooding into Vanier's apartment, and he was feeling good. After watching the sunrise over the river, he had taken a long shower and dressed in a clean suit and ironed shirt. He sat on the couch, his face bathed in the light of the rising sun, and closed his eyes. There was no alcohol fuzziness and no fatigue from sleeping on the couch. Christmas was over.

He focused on his breathing, belly out for the inward breath, in for the outward breath, and relaxed. Thoughts bubbled up from the depths, and he acknowledged them as he had been taught, and let them continue their upward journey out of consciousness. After five minutes, there were no more thoughts, just steady breathing, awareness and a sense of wellbeing. He let twenty minutes roll into thirty, like a child refusing to come out of the pool in summer, and finally surfaced with an unconscious smile on his face.

He got up, stretched, and went into the kitchen, cut chunks from a block of extra-old cheddar, and put an English muffin in the toaster. The kettle boiled, and he made a cup of instant coffee, then sat at the table eating and looking at downtown through the picture window. The phone rang.

"Vanier," he said.

"Luc," said Dr. Anjili Segal.

"Anjili. How are you?" said Vanier, happy that he didn't sound like he had been drinking all night.

"I'm well Luc. So, you survived Christmas?

"It was wonderful," he lied. "And you?"

"The same, Luc. But I'll be glad to get back to work. I'm booked for the fourth and fifth autopsies of your Christmas Eve victims. If you want to be there, I am starting at 11.30 on the first. Probably three o'clock on the other one."

"I'll be there, Anjili. I wouldn't miss it for anything."

"You don't have to be facetious, Luc. I just thought you would be interested in attending."

"Anjili, I didn't mean it like that. I'll be there. I may even bring a guest."

"I'll see you then, Luc," she said and hung up.

## 9 AM

St. Jacques put the phone down as Vanier walked into the Squad Room. She didn't look happy.

"The Santa suits are a dead end, sir. We checked the rental stores on the Island without any luck. There are only four stores that rent them out, but there's any number of other places that sell them.

Even Wal-Mart sells them. Of the four rental places, only two rented suits with fur trim on the bottom of the pants. Apparently, it's a premium item, and our Santa had fur on the hem of his pants. Only eight of those suits were still out on Christmas Eve. It seems that the big trade in rentals is for parties before Christmas, not for the night itself. Anyway, all but eight of them were returned before Christmas Eve."

"Have we tracked them down?" asked Vanier.

"Seven were accounted for, and both the owners and their suits were far away from downtown on Christmas Eve. The eighth was rented by a Tony Martino, who was at home Christmas Eve, but he left the suit in his office. He was supposed to have returned it on December 23 but didn't. He was nervous during the interview with the uniforms. He said he left the suit in the office after the Christmas party because there was a stain on it and he wanted to wash it out before giving it back."

"He couldn't bring it home for the wife to wash, I suppose?" said Vanier.

"Exactly, sir. Human frailty," said St. Jacques. "The stain seems to have been semen, his own, the result of an encounter with one his staff that got out of hand, so to speak. Kind of like the Lewinsky dress. He wanted to clean it up before he brought it back, but didn't have time, so he left it in the office. He told the officers where he left it, and that's where it was when Martino brought the officers to the office. Martino says that nobody could have got into the office after it closed, and he was with his family on Christmas Eve."

Vanier sighed. "So no easy trail to Santa. The perfect disguise at Christmas. Everyone sees it but there's nothing special about it."

St. Jacques continued her summary. "Two ticket sellers at the métro remember seeing Santa entering. He used tickets to clear the turnstiles, so we can't check monthly pass information. Only one of them remembers seeing him leave. He said he was moving quickly and not looking around him. But there was nothing to distinguish him from any other Santa. From the camera images, we know he didn't use the métro to go from one station to the next. He entered and left each station he visited. From the timing of his appearances, he didn't have time to walk or take a bus either. We checked the taxi companies, and none of the drivers remembers picking up any Santa. He wouldn't have been riding a bike in that weather. So that leaves a car. He must have driven from station to station. From the camera images, Santa was six foot two and, from the way he walked and filled out the suit, he was in good shape. Hard to tell an age, but probably under forty."

"OK, St. Jacques. Keep looking at the films. What else do we have?"

D.S. Roberge spoke. "Dr. Grenier's alibi checks out. I spoke to his wife, and he was home Christmas Eve. As for Drouin's return to the Cathedral, I spoke to Monsignor Forlini, he was the senior priest at Midnight Mass. He wasn't sure of the exact time when he first saw Drouin, but said that it could have been between 10.45 and 11.15 p.m. He said that Drouin was rushing to get into his vestments, and Mass started at 11.35."

"And what was the last sighting of Santa?"

"10.30, sir, at the Berri Métro. I had them go back and confirm," said St. Jacques.

"That's tight, but possible. If he had a car he could get back to the Cathedral by eleven easy. But Drouin said he left his car at the Cathedral."

"He could be lying," said Laurent.

"Would be lying if it were him. Did we check out parking tickets in the area?"

"I'll do it," said Roberge.

Vanier noticed Laurent shuffling papers, getting ready to speak. "Laurent, we can talk about the Holy Land Shelter in the car. We have an opening to go to."

A tired joke. Laurent sighed. "You drive or me?"

"I'll drive," said Vanier. "Give me a few minutes." He turned to the group. "Everyone have something to do?"

Heads nodded, and Vanier picked up the phone.

# THE DEAD OF WINTER

## 11 AM

The drive to the Coroner's building was easy. Most people were still on vacation, and the only serious traffic was caused by giant trucks loaded with snow going to the dump or returning empty for their next load. Vanier drove fast, speeding up through yellow lights and anticipating the greens.

"So what's the story at the Holy Land Shelter?" asked Vanier.

"Well, up to last March, Father Drouin was on the Board." Laurent was leafing through his notebook. "Then there was a huge turnover in March, seven new members on a ten-member Board. That means seven resigned or were kicked out. That has to be pretty disruptive for the organization. I've started to get the stories on the ones who resigned first. I figured, if there was a problem, the outgoing members would be more inclined to talk."

"Who can we talk to besides Drouin?"

"I'm running through the names, trying to figure out how to get in touch with them. A likely one is Pascal Beaudoin. I found a listing for Pascal Beaudoin as the Secretary of the Board for the last four years. And I found a lawyer downtown called Pascal Beaudoin with Henderson & Associates."

"How do you know it's the same Pascal Beaudoin?"

"The new Secretary is a certain Gordon Henderson, the same name as the main guy in Henderson & Associates. I figure it's not a coincidence."

"So why don't you call this Beaudoin and see if we can go to see him after the autopsies."

Laurent got on the phone and had an appointment confirmed with Beaudoin by the time they were pulling into the parking lot. The Coroner's building sat on rue Parthenais in the East End, in a poor residential neighbourhood. A typical 1960s government building, unimpressive in form, style, and functionality, someone's idea of building up the local economy by dumping a government building in the middle of a depressed area.

The autopsy viewing room was a small, utilitarian space designed to allow students to watch and learn; wooden benches and a large picture window overlooked the business area. On December 27, the students had found better things to do, and the detectives were alone.

Vanier and Laurent settled in and looked down on a theatre of three ribbed stainless steel tables. The naked body of an emaciated woman lay on one of the tables, dwarfed by its size. The table had been raised at one end to allow blood and other fluids to drain down into a collecting bottle. Vanier guessed it was Edith Latendresse from the Berri Métro, with her empty breasts nothing more than flaps of skin draped over a protruding ribcage. More bones than flesh, the skeleton wrapped in skin was a stark contrast to the plump cocoons of blankets he had seen on Christmas Eve. She had looked full then, bundled in layers against the cold.

Laurent perked up as Anjili Segal entered the room below them. Her dark hair was held tight by a headset that supported a microphone in front of her mouth, and her surgical uniform couldn't hide the curves of a woman in good shape. She looked up to the viewing gallery and caught Vanier's eye. They smiled at each other. Then, for Laurent and the transcript, she said, "Inspector Vanier, how good to see you, and you, too, Sergeant Laurent. A very Merry Christmas to you both. I was just getting ready to begin. So glad you could come."

"Always a pleasure, Dr. Segal. Any word on the others? Anything unusual?"

Segal seemed to deflate as she thought about her response.

"Inspector, I did not perform the earlier autopsies, but I've looked at the initial reports. The first three victims were very sick, probably terminal. If it hadn't been Christmas Eve, it could have been tonight, or next week, who knows? My colleague guessed at three months, maximum, for each of them. But you never know. A guess is a guess.

Maybe with care one or two of could have lasted longer. But out on the streets, nature takes over, and nature hates frailty. These were all the walking dead."

"Is there a cause of death?" asked Vanier, forcing himself to look away from Segal and stare at the body on the table. Naked is how we arrive and leave, naked and alone. Protocol demanded nothing be done to the body before the autopsy, and the grime of the street was obvious, even from a distance.

Segal picked up a clipboard and began reading from the reports: "The first, a male of about 63, had a stomach tumour as big as a full term baby. The second male was about 60 years old. Both his lungs were locked solid with emphysema. It does not say why, but it's probably from smoking the discarded butts of more affluent smokers. The last, a female of about 50, had a liver that was close to non-functioning. Probably an alcoholic, drinking too much cheap wine from the dépanneur for too long. Her blood alcohol level was elevated. For some reason, I don't expect much different from Madame Sans-nom," Segal said, gesturing to the naked cadaver on the table.

"She's no longer nameless, Dr. Segal" said Vanier. "Her name is Edith Latendresse."

"Thank you, Inspector." She wrote the name on her clipboard and returned to reviewing the notes from the earlier autopsies. "From what I can see, my colleagues will probably conclude that death was from natural causes, Inspector. As if all this is natural." She looked up at her guests. "I'm sorry, gentlemen, I'm getting carried away. Perhaps it's the season."

"No excuses. This isn't natural, Doctor," said Vanier, meeting her eye. "It's an affront. Let's do them a service. If they did happen to die by the so-called grace of God on Christmas Eve, at least give them the best damn reports we can, write a few pages of details for them."

"What are you asking for, Inspector?"

"The star treatment. Pretend it's the Mayor or one of his buddies who turned up stiff. All the tests your people can think of. Every detail. It's all we have. If we're all letting this happen every day, at least we can record the details," said Vanier.

"We will do our best, Inspector."

"Thank you, Doctor. I am sure that Madame Latendresse would thank you too," he said nodding in the direction of Edith Latendresse.

"That's something, isn't it?"

"What?" asked Vanier.

"It's something to have a name."

"That's all she has now."

Dr. Segal turned to the emaciated body and began talking into the headpiece, bending over to inspect the body. After a fifteen-minute tour of the outer shell, always talking into the microphone, she reached for a surgical knife. Soon she would need sturdier cutting tools. Her first slice was clean, from just below the throat all the way down to the pubis. Vanier was getting squeamish when she sliced and pulled at the skin to expose Mme. Latendresse's organs. He looked to the floor as she picked up the electrical tool and began to cut through bone. There was no reason for him to be here. Everyone knew it. But Vanier still kept coming. Three or four times a year he would sit through an autopsy and force himself to watch bodies being taken apart.

## 2.30 PM

The offices of Henderson & Associates were located in a tired high rise on University Street, reasonably well situated downtown but well past anything resembling its prime. Vanier and Laurent went up to the fifteenth floor and followed the arrow to an incongruous set of mahogany doors with gold handles that contrasted with the industrial carpet and painted gyprock of the hallway. Inside the heavy doors their feet sank into thick carpet in front of a fortysomething receptionist who was winning the war against age. She was wearing a headset and working a console like a D.J.

"Henderson and Associates. Can I help you?"

"Yes," said Vanier, leaning towards her and getting lost in the faintest hint of perfume. "We're here to see Maître Beaudoin."

She held her finger up and smiled at Vanier, pointing to the phone.

"Yes, and who can I say is calling?" She pushed some buttons and said, "Madame Delorme for you, sir." She listened for a few seconds, pushed another button and said, "I'm sorry, Madame Delorme, Mr. Henderson is in a meeting at the moment, may I take a message?"

Vanier stood at the desk, imposing his bulk. She was used to the difficulties of the double duty and she held up her finger again, giving him another heartbreaker of a smile.

"Henderson and Associates. Can I help you?"

Vanier took a step back and then walked around the receptionist's desk to the hallway leading to the offices. The impact was immediate. She took off her headphones and dashed after him, taking his elbow delicately and walking him back to the reception area like they were both looking for the dance floor. Vanier was enjoying it.

"I am so sorry, Mr...?"

"Detective Inspector Vanier."

"I am so sorry, M. Vanier. Sometimes it gets so busy that I completely forget my manners. I'm Julie. Please excuse me." She led him back to reception, holding his elbow.

"Not at all," said Vanier, thinking that he could forgive her a lot under the right circumstances. "This is Detective Sergeant Laurent. We're here to see Maître Beaudoin. He's expecting us."

"Of course he is. He asked me to seat you in the main boardroom," she said, still holding his elbow, like he might try to escape again. Laurent followed them through the glass doors of the boardroom, its tall windows providing a perfect view of the building next door. "Some coffee?"

"Wonderful," said Vanier.

"Please take a seat," she said, gesturing to the long, dappled green marble table. The room was decorated in an Oriental style with a large Chinese gong on one side table and several Chinese vases on another. The floor was polished hardwood, with a Persian carpet under the table. The walls were clear glass.

Julie returned a few minutes later with a tray holding a full pot of coffee, cream, sugar, china coffee mugs, and a plate of biscuits.

"Please, gentlemen, help yourselves, and call me if you need anything. Maître Beaudoin should be here in a few moments."

Vanier watched her leave, as Laurent poured two cups of coffee, handing one to Vanier. Vanier sat with his back to the window, facing out of the boardroom through the glass wall. Laurent was at the end of the table, which would make it impossible for Beaudoin to find a spot where he could look at both of them at the same time. They saw him approach and break into a smile even before he was through the door.

"Gentlemen," he said, reaching out to shake Vanier's hand and then Laurent's. "Sit down, gentlemen, sit down. I'm always glad to help Montreal's finest. Now, what can I do for you?"

Beaudoin exuded the good humour of a welcoming host, and wariness only broke through in the shortest of flashes. His short frame was carrying too much weight, and he sat down. They exchanged cards.

"We'd like to ask you a few questions about the Holy Land Shelter," said Vanier.

"The Holy Land Shelter? That's police business?"

"We're investigating the deaths on Christmas Eve and trying to understand the lives of the homeless. We're just looking for background. You were heavily involved in the Shelter's Board, and we thought you could give us some insight."

"Well, yes, I was involved with the Shelter, but it was mostly legal and administrative work. I'm not really an expert on the homeless. All I know is that it's a tough life."

"You'd be surprised what can help in an investigation like this."

"I suppose."

"For instance, so much of the work is done by volunteers. What brings people in? What makes people leave? We've heard that there were big changes last year at the Shelter. I understand that most of the Board resigned. Why was that?

"Well, I can't speak for the others but for myself, I was tired. Simple as that. Five years is a long time, and I needed a rest. And the Board needed fresh blood. There's nothing wrong, is there?"

"I didn't say there was a problem. We're just interested in understanding how these places work. Just a little curious, that's all."

Beaudoin looked down at the business cards. "Chief Inspector, you must be a busy man, and these latest murders must be taking up a lot of your time. Are you working on those, Inspector, or are you just interested in the Shelter?"

"Maître Beaudoin, I have the best job in the world. When something interests me I can look into it. Luckily, not everything interests me, so I have time to do my job. Right now, I am simply trying to understand what it means to be homeless in Montreal. How they live, where they go, who they have dealings with. So the Shelter is a good place to start, isn't it? After all, it takes in, what, 300 people a night?"

"The Shelter does great work, Inspector. It fills a desperate need. I enjoyed my time there. You have no idea what kind of a feeling that gives you. It's rare, especially in this business. I didn't do hands-on work with the homeless, but I think what I did was helpful. In a lot of ways I miss it."

"So why quit?"

"Like I said, five years is a long time. I needed a rest. And they probably needed a rest from me."

"What about Father Drouin? Did he need a rest too?"

"Ah, Father Drouin. A great guy, a great human being. He could be difficult, but it's because he's so shy. It took me over a year to get to know him properly, but when you do, you can't help but love him."

"He got tired too?"

"Perhaps. Yes. He was tired too." Beaudoin's answers were slowing down, like he was trying to guess where Vanier was going. "It's not easy you know, it can take a lot out of you. And he had other things to do. He's very busy for a priest. He's involved in a lot of things."

"In all, seven of the ten members of the Board from last year are no longer there. That quite a turnover isn't it? It must be difficult for the organization to survive that sort of …turmoil?"

Beaudoin looked uncomfortable, but before he could answer, the conference room door opened, and a tall gaunt man walked in. He was dressed to announce his importance, peacock style. He looked straight at Beaudoin, ignoring the policemen.

"Pascal, I heard that you were having a meeting with some policemen. I thought you might need some back-up," he said with a humourless chuckle, then turned to the two officers, with a broad smile that stopped well below his eyes. "Gentlemen, I am so pleased to welcome you to my offices. I am Maître Gordon Henderson," he said, emphasizing the honorific title for Quebec lawyers.

Vanier and Laurent introduced themselves, and they exchanged cards with Henderson.

"What is it we can do for you? Are you selling tickets for the annual ball?"

"The annual ball is a thing of the past, but if it is ever revived, I'll put you down for a table, shall I?"

"Absolutely."

"We were here to speak to Maître Beaudoin about his work with the Holy Land Shelter."

"Well, there are no secrets in this office. We supported Pascal's efforts to help the needy. He has a big heart. But you know how it is Inspector, business comes first. After five years, it was time for him to direct his efforts elsewhere. We live in a very competitive world, and there are limits to how much time can be wasted. We are all slaves to the billable hour; the clients are more demanding by the day."

Beaudoin looked down at the table, scratching notes on a yellow pad.

"And talking of the almighty billable hour, Inspector, it would be more efficient if you would write down your questions to Pascal and send them to us. We would be happy to provide you with answers to any questions you might have. But right now, I need Pascal on a call to Japan that I promised would begin in five minutes," said Henderson, looking at his watch.

Vanier took the cue, hoping he could come back some day with a good reason to question Henderson. He'd been thrown out of bars with more subtlety. The two policemen stood up and exchanged handshakes with the lawyers. Beaudoin left them at reception, but Henderson waited to see them leave. Vanier cast a goodbye smile at the receptionist, who gave him one of her own and a small wave.

"Fucking bastard," said Vanier as the elevator doors closed.

## 3.45 PM

When the door closed on the departing policemen, Gordon Henderson walked into Beaudoin's office.

"Pascal, why didn't you tell me that you were meeting with police inspectors? I don't like having to find out things like that from Julie."

"Well, Mr. Henderson, they just called this morning and asked if I would have time to give him some background on the Holy Land

Shelter for their investigation. They're the ones on the Christmas Eve deaths. I didn't think anything of it, they just wanted background information."

"Just background information? Pascal, you know that the Shelter is a very sensitive file. We can't go around discussing it with just anyone, and particularly not with policemen. We have a duty to our client. I really am disappointed, Pascal."

Beaudoin swallowed. "I'm sorry. You're right. I should have spoken to you first. It's just ... well, you're right."

"Just see that it doesn't happen again. Now, where are you on the Blanchard letter? I need to send that out first thing tomorrow morning. Is it ready?"

"Almost, Mr. Henderson. Almost," Beaudoin said. He hadn't even started it. "It will be on your desk before you arrive in the morning," he added, ruining not only his evening, but a good part of the night.

"Wonderful. I'll leave you to it then," Henderson said, and left.

Beaudoin pulled a file from the pile on his desk and began to focus on the problems of M. Blanchard, who wanted to double the size of his Westmount house over the objection of his neighbours and the city council. He began typing into the computer, drafting objections to the reasonable arguments of the city and the neighbours that the plans ignored the by-laws and the character of the neighborhood, and would be a palatial monument to bad taste. He would get to the threats against the individuals and the council later; it was always better to close with the threats. At 7.30 p.m., he stopped writing, picked up the phone and punched numbers.

"Hello?" a young voice, a girl.

"Hey, Chickadee!"

"Papa," she squealed. "Where are you? Maman made shepherd's pie, your favourite."

"I'm still at the office, my love. I have to work late. Can you pass me Maman?"

"Maman," she yelled into the phone. There was silence. Then she said, "Maman says if you're going to be late, you can heat up your supper in the microwave. Are you going to be here before I go to bed? I can wait for you."

"No, my love. It's going to be late. Tell you what, though, I'll see you in the morning. Tell Maman and David good night from me, and give them both a big kiss and a hug. I love you, Chickadee."

"Me too, Papa. But I gotta go. Dinner's on the table. Bye."

He heard the click of disconnection and put the phone back in the receiver. He turned back to M. Blanchard's problem, which was quickly becoming Westmount's problem.


## 5 PM


From where he sat, Vanier could see the back of D.S. Fletcher's head. Fletcher had just returned to work and was catching up. Vanier had spent the last hour reading interview reports and watching Fletcher. Eventually, Fletcher pushed his chair back and rose from his desk, stretching. "Anyone want coffee?"

"Sure," said Vanier, fishing for change. "Regular Colombian, milk, no sugar."

Fletcher took the coins and three other orders and left. His jacket was still on the chair, and Vanier was on his feet immediately, walking towards the wall that held the maps, photos and notes of the investigation. As he passed Fletcher's desk, he bent slightly and pulled Fletcher's cell phone from his jacket pocket. Back at his desk he quickly scribbled the numbers in the call log since Christmas Eve, along with the times and duration. He looked up from time to time and scanned the room, but if anyone had noticed, they were not saying anything. When the list was done, he wandered back towards the photo wall and slipped the phone back into Fletcher's pocket. He was studying the wall when Fletcher returned with the coffee.

"So what do you think, sir?" said Fletcher, handing him the coffee.

"Thanks. Don't know what to think. Maybe we're wasting our time."

"We won't know till we get the cause of death, I suppose."

Fletcher went back to his desk. An hour later, he went to the bathroom, and Vanier approached St. Jacques and handed her a paper.

"I have a job that needs discretion."

She looked at the list.

"I want all these numbers identified, but don't do the checking from here, and don't tell anyone what you're doing."

She couldn't help glancing at Fletcher's desk.

"Yes, sir. When do you need this?"

"Soon as you can, Sergeant."


## 11 PM


Vanier was wandering fitfully around his apartment, picking things up and putting them away, keeping busy. An unopened bottle of Jameson was calling to him, and he was doing his best to resist. It was late, and he wasn't tired, but sleep would be the only way to quiet the bottle. The phone rang.

"Luc?"

"Anjili. What's new?"

"Bad news. The five victims from Christmas Eve all died of poisoning. Potassium cyanide."

"Are you sure?"

"Normally toxicology can take weeks of tests, if you don't know what you're looking for. There are just too many variables. But we decided to test directly for potassium cyanide. All the victims were flushed."

"Flushed?"

"Pink looking. First, we put it down to alcohol, but one of the doctors reported smelling almonds, which is typical with potassium cyanide poisoning. So we got one of the bottles from your people and tested the residue. It showed positive for potassium cyanide, along with rum and eggnog. Then we did blood tests and found significant concentrations in each of them. Luc, each of them had ingested enough to kill a horse. These people were poisoned, Luc."

"Shit. What exactly is potassium cyanide?"

"It's the same poison that Jim Jones used for the mass suicide of his followers. Remember Georgetown?"

"That was a cult, right?"

"Yes, it was a cult. He killed himself and 600 of his followers with potassium cyanide dissolved in Kool-Aid. Apparently, Kool-Aid hides the taste. It's a gruesome death. It kills by inhibiting aerobic respiration. The blood cells can't absorb oxygen and all of the body's organs become oxygen deprived – it's like smothering someone, cutting off their air supply. The victim goes into a coma in minutes, and then suffers cardiac arrest. We're writing up the reports now, Luc, but I thought you would want the news early. You have a murderer out there, and you need to find him."

"How much of the stuff do you need to kill someone?"

"It doesn't take much, less than a gram will do it for a normal adult, and it's very soluble in water."

"So they all drank poison?"

"That's what it looks like."

"How do you get this stuff? Can you buy it in the pharmacy?"

"No. But it's a common industrial chemical. It's not rare, it has several industrial uses, and plating jewelry is a big one. There are probably dozens of businesses in Montreal that keep stocks of it."

"That's nice to know. Isn't it controlled? Isn't there a central list of everyone who keeps the stuff?"

"I had someone check. Seems that there are rules for how you have to deal with it in workplaces, health and safety rules, that sort of thing. But there's no central registry."

Vanier was thinking, first start with the Canadian manufacturers, then the importers, then onto the distributors and end-users. "It sounds like a big job, tracking it down."

"Isn't that what you guys do best?"

"Yeah, if I had unlimited resources. This could take days. Anjili, listen, I have to go. Thanks for this. I'll be talking to you. Can you fax the preliminary findings over?"

"First thing in the morning. Luc, you have to find this person."

"I know Anjili. I'm working on it. Thanks," he said, as he hung up the phone.

He remembered Santa Claus handing Edith Latendresse a gift and then bending down to kiss the old woman on the head. Santa Claus as executioner. That was a new one, even for Vanier. He checked the time, it was probably well past Bédard's bedtime. He smiled as he punched the Chief's number on his cell phone.

"Huh?"

"Chief Inspector? It's Vanier here."

"Inspector Vanier, do you know what time it is?"

"Yes, sir. But you said that you wanted to be kept informed of developments. We have confirmation that it's murder. All of the victims were poisoned. Potassium cyanide. Apparently, it's the same stuff that Jim Jones used."

"Who?"

"Jim Jones, sir. Remember the mass suicide in Guyana?"

The Chief Inspector was awake. "What? Jesus, he killed hundreds, didn't he? You're telling me that we have a lunatic loose poisoning people?"

"Looks like that, sir."

"I have to talk to communications. We have to manage this properly. Christ, a mass murderer, that's all I need."

"Sir, you said that I could go off budget, get more people. Well, I think that we need to ramp this up. Apparently, there's lots of potassium cyanide lying around. If we need to track it down, I'm going to need resources."

"Luc, you need overtime and extra people. I'll give you the overtime; I'll see what I can do about the extra people. I have to make some calls. How do we know this?"

"I just had a call from Dr. Segal."

"OK, so it's reliable. Let's keep this quiet until we can talk to communications. Jesus, this could set the city into a panic. Do you have any leads yet? Do we have a suspect?" He was pleading.

"Not yet, sir. No suspects. But we're following up some ideas. Sir, I need more people."

"Yes, Inspector, I'll get back to you on that. Listen, thanks for calling. Keep me informed."

The line cut before Vanier could answer. "Yes, sir," he said to a dead line.

# PART TWO

# SIX
## DECEMBER 28

## 8 AM

**Only five officers were at their desks** when Vanier arrived: Laurent, St. Jacques, Roberge, Fletcher, and Janvier. Vanier stood in the middle of the room and had their attention.

"Listen up. It's officially a murder investigation. All the victims were killed with potassium cyanide." He spelled it out and they scribbled it down. "It's a common industrial chemical and a lethal poison. Santa mixed it in rum and eggnog and sent them on their way."

Laurent raised his big head. "Isn't that what Goering used?"

"Goering?"

"In the Nuremberg trial. I saw the film. Somebody smuggled him a cyanide pill, and he killed himself."

"Christ, you learn something every day. So we can take Goering off the list of suspects. We're making progress. And I don't think that we're looking for pills. Our guy is serving it up in liquid, so we can start by assuming that he has a stock of powder. So here's what I want. Start with the manufacturers and importers, anyone who makes the stuff, and anyone who has imported it in the last three years. Have them check to see if any is missing; any recent thefts; disgruntled employees; employees who've quit recently – you know the sort of thing, anything unusual. You find anything, let me know immediately. Once you've got the sources of this stuff, start working on the customers, all the way down to the last buyer. We have to check them all, and as quickly as possible. Any questions?"

"Any suggestions on customs, for the importers?" This from Fletcher.

"Good question." In the last few years they'd had problems getting information quickly from customs. They weren't keen on sharing unless there was some joint task force, and even then, they liked to hold back. Something about the privacy rights of importers. Vanier flipped open his phone and scrolled through his address book. "Call Danielle Sabbatini, she's an investigator in Laval, and she owes me. 450-363-2082. If she gives you grief, tell her you're cashing in a marker from me. If she still won't help, call me."

"Sir, what about the government agencies?" This from St. Jacques. "Maybe you need a licence to keep potassium cyanide. So maybe there's a list somewhere."

"I was told that it's unlikely, but it's worth a try. See what you can get. Anything else?"

"Yes, sir," said Fletcher. "We checked the parking tickets. They weren't giving tickets Christmas Eve, they were towing cars away to make way for the snow clearing. Anything that was parked illegally, or that was in the way of the clearing, was towed. Thirty-six cars in all, and I'm working through the list. Nothing so far, but it could take another two days, sir."

"Well, keep it up."

"Are we getting extra help, sir?" asked St. Jacques.

"The Chief is considering my request for additional resources and will get back to me when he has time to think. So don't hold your breath. In the meantime you'll be glad to hear that you can all work as much overtime as you like. The Chief has generously agreed to open the purse on that one."

That news was greeted with groans.

"Right. If you've all got work to do, let's get to it. Laurent, you come with me, we're going to church again, separate cars."

As they were pulling on their overcoats, St. Jacques passed an envelope to Vanier. Laurent was watching but said nothing.

"My lottery winnings," said Vanier.

"So where's mine? I'm in the pool too," said Laurent.

"You didn't win."

"Fuck."


## 9.30 AM


Laurent ignored the clutch of men waiting with outstretched paper cups, and pulled open the steel and glass doors to the Cathedral. Vanier followed, watching Laurent dip his fingers in the holy water font, then bless himself before opening the second set of doors. Old habits, thought Vanier.

It was dark and cold inside, a sacrifice to the cost of lighting and heating the empty granite space. An attendant told them that Father Henri was conducting a service in St. Jude's Crypt, and pointed the way. They approached to see the priest on his knees facing the altar and leading about twenty people in the Rosary. Vanier checked the beads being handled by the devout, and saw that they were almost halfway through the last decade. He knelt. Laurent blessed himself again and knelt beside him.

"*Hail Mary, full of Grace. The Lord is with thee. Blessed is the fruit of thy womb Jesus,*" Drouin intoned.

"*Holy Mary, Mother of God, pray for us sinners now and at the hour of our death. Amen,*" the devout replied.

Vanier joined in the response loudly enough to be heard, and Drouin, his back to the faithful, raised his head slightly as if trying to pick out the new voice.

When the Rosary ended, Drouin left a little time for silent prayer, then stood and turned to survey the group. His eyes fixed immediately on Vanier, who returned the look with the face of a cherub.

Drouin addressed the devout with difficulty. "That brings us to the end of our session. Let us give our problems and concerns to the Lord in prayer, and to the Blessed Virgin, and to our beloved St. Jude. Again, I invite any of you who need the Lord's intercession to write your needs on one of the cards provided and drop it in the box."

The crowd began to shuffle out, some stopping to whisper to Drouin, a few stopping to drop prayer cards into the box. While waiting for the shepherd to finish ministering to his flock, Vanier moved over to the table and picked up a blank card. Laurent followed, and Drouin eyed the two men with concern. The cards were only scraps of recycled paper. Vanier took out a pen and was still writing when Drouin approached.

"It's curious, Inspector, but you didn't strike me as a religious man. Do you have a need that you wish us to pray for?"

"Religious, me? Not really. But it's like the lottery, isn't it? If you don't play you don't win."

"Well, I never play the lottery, Inspector."

"I suppose not. It wouldn't do for a priest to collect twenty million from the 6-49 jackpot. People would think he had some divine help. But maybe prayers are the Church's lottery. What do you think, Father Drouin?"

"Prayers are a much better investment than the lottery, Inspector. Prayers are answered every day."

"So there's hope for me?"

"And what is your prayer, Inspector?"

Vanier held up the card for Drouin to read: *Help me catch the bastard who killed the innocents.* "Oh, excuse me, Father," he said, taking the pen to cross out *bastard* and scribble something else. "This should do it," he said, handing the card back to Drouin.

*Help me find the people who killed the innocents.*

"I can't help noticing you changed a singular for a plural."

"Yes. Strange that, isn't it? And I think we're dealing with one killer. But in my job we're always fighting several people, people who know something but don't come forward. People protecting the killer or people who just can't be bothered."

"You really believe those poor people were killed?"

"They were killed, Father. Murdered. What do you think of that?"

"It's beyond belief. Who would do such a thing? Who could possibly have a reason to kill them?

"That's my job. Nobody kills without a reason. When I find out why, I'll have the killer."

"I can't think of anyone who would have a reason to kill these people."

"Well somebody did. Just because you can't think of a reason doesn't mean that the killer didn't have one, does it? So, any ideas? Anyone come to mind?"

"It would have to be a maniac. It doesn't make sense."

"Do you know any maniacs?"

"I know a lot of people. But nobody who is capable of killing."

"Yesterday you said these people didn't have friends. Did they have enemies?"

"No, Inspector, just because you don't have any friends doesn't mean that you have enemies. The truth is, nobody cared about these people, and certainly nobody cared enough to kill them."

"There was nothing that struck you as odd in the last few weeks?"

"No, nothing. The usual grumbling and complaining about their lot." Drouin semed to have a flash of memory and Vanier waited.

"There is something. George Morissette was particularly troubled about money recently."

"George?"

"Yes, George Morissette, he used to be a notary, very smart when he's sober. He kept saying that the shelter was cheating him. Every time we talked, he would bring it up. I thought nothing of it. I know M. Nolet, and he is a dedicated man. I just thought George was confused."

"We're going to need a full statement from you, your dealings with the victims, the last time you saw each of them, who they knew, that sort of thing."

"Of course, I am happy to tell you everything I know. I just don't know that it will be of any help."

"You never know, Father. Laurent here will drive you to the station."

"I just need a few minutes to close up."

Drouin began to close down the shop, extinguishing candles and folding the linen that lay across the altar.

"So what was the service? Benediction?" Vanier asked, remembering childhood Sundays, mass in the morning, and benediction in the afternoon.

"No. A simple prayer service. People who come together in faith to seek the intercession of the Saints, in this case, St. Jude. As I said, Inspector, prayer is a wonderful thing. Prayer works miracles." Drouin touched the box of cards. "After every service I put a date on the new cards, and we pray for the request for ten days. We meet three times a week, Mondays, Wednesdays, and Fridays. That comes to about two-and-a-half weeks of prayer."

"So if I put my card in the box, you'll pray for me?"

"Yes, Inspector, but if you want the Circle to pray for you rather than your request, perhaps you should fill out another card."

"The Circle?"

"The Circle of Christ. That's the name of the group. People like to belong, Inspector. It helps if the group has a name. If you put your card in the box, it will be read and the Circle of Christ will pray for your intention, or for you, at our next meeting."

"I feel better already, Father. Could I ask you a favour?"

"Of course."

"Could I borrow this box for a day? See what people are praying for? I'll have it back, with its contents, in time for the next meeting." Vanier was already holding the box.

Drouin hesitated. "It's private. It's the prayers of sincere believers. I can't see what possible relevance it can have to your investigation."

"Father, it's going to sit here untouched overnight. Indulge me."

"Well, I suppose so," said Drouin.

"Great," said Vanier, putting the box under his arm.

As they took the step down out of the crypt, Vanier turned to Drouin.

"We'll find him, Father. And when we do, we'll find everyone who put obstacles in my path, or who failed to raise their hand and point him out. If there's anything on your mind, Father, call me," he said, handing him a business card and turning to leave. "Laurent will wait for you and take you to the station."

## 11 AM

Vanier was running the engine to keep the car warm. He pulled St. Jacques's note from the envelope and scanned the list of numbers,

names and comments. One name stood out, René Gauthier, a journalist with the *Journal de Montréal*. Vanier recognized the name from
the *Journal's* coverage of the Christmas Eve murders. He punched in
the numbers and it picked up after two rings.

"Oui?"

"M. Gauthier?"

"Yes. Who's this?"

"Detective Inspector Vanier."

There was a brief pause, then, "Detective Inspector, I'm hon-
oured. What can I do for you?"

"I just wanted to congratulate you on your coverage of the homeless deaths. You must be working very hard on the story."

"Very kind of you, Inspector. I do what I can."

"You seem to be in front of the pack on this one. You always
know more that your competitors."

"I work harder than them. Simple as that."

"Tell me, do you know my colleague, Detective Sergeant Fletcher?"

Another pause. "Of course I do. He's my brother-in-law."

Vanier looked at St. Jacques' list again. Fletcher had been calling
two Gauthiers, the list said: the other was Marie-Chantal Gauthier,
Wife. "Marie-Chantal is your sister?"

"Correct."

"And what are you going to tell Marie-Chantal when her husband gets his ass kicked off the force?"

"What?"

"Simple question."

"Listen, Inspector, if you think that David is my source, you've
got it dead wrong. In fact, he's been pissed at me for the last few days.
Every time I do a story that's a bit too accurate he's on my case wanting to know where I'm getting my information. He was worried. He
knew someone would make the connection soon enough."

"So what did you tell him?"

"What I told you; that I work harder than the others."

"You expect me to believe that?"

"Believe whatever you like, Inspector. I have a job to do, and just because my brother-in-law is on the investigation doesn't mean I stop working. But don't think that he's feeding me information. He's not."

"Just so we're clear, M. Gauthier. If you have a source in my division, he or she is finished. Understand?"

"Good day, Inspector."

## 3 PM

Vanier was sitting with his back to a wall in Magnan's Tavern, his attention divided between watching the door and watching highlights of last night's hockey game on the big screen. Magnan's was almost empty, the lunch crowd long gone and the evening crowd not yet arrived. Only the serious drinkers were bridging the gap. Beaudoin walked in and quickly spotted Vanier. As he sat down, a waitress close to retirement age appeared behind Vanier with a tray in one hand, the other resting on Vanier's shoulder. Beaudoin ordered a beer and Vanier a refill.

"I wanted to follow up on our conversation. We were interrupted," said Beaudoin.

"Yes, I noticed. It must be hard."

"What?"

"Becoming a professional, and then finding that you're not in charge. You're still taking orders."

"Are you in charge, Inspector?"

"Ha," Vanier's eyes brightened. "Good question. Can we ever be independent?"

"Win the lottery, I suppose."

"No. Not even then. So what else is there?"

"What?"

"The Shelter. What should I know?"

The waitress put two frosted drafts on the table and walked off, and Beaudoin started talking. There was a company, Blackrock Investments, and they were interested in acquiring the Holy Land property. Not acquiring exactly, because acquiring implied buying it, it implied a cost. They were interested in having the Shelter's land and a lot less interested in paying for it. Henderson got wind of it somehow and, all of a sudden, Blackrock became a client. Henderson concocted a plan. It was a land swap. Blackrock owned land on the fringe of the fringe of the lower island under the expressway, a worthless patch of land good for nothing but low-rent warehouses and chop-shops. It was known as The Stables, because people had once kept horses there, maybe a hundred years ago, but it was now one of those useless, polluted urban islands, rendered inaccessible by highways and train tracks. The plan was to swap the Holy Land property for The Stables, along with a promise to build a state-of-the-art refuge for the homeless. Because promises and plans are cheap, no expense was spared. It would be a comfortable home for the destitute, designed for rehabilitation, retraining and reintegration; an ambitious plan to bring the homeless back into society instead of just warehousing them for a night.

Beaudoin explained that he didn't grasp the swindle immediately. He thought it was a great idea to upgrade the shelter. But within weeks, he realized it was all bullshit. The Stables was owned by a shell company, an empty shell that was ready to fold as soon as the swap was done. Everything was planned, even the excuses: the land was polluted, they couldn't get planning permission, financing didn't come through, it wasn't the ideal place to house the vulnerable. Nothing mattered, not even the excuses. There would be no new building, no new shelter. Blackrock would get the Holy Land property and make a fortune. The homeless would lose what little they had and end up, well, homeless. It would be tragic, hands would be wrung, but in the end, nobody would care. It was a brilliant plan.

But to get the swap accepted, they didn't just need the approval of the Board of Directors of the Shelter; they had to get the Holy Land Foundation to approve it. The Board ran the Shelter's day-to-day operations, but the Foundation owned the Shelter and the land underneath. It was run by a group of solid citizens whose job was to look after the Holy Land's core assets.

"The Foundation's members are all getting on in years, the average age must be 85," said Beaudoin. "It's easy to flood the Board of Directors with hand-picked yes men, but you can't do that with the Foundation. The way it's set up, the members of the Foundation choose their own members. To serve on the Foundation, you have to be asked by the current members of the Foundation. So that was a major problem. The current members of the Foundation would never agree to the deal without the kinds of guarantees Blackrock was not prepared to offer.

"So, brilliant as it was, the plan had a major problem: the Foundation. That's where I came in. After years on the Board, I knew the members of the Foundation, and they trusted me."

"So you went along?" asked Vanier.

Beaudoin looked down at the table and continued, trying to leave himself with some excuses. He couldn't.

"More than that, I became the key to the whole plan. Henderson told me to start courting the members of the Foundation and to start collecting proxies, the right to vote on behalf of the Foundation members. So I did. I took them out to dinner, to the hockey game, and then things started to happen. At first, it was only proxies for easy decisions at single meetings. But gradually I built up trust. I would call the members before meetings to get their instructions on how to vote on specific issues. After a while, they started asking me how they should vote. Eventually, some members were offering me general proxies. Like I said, they trusted me. They thought I was doing them a personal favour. To make matters worse, the proxies were always in the name of Henderson, my boss. I told them, well, I told them what I was told to tell them, that it was to preserve independence. So now Henderson's holding general proxies for more than two-thirds of the votes of the Foundation, and he intends to use them to approve the swap. And his ass is covered because the Board will recommend the swap. It's loaded with Blackrock appointees."

Beaudoin finished his beer, and Vanier gestured for two more.

"So how much do they stand to make?"

"Hard to tell. I've seen studies that value the condo project at $400 million. The land alone, free and ready to develop, is worth about $80 million. It's three city blocks, about ten minutes walking distance from downtown."

"When's the vote?"

"That's what I haven't been able to figure out. Even though Henderson is sitting on enough proxies to carry the vote, he still has to do things by the book. He needs to give notice to all the Foundation members and tell them what business is being considered. I've drafted and redrafted the notice a dozen times, and Henderson keeps giving it back to me. He says it's too clear, that I should make it obscure. I've drafted fine print that would make you go blind. That notice will go out soon, and then it's fifteen days to the meeting."

The beer arrived, and Beaudoin took a deep gulp. Vanier looked at him, trying to make up his mind, thinking that maybe a late conversion was better than none.

"How do you feel?"

"How the hell do you think I feel? I feel like shit. I'm betraying the one good thing I've done in the last five years. I try to justify it. I didn't really have a choice, I have to support my family."

"That justifies it?"

"No, that's not it. But I've got responsibilities. I've got two beautiful children and a wife who still loves me. Somebody has to put bread on the table."

"If only life were that easy, Pascal. The reason why you screw people doesn't matter, you're still screwing people. And who says you're entitled to use your family like that, to justify something they wouldn't agree with anyway."

"You're right. It's just bullshit self-justification. It's just me. I'm responsible. My family's not involved."

"Oh, they're involved. If you're involved, so are they. It's just not their fault. But you didn't call me for forgiveness or for a blessing. What is bothering you?"

Beaudoin stared into his beer and said nothing.

Vanier tried again. "What does your wife think of all this?"

"She doesn't know."

"You sure?"

"No. Maybe that's why I called you. Something's got to give. Letting this happen is a betrayal of who I am, of who I see myself as. I won't be the person she married, and she'll know. If she accepts it, we'll both be different people. And I don't think I would like either of us."

"People change all the time," Vanier said.

"No, they grow, they mature. But what's at the core stays the same."

Vanier thought about what he had said about Marcel Audet never changing. "Maybe you're right."

"So, what should I do?"

"I'm the last person to ask for advice. It's your decision. You have to make it."

"But I'm not alone."

"Then talk to your wife. They tell me that communication is

good; it's a healthy part of every marriage." Vanier sounded like he believed it.

Beaudoin was silent.

"So, what's Marcel Audet doing at the shelter?"

"I've thought about that. Blackrock has something on Nolet. He used to be a solid guy, but he's shut down for the last six months. He knows what's going on, but says nothing, like he's scared. I think Audet is there to keep an eye on him, to keep the pressure on. From what I've heard, Audet seems to have started a personal business, kind of a pay-day loan scheme. If you're homeless, you can use the Shelter's address to receive social security checks. I think Audet cashes them, for a price, and pockets a percentage. He's a nasty piece of work."

"I know. So why did you call me? What can I do?"

"Nothing, I guess. It's just, when you showed up at the office, I was hoping that the deal would be sidetracked. It wasn't. Henderson's still pushing."

He looked at Vanier, his hands opening up on the table. "This isn't police business, is it?"

"Not that I can see. Just another deal where good people get screwed over and everything is perfectly legitimate."

"This isn't where I wanted to be. You start by making small concessions, and before you know it, you've sold out. Your visit shook me. It made me think." He took a long slug of beer and looked at Vanier. "Maybe I just wanted a sounding board. No, it's more than that. I wanted you to know what's going on."

"Like I said, I don't normally give advice," said Vanier. "You lawyers have that all sewn up. But I'll make an exception in your case, Maître. Things can get ugly when there's a lot of money involved. Be careful."

Vanier wrote his cell phone number on his card and handed it to Beaudoin. "Call me. If you're worried. If something comes up. Call me."

Beaudoin put the card in his pocket, and Vanier stood up.

"So, when I go to see Blackrock Investments, who should I ask for?" said Vanier.

Beaudoin looked up at the policeman, surprised, and told him.

## 4.30 PM

Blackrock Investments had its offices on the top floor of a building on Chabanel, the centre of Montreal's garment district until the industry abandoned Montreal for the sweatshops of China, Vietnam and Bangladesh. With the industry gone, Chabanel became a honeycomb of empty spaces. That's where Blackrock came in. Backed by generous subsidies of other people's money, subsidies from all levels of government, they began buying the empty shells and reinventing the area as the creative and artistic centre of Montreal. Even with the subsidies, it was hard going, but eventually the neighbourhood started to fill up with designers, artists and software producers. Rents were cheap, because everyone was subsidized.

Vanier and St. Jacques sat in the steel-themed reception area on oversized chairs that looked like they were designed by a club-hopper whose idea of furniture was a place to perch for a few seconds before flitting to the next flower. The receptionist, a tall Haitian beauty, was dressed for a fashion shoot and thumbing through a magazine like they weren't there. Chill-out music, the kind Vanier hated, played from expensive speakers hidden somewhere in the décor. St. Jacques shifted uncomfortably on her perch.

The thick carpeting masked the sound of the approaching men, and Vanier sensed movement only at the last minute. Two men stood in front of them in suits that looked like they had been sprayed on. The shorter of the two reached out his hand to Vanier, "Inspector Vanier, I am Vladimir, Vladimir Markov. Please call me Vladimir, everyone does.

And this is Mr. Romanenko. He prefers to be called Mr. Romanenko."

Vanier found himself being polite. "Gentlemen, this is Detective Sergeant St. Jacques."

Markov's eyes made a fairly obvious tour of St. Jacques's body. "Detective Sergeant, I am charmed to meet you. Tell me, do you wear a gun? I would find that so exciting," he said, turning on what might pass for charm in Eastern Europe.

"Gentlemen, we have a few questions we would like to ask," said Vanier.

"Follow me, Inspector," said Markov, turning to the boardroom. "Ayida," he said to the receptionist, "could you whip up some coffee for our guests?"

"*Au lait* would be good, messieurs?" she asked.

"*Au lait* would be perfect."

Markov led them into a boardroom dominated by a huge conference table of grey polished steel that contrasted with the white walls and black-framed prints. *Not IKEA*, thought Vanier. Markov made a show of pulling a chair out for St. Jacques, and she tried her best not to look surprised. While they waited for coffee, Markov gave the officers a capsule history of Blackrock's achievements, its dedication to the revitalization of Montreal, its support for a litany of charitable works, its support for politicians of all parties, at all levels of government. The message was that Blackrock was an untouchable community asset, well beyond the reach of lowly police officers.

Eventually Ayida reappeared with a tray and four china cups.

"Ayida used to be a barista, and she cannot resist showing off her talent," said Markov. "Isn't that right, Ayida?"

Ayida acknowledged that he was right with a faint smile, and withdrew without a word.

"The coffee is roasted by 49$^{th}$ Parallel in Vancouver. Without a doubt, they are the best coffee roasters in North America, true artisans. Cheers!" Markov said, as he raised his cup.

Vanier reciprocated with a nod despite himself; he had to admit that the coffee was a huge step up from the machine at headquarters, even down to the palm tree pattern traced into the foamed milk. St. Jacques stared at the palm tree in her cup. Vanier pulled out a notebook and placed it on the table, a simple act of intimidation that seemed to be lost on Markov. Romanenko stared at the notebook.

"Now, Inspector," said Markov, "how can we help you?"

"We're looking into the deaths of five homeless people on Christmas Eve."

"I heard about that," said Markov. "It's tragic. As a member of the community, I feel that we really must do more for the less fortunate in society. But how can we help you with this, Inspector?"

"We're looking into Blackrock's relationship with the Holy Land Shelter. You're familiar with the Shelter, I assume?"

"Of course I am, Inspector. Isn't every Montrealer? It's a wonderful institution. In fact, I believe that we made a substantial donation to the Shelter last year. As I said earlier, we at Blackrock are very cognizant of our civic duty."

"What is your involvement with the Shelter, apart from the donation, of course?"

Markov sat, perfectly composed. He didn't look like he was forming an answer, and that was Romanenko's cue.

"Could you be a little more specific Inspector? That's a fairly vague question," said Romanenko.

The gloves were coming off, and Vanier felt more at ease.

"Is Blackrock interested in acquiring the Holy Land Shelter land?"

"Inspector," said Romanenko. "I can't see how Blackrock's investment plans have anything to do with your inquiries."

"Let me decide that. It's a simple question, yes or no?"

"Simple, I agree," said Romanenko. "But you are asking a question relating to the confidential business plans of a private corporation. A question, I might add, that has no apparent bearing on your investigation. If people knew what we plan to do, anyone – even a policeman – could make a fortune. Confidentiality is a critical part of our business. I am sure you understand, Inspector." He turned to face Markov. "I am advising my client not to answer any questions relating to the business plans of the company."

"He's strict, Inspector," said Markov. "Perhaps that's why he's so good. But I must follow my lawyer's instructions. Is there anything else you wanted to know? Perhaps something related to your investigation?"

Vanier was outgunned but tried again. "I've noticed that many of the current Board members of the Shelter have ties either to Blackrock, or to you. Why would that be?"

"Inspector," said Romanenko, "I believe that the usual objection to your question is that it assumes facts that have not been proven. And, again, that it does not appear to have any connection with your investigation."

"He is good, isn't he?" said Markov, smiling like an insurance salesman.

"So you won't help us with our investigation," Vanier said, looking at Markov.

Markov moved forward in his chair and looked Vanier in the eye, dropping the all-good-friends pretences.

"Inspector, if you come to me with a question relating to your investigation, any question at all, you will have my full cooperation. But don't think for one moment that you have a licence to come wandering in here with your wonderful assistant just because there is something about the modern world that you don't understand. Catch the madman who committed these murders, and I will have a word with the Mayor about a commendation. But I recommend that you stay with the job at hand, Inspector."

"Tell me, Mr. Markov, do you know a Michel Audet? He works at the Holy Land Shelter."

"Who?"

"Michel Audet. Name ring a bell?"

"Honestly, I can't say that it does. But you know how it is, Inspector. I meet so many people, sometimes names escape me."

"Even though your Board members hired someone with a criminal record for security?"

Markov said nothing. "Inspector, the Board does what it thinks is best for the shelter. Who am I to second-guess their decisions? Anyway, all I can say is that I don't recall this Mr. Audet. Perhaps I met him, perhaps not."

"Thank you, sir. I think that is all then," said Vanier, standing to leave. He waited for St. Jacques to join him, standing next to a perfect scale model of Blackrock's latest project, perfect, even down to the tiny people and shrubbery. As St. Jacques approached, he took a step back towards the maquette, and St. Jacques saw that a collision was inevitable.

Markov yelled, "Stop," but Vanier continued, colliding with the table, and sending the maquette crashing to the floor where it broke into pieces. Vanier looked up from the pile of rubble.

"So sorry. Accident."

Markov was angry and doing his best to contain it. He walked over to Vanier and said quietly, "Hey, policeman, chill. I'll have Ayida show you out."

"No need, we know the way."

St. Jacques joined Vanier as he walked to the exit. Vanier wondered how long it would be before the complaint reached Bédard.


8 PM


The city was half way through the job of clearing the snow from the last storm when another rolled in, promising to drop 25 to 39 centimetres. It had started around 5.30 p.m., and the snow was inches deep. Despite the storm, rue St. Denis was still crowded with bar-hoppers. At every corner, teenagers, refugees from small towns in the country and crap neighbourhoods in Montreal mumbled to anyone who would listen, "Hash, coke, Ex?" The market was open, and business was brisk.

Vanier was walking north, amusing himself by swerving into the pushers and their customers while he scanned the perimeter of the crowd. The pushers and their clients always scattered, looking at him like he was drunk, but not sure enough to do anything about it. He spotted Degrange standing in the entrance to a rooming house five steps up from the street, keeping an eye on his vendors. After years of loyal service, Degrange had been promoted. It wasn't much of a promotion, but enough so that he didn't touch the drugs or the money anymore. His job was to make sure that the pipeline kept flowing in both directions, drugs to the street and money to his boss, with no leaks in either direction. He was wearing a red lumberjack coat with a  Montreal Canadiens toque pulled tight over his ears. When he spotted Vanier bumping his way up the street, he pulled back into the shadow of the doorway. He had nowhere to go when Vanier climbed the steps.

"Inspector Vanier, great to see you again," he lied. "What can I do for you?"

"Let's take a walk"

"I can't, Inspector. I can't be seen walking down the street with someone like you. You understand".

"Shut up shop. Right now. I'll be in Harvey's, up the street. You better be there. Ten minutes."

Vanier walked down the steps and turned in the direction of Harvey's, continuing to weave through the pedestrian traffic, bumping into the vendors and disturbing the market.

He ordered two coffees at the counter and found a quiet table, glaring at anyone who approached to keep the surrounding tables remaining empty. Some customers recognized him and left without ordering. The coffee was getting cold when Degrange sat down and reached for the paper cup. He pulled four sachets of sugar out of his pocket and tore them open, two at a time, before tipping them into the coffee.

"You shouldn't do that, Inspector, scaring away the customers. It's bad for business."

In the heat of the restaurant, Degrange stank of mildew, sweat and cigarette smoke.

"You owe me, Michel. Don't forget."

"Did I say no? I'm just saying, I have to keep my credibility. I won't be any use to you if I lose my credibility, will I?"

"I want to know about Marcel Audet. He used to be with the Rock Machine. What do you hear about him now?"

Degrange's eyes lit up. "Audet? I remember him. Bad fucker, like all of them Rock Machine bastards. Don't know why they wanted to go up against the Hell. Never made sense. I don't hear of him these days. Wasn't he sent up for assault?"

"He's been out for four months. Did three years."

"He's not a player. I didn't even know he was around. Know what I mean?"

"Well, there's $50 for good information, not bullshit. Who's he working for? What's he doing? And an address. An address would be very useful."

"Well, Inspector, I can ask around. See what I can find out. But $50, that's minimum wage."

A couple was about to sit down, and Vanier gave them a look that sent them looking elsewhere.

"I want to know who he's working for. See what you can find out." Vanier dropped a  twenty on the table and left. Degrange reached for it quickly, like it might disappear.

## 9 PM

Beaudoin clicked the lights off in the children's rooms, slowly closing the doors, one after the other, and walked down the carpeted stairs. Caroline was sitting on the couch watching the hockey game on a muted television. Beaudoin sat on the chair opposite the couch. She didn't look up, feigning interest in the game while she used the remote to raise the volume just enough to discourage conversation without disturbing the children. She didn't react when the phone rang. Beaudoin got up.

"Hello."

…

"Yes, sir, I know."

…

"Mr. Henderson, the regulations say that the notice has to give a clear explanation of the business to be conducted at the meeting. If it's not clear, anything done at the meeting can be challenged later on the basis of an invalid notice." Beaudoin walked into the kitchen with the cordless phone pressed to his ear.

"I know that, sir. It's a delicate balance. But you have to protect yourself from future challenges. There's no point of winning a vote if it's overturned by the courts."

…

"Yes, sir. I'll do what I can. Obtuse, I'll aim for obtuse, as you say."

…

"Tomorrow. I'll have a redraft ready for you tomorrow."

He walked back into the living room, dropped the phone into its cradle, and sat down heavily on the chair.

"Caroline. We need to talk."

The most feared words of any relationship. She didn't say anything.

"This is not where I wanted to be. I thought I could do something, achieve something."

136

She continued watching the screen.

"I'm ashamed of who I am, Caroline. I don't like me. I don't like what I've become."

She pushed the mute button. "And you think it's my fault?" she replied, looking at him for the first time.

"No, I don't think it's your fault. But you've noticed?"

"Pascal, I love you, but you weren't made for this. You weren't made for compromise. And that seems to be all you do these days. And the compromises are killing you. You used to believe in things, and now it's just about earning money."

"I don't have the luxury to be an idealist, Caroline. We have two kids. They need a good home."

"They need a father more. They need a father they can look up to. I married you because of what you were, a caring person with principles. Pascal, look at you. Any time Henderson calls, you jump. You'd do anything he asks."

"That's what I mean, Caroline. I think I've reached the end."

Beaudoin explained the whole story. And his wife listened to the boy she had married years ago and hadn't seen in years. Was the person she married really coming back? She didn't know what to think, but she knew that if he was, she didn't want to lose him again. They made plans. How life would be. How life didn't have to be a series of compromises. She told him she didn't need the big house, didn't need the chalet up north, she needed him. And the kids needed him.

## 9.30 PM

Vanier poured the amber liquid over two ice cubes and swirled it around before sitting down in front of the pile of Prayer Cards that weren't even cards, but recycled scraps cut from sheets that had been used to print the Cathedral's newsletter, a sign of Mother Church's schizophrenia. The Church wallows in opulence one moment and is as parsimonious as a Scottish pauper the next. No expense is spared on costumes and props for the theatrics, and the trust funds are nurtured with a mother's concern, but messages to the saints must be scribbled on used scraps of paper, and the pious must pay for the candles burned in offerings.

Each rectangle of paper was dated in the top left-hand corner and had a hand-written note on one side. Printed scraps of unintelligible information from the newsletter filled the other. Most started with a variant of *Dear St. Jude,* and were signed, some with full names and others with abbreviated signatures: Mme. H, JP, or M. D. Each card was a postcard monument to the human spirit's inability to accept the brutal unfairness of life.

Vanier sipped on his Jameson and began to read:

> *Dear St. Jude,*
> *Our daughter Caroline has disappeared.*
> *Please give us a sign that she is alive. Help her*
> *understand that we love her. Help her find her way*
> *and, the Lord permitting, to find her way back to us.*
> *G.H.*

He counted them. There were 131 in all. He arranged them in chronological order. The earliest prayer was nine months ago, looking for a miracle to conquer inoperable cancer. The most recent was signed December 23. It read:

> *To St. Jude,*
> *My husband is the only man I have loved*
> *for 35 years, and he left me two weeks ago. Please*
> *restore him to me.*
> *Mme. G.*

He grouped them by subject: financial, matrimonial, medical, and a single rectangle praying for scholastic achievement. He tried to order them by the colour of the ink, and quickly realized that Drouin had probably supplied a cheap blue Biro along with the papers. Sometimes a prayer would set him back.

> *S.J.*
> *Michael has started hitting me again.*
> *Please put love back in his heart. Help him to stop*
> *drinking. Let him know that I love him.*

It was signed with two crosses, symbols of sacrifice. Vanier knew where that prayer had come from. He had often prayed something similar for his mother while pretending to be asleep when his father came home drunk and angry. He had prayed it in army bases across Canada, and his prayers were answered a couple of times when his father was shipped overseas. But no sooner were they answered than his mother would lead an assault on the saints pleading for his safe return.

He refilled his glass and started again. This time he laid them all out on the table and stood up for a bird's eye view. In a moment he saw it. He sat down and began selecting the squares that had names on them. Ten of them had first and second names, and each one was signed with an A. Each was a plea for a peaceful death, for an end to pain. They formed a single prayer mosaic. Five of the slips of paper had names he knew:

> *That the tormented suffering of Joe Yeoman be*
> *soon over and that he join his Holy Father in*
> *everlasting life.*
> *A*

> *For Edith Latendresse, that her inhuman*
> *suffering may end peacefully.*
> *A*

*That the Lord welcome Céline Plante into His*
*arms. A spirit too beautiful for this world.*
*A*

*Dear St. Jude.*
*Your servant George Morissette has suffered*
*enough. Give him release. Allow him to escape*
*his suffering and join you in everlasting life.*
*A*

*For Pierre Brun, during his last days on earth.*
*May his pain be short and the joy of everlasting*
*life be his.*
*A*

That left five cards in the pile with names. Vanier read the
remaining cards.

*For Antonio Di Pasquale, ease his suffering and*
*make his transition peaceful.*
*A*

*Mary Gallagher's time is coming soon. Accept*
*her into your arms Lord, and test her no more.*
*A*

*Duane Thatcher, a young man who will never*
*know middle age deserves your intervention to*
*ease his pain. Let him not suffer any more. Settle*
*his mind and give him peace.*
*A*

*For Denis Latulippe, may fate – and this world –*
*be kind to him in his last days.*
*A*

*My fellow man, Gaëtan Paquin, deserves better.
He has been sorely tried by life's hardships and
continues to struggle to overcome them. May his
final days be free of pain. And may he finally
realize your love.*

*A*

He stared at the five new names, wondering who they were, or
even if they were still alive. He picked up the phone and punched the
speed-dial. It picked up on the third ring.

"St. Jacques."

"Sylvie, it's me." He could hear ABBA playing in the background.
"ABBA?"

"It's a documentary on TV, sir. I was surfing the channels."

"I wouldn't have put you down as an ABBA fan."

"I'm not. Like I said, I was surfing. But I'm sure you didn't call to
discuss my musical tastes."

"You're right. But we'll pick up on this later. You were looking
into the typical number of homeless deaths in a year, right?"

"Right. But nobody keeps numbers. All we have are estimates
and they vary like crazy."

"And?"

"Well, the Coroner's office says there are about ten to fifteen a
year. But GimmeShelter, a group that lobbies for the homeless, says
the number's closer to 40. Seems to be a question of definition."

"So that's not going anywhere. Could you check some specific
names with your contacts? I need to know if they're alive or dead.
They could be on Santa's list." Vanier explained about the prayer
cards and gave her the five names. "And I think we should go and see
the priest first thing in the morning."

"The priest? Drouin?"

"Yeah. I'll pick you up at eight."

"Ok, sir. I'll see you then."

"Oh, and by the way."

"Sir?"

"I love ABBA. Enjoy."

"Thank you, sir."

Vanier flipped through the channels looking for the ABBA documentary but there wasn't one. Maybe she has satellite, he thought, and pulled out their Greatest Hits CD and put it on. Then he started sorting through the piles of newspapers and magazines that lay in the hallway waiting for recycling. They had been waiting for months. He pulled an old copy of the *Journal de Montréal* from the pile and went to the table; he only bought the newspaper when there was something of interest in it – which was rarely. The front page carried a large photograph of Vanier walking into police headquarters, guiding a handcuffed piece of shit with his hooded jacket pulled over his head. There was also a small photograph of Carole Thibodeau that the piece of shit had raped and strangled two days before. Vanier turned to the classified ads in the back pages and found what he was looking for: two columns of small ads thanking St. Jude for his intervention, often with a small photo of the man himself. The deal was, if St. Jude answered your prayers, you had to publish your thanks, and the *Journal de Montréal* gave them a special place every day. St. Jude had been busy, Vanier counted fifteen separate ads. All were more or less the same, no details of the answered prayers, just a standard thanks for intervention.

# SEVEN
## DECEMBER 29

8.30 PM

**Vanier and St. Jacques were sitting** in a pew close to the back, waiting for Drouin to finish his eight o'clock Mass. When it ended, they followed him and two altar boys through the side door and into the sacristy. The boys bowed with the priest towards the crucifix on the wall and then went off-duty, dashing on either side of the two officers as though they were avoiding furniture, trying their best not to break into a sprint in their rush to get out of the room and back into their street clothes. Drouin stood in his mass regalia and tried a wan smile.

"What can I do for you, Inspector?"

"I've looked through your cards, Father."

"My cards? They're not my cards. I don't own them. They are simply the prayers of the faithful."

"Did you know that all five of the victims are named in your prayer cards?"

Drouin's face lost what little colour it had, and he stared at Vanier, as though willing him to say more. Vanier looked back. Drouin turned to St. Jacques and saw he wouldn't get anything better from her.

"I'd thought about that. I don't remember all of the cards, there are so many. But I recalled praying for some of the victims."

"You didn't tell me that."

"It didn't seem important." Drouin removed the stole, absent-mindedly kissed its cross and hung it on a wooden valet.

"The prayers call for their release from suffering. Could that have been a message? Could someone have acted on it?" said Vanier.

"You think that someone in our group took it upon themselves to ensure that our prayers were answered? That can't be true. It must be a coincidence, Inspector."

The priest reached down and grabbed the hem of his white and gold chasuble, pulling it up over his head and draping it carefully over the valet. He turned back to them standing in his white alb, a symbol of purity.

"This is the Church. Human life, all human life, is sacred. You must know that, Inspector. It is inconceivable that any Catholic would do such a thing. Inconceivable."

"So you think it's a coincidence that your group has prayed for five people in the last few weeks and now they're all dead? That's some coincidence, Father."

"Inspector, I don't know what it is. All I know is that I cannot think of any connection between our prayer group and the kind of person who is capable of such an atrocity."

"And if I told you that some prayers haven't been answered yet? That we're trying to track down five other people who've been singled out for divine intervention in your prayer sessions?"

Drouin was in the process of pulling the alb up over his head, revealing his civilian clothes beneath, but he stopped and stared at Vanier. His hands were shaking.

"Dear God. What's going on? Tell me I can help."

"You can help, Father. There's nothing wrong with voicing your suspicions, no matter how far-fetched. In my job I see the far-fetched and ridiculous every day. How many newspaper stories have you read that start with, *"The neighbours were surprised. He seemed such a nice family man"*?

"What are you asking me to do? If there were anyone in our group I thought was capable of such acts, you would be the first to know. But there isn't, Inspector. You're asking me to imagine, to speculate, who might be capable of this. Well, I have no idea. But I will think hard about it, and I will pray for guidance."

"While you're doing that, why don't you pray for the next victims?"

Drouin clutched the edge of the wooden countertop.

"Mary Gallagher. Know her? What about Denis Latulippe? Or Gaëtan Paquin? Antonio Di Pasquale? Duane Thatcher? Know them? I have men looking for them right now. But I'll bet someone else is trying to track them down as well. Pray that we get there first."

The two officers couldn't help but hear the intake of breath. Drouin sat down.

"Mr. Thatcher died in late November. He died of exposure one night in the entrance to the Simons department store on St. Catherine. And Antonio hasn't been seen in months. People have been asking after him."

"When in November?"

Drouin looked at the calendar on the wall. He got up and flipped it back a page. "November 20. I remember it was a horrible night. It was cold, not cold enough to freeze, but too cold to sleep outside. It had been raining, and the poor man was soaked, trying to sleep in a doorway. Everyone assumed he simply died of exposure. It's more common than you think."

"He may have been helped on the way. Father, anything you can think of that might be useful."

"Inspector, I will go through all of the people that have attended the prayer services. If I can think of anything that might be helpful, I will call you."

"How many people are we talking about?"

"Fifty, perhaps sixty."

Vanier was surprised. "Do you have names, addresses?"

"No. This isn't an organized group, nobody has to give their name. Some people show up every few weeks. Others are more regular. Please, Inspector, let me sit quietly and think about it. I'll write a list of everyone I can think of and bring it to your office this afternoon."

"That would be helpful." Vanier reached into his pocket and pulled out two sheets. One was a photocopy of the prayer cards from the five victims on Christmas Eve. The other had the cards for the five remaining people. "Who wrote these?"

Drouin sat down with a sheet in each hand and scanned the cards. "Alain."

Vanier could barely hear. "Who?"

"Dr. Alain Grenier. They're all signed by the initial A. I've noticed he does that. But he couldn't have anything to do with this."

"Perhaps. Perhaps all he's doing is giving directions. But you have no doubt that these, these prayers, were all written by Dr. Grenier?"

"He wrote these," he said, handing the sheets back to Vanier.

"And you'll bring the list over this morning?"

"I said this afternoon, but as soon as it's done. I promise."

Vanier handed him his card. "Just in case you lost the last one."

He turned to leave, followed by St. Jacques.

Drouin sat down heavily on the wooden chair. Fifteen minutes later he was still there. He pulled up the hem of the alb, and reached into his pants pocket for his phone. Typing the first three letters of Grenier, the screen gave him a choice and he selected Call Home. It picked up immediately.

"Alain?"

"Father Henri, how good to hear from you. My best wishes to you for the season."

"I've just had a visit from Inspector Vanier."

"Yes. He came to see me on Christmas Day. A terrible business."

"Alain, he says that the names of the victims were all on the Circle's prayer cards." There was silence on the other end of the line.

"He says that they were all on cards written by you, Alain. How can that be?"

"They were my patients, Father Henri, and they were all desperately ill. I don't remember, but I could have asked for prayers for them. There was nothing else I could do for them but pray."

"So there might be a connection. It's not simply the Inspector's imagination."

"Father Henri, I'm not sure I would go that far. There's nothing wrong in praying for those in desperate need. But that's a long way from making a connection to murder. These people led very dangerous lives. If you ask me, it's just coincidence."

"The Inspector doesn't seem to believe in coincidence, Alain. And, quite frankly, I find it hard as well. What if someone in our group took it upon themselves to kill them just to ease their suffering? Isn't that our responsibility?" Drouin said, as though he were practising walking through the thoughts that were clouding his mind.

"I suppose it's possible, anything's possible, but it's unlikely. Anyway, let the police do their work, and they'll get to the bottom of this. Do what you can to help, but this is for the police. Let them do their work."

"I suppose you're right, Alain. But they said that there were five other names. One's dead, one's disappeared and the three others, who knows? What about them?"

"Do you know them?"

"I know one fairly well, Mary Gallagher, poor soul. The others

I know vaguely. The Inspector gave me the names, but they're not people that I've worked with. But it wouldn't take me long to track them down. I didn't tell him that. That's strange, Alain. I should have told him I could help him to find them. But I didn't." Drouin fingered Vanier's card.

"So why don't you call the Inspector and tell him that you can help. If they're in danger and you can help to locate them, let him know."

"Yes, Alain. I'll call the Inspector."

Drouin clicked disconnect on his phone and started punching another name into his address book. Just one number showed up. He pushed the Call Mobile button.

It picked up on the fifth ring.

"John?"

## 10 AM

Vanier and St Jacques were in the car driving north to Outremont, St. Jacques was on the phone to Laurent, and Vanier was brooding. When she finished, she turned to Vanier.

"You're very quiet," she said.

"The usual woman's opening. The all-time classic open question."

"I just said, you're very quiet. And it's not a question."

"You were on the phone."

"Right."

"What do you make of him?" she asked.

"Who?"

"Drouin, of course. You were thinking of someone else?"

"He's strange, locked down. Like his inner life is running on speed, and real life is an accident. Make sense?"

"A little," she said. "Think he's a suspect?"

"He has to be, but I'm having trouble with the idea."

Why?" She turned away to look out the passenger window.

"I don't know. It's not just the timing, although that should be enough. But he seems like he's struggling with himself too much to take on murder. Like he's carrying some personal burden that has all his attention. But he's not telling us everything."

"I doubt he's telling anyone everything. But I get your point. He's focused, but it's inward."

"So how do we get him to open up?"

"Good question. We turn left here." St. Jacques was reading the street signs. They parked in the driveway, and St Jacques looked at the façade of the big house.

"Strange," she said, as they walked up the steps to the front door. Vanier agreed. It was one of those houses that tried to make a statement but didn't manage it, leaving you wondering about the architect, but not in a good way. It was a Frank Lloyd Wright imitation with all of the lines but none of the flow; concrete and glass without the poetry. She rang the doorbell, and a mouse of a woman in a blue nylon dressing gown and matching blue slippers answered the door, holding onto it for protection.

"Good morning, I'm Detective Inspector Vanier of the Montreal Police, and this is Detective Sergeant St. Jacques. Is Dr. Grenier home?"

She looked at Vanier as though he was speaking Farsi. She was saved by a voice from within asking who it was. She stepped back, opening the door wider to give a better view of the visitors, "It's the police," she said, almost an afterthought.

Dr. Grenier appeared behind her, clutching a newspaper. He put his free hand on her shoulders, and she moved out of the way.

"Thank you, Evelyn. I will see to our visitors."

"Good morning, Doctor. I wonder if we can bother you with a few questions," said Vanier.

"Certainly," said Grenier, taking up a position in the doorway that said there would not be an invitation to come in.

"Can we come in?"

"Oh. Of course," he said, backing away from the door. "If you would take your shoes off and leave them here."

Vanier thought about keeping his on for show, but relented. St. Jacques was already shoeless. Grenier handed them each paper, disposable slippers, the kind they give out in dentists' offices, and led them into a study that was as bare as his office.

He sat at the desk and beckoned them to sit down.

"I hope your investigation is progressing. It's a terrible business."

"Police business?" said Vanier. "It's not so bad."

Grenier looked him in the eye. "I meant the deaths of these poor souls."

"Oh. Yes."

"What can I do for you?"

"We're interested in Father Drouin's Circle of Christ. You were an active member, I believe."

"Well, that depends on how you define active, doesn't it? But I suppose you could say I am a regular member. I participate as much as my work permits. I find prayer is good for the soul."

"Don't we all," Vanier lied. "But what did you pray for?"

"I don't see what this has to do…"

"Humour me, Doctor. What did you pray for?"

"Like everyone else, I prayed for the intentions that were expressed. They were varied, Inspector, success in school, family troubles. People used to bring …"

"What about your own prayers, Doctor? Did you ask the group to prayer for your wishes?"

"I filled out cards from time to time, like everyone else. That was the purpose of the group. And, yes, I asked the group to pray for the five individuals who died. You already know that."

Vanier and St. Jacques exchanged a glance. Drouin had called Grenier after their visit. Vanier took an envelope out of his pocket and pulled out five prayer cards. Each was sitting inside its own plastic bag. He laid them face up in front of Dr. Grenier. "So you acknowledge that you filled out these cards?"

Grenier looked up, past the two officers. "No."

St. Jacques turned to see Mme. Grenier reversing out of the room, a tray in her hand. She stood up and followed the woman.

"You didn't write these cards, Doctor?" said Vanier.

"No. I mean, yes. I was confused. My wife was bringing coffee. They are the cards that I wrote for the prayer circle. Yes."

Grenier looked at them, his hands palm down on the desk, not wanting to touch them.

"Do you see the names?"

"Of course I do. They're the five victims from Christmas Eve," he said, straining not to shout. "Of course I see them."

"Do you think that your prayers have been answered?"

"What are you suggesting? That I prayed that they would be killed? Are you insane?"

"No, Doctor. I'm not insane. I see five cards begging St. Jude to deliver five people from their suffering, and I've got five corpses lying in cold drawers in the morgue. They're not suffering any more. Haven't your prayers been answered, Doctor?"

"I didn't pray that they'd be killed. I prayed that they would be spared the suffering they were enduring. I didn't pray for more suffering. Have my prayers been answered? Who knows?"

"Who knows?"

"Inspector. You can't understand. You don't know the pain that these people were enduring. You have no idea. You see someone pushing a supermarket trolley full of their possessions, and you think you understand."

"So death is better?"

"Don't put words in my mouth."

St Jacques walked back into the room with two mugs of coffee.

"You wife was coming in with a tray and turned around. Thought I'd salvage some coffee. We haven't had breakfast."

She put a mug of coffee before Vanier. He picked it up and leaned back.

"Sergeant, while you were away, Dr. Grenier admitted that he wrote the five prayer cards that name our victims, but he's not sure if his prayers have been answered. Now, you were saying that I shouldn't put words in your mouth, Doctor."

"That's right. Who are you to accuse me of being involved in this?"

"I'm not accusing…"

"I've spent thirty years bringing comfort to destitute people. I tended them, loved them. What I did, I did out of love, and with God's blessing. You, Inspector, you might toss the occasional dollar in the direction of someone who holds his hand out in the street, but I live with these people every day."

"What I was saying, Doctor—"

"Let me finish, Inspector. I'm not the one who decided to empty Quebec's mental health institutions and force the sick and dysfunctional into the streets. I wasn't the one who waved them goodbye and sent them off to fend for themselves with nothing but a bottle of pills. Blame the politicians, the liberals in the universities. Blame society. Those people who sit safe and warm in cozy houses, far away from the street, those who decided that the state shouldn't pay to look after the sick and broken. They said, *Put them into the community, and we can take better care of them there.* Yes, a great idea. A great idea if we lived in a community of saints. But we don't. We live in a community of isolated, self-absorbed individualists who don't give a damn about their fellow man."

Vanier and St. Jacques stared as Grenier continued as though a long-sealed tap had been opened. He was the one trying to ease the suffering caused by others, and it was an affront to think that he could do harm.

"We poured them out of the institutions like shit from a bucket to float away God knows where; but not into my neighbourhood. As soon as they stop in my street, or collect in my parks, well flush them away somewhere else. Make them move on. Sure, we buy virtue by writing cheques to charity, a cheque for little Angelica in some god-forsaken hole in Africa, or Juan in a hovel in the Dominican Republic. And maybe we get a yearly photo of our good works that we can stick on the fridge and tell our friends about our adopted kids in the Third World. But we turn away from the sick, destitute, beaten and just damn poor that live right here. Every day, we cross the street assuming that a Samaritan will turn up to help the broken man lying on the ground."

His eyes were getting cloudy.

"These are my people, Inspector. Praying for them, and asking others to pray for them, doesn't make me a murderer. I cared for them."

Vanier was taken aback. St. Jacques spoke up.

"Dr. Grenier, in the prayer cards, we found five other cards that we'd like to ask you about."

Vanier took out the second envelope from his pocket and laid the last five cards on Grenier's desk. Grenier looked at them.

"Oh my God." He reached out his hand and touched one with his finger. "Duane Thatcher died in November."

"We know that, Doctor."

"I haven't seen or heard from Antonio Di Pasquale in, what, six to eight weeks." He shifted his eyes to the third card. "Mary Gallagher, a lost soul in need of help, but what's the point. She's dying, like Denis Latulippe and Gaëtan Paquin. They all know it. They know they are on their way out, and I think they accept it. Like it's the natural trajectory of their lives. But don't think for a moment that I wanted them to die. Nothing is more ridiculous. I put their names on these cards because, deep down, I want to have some grain of hope for them."

"If four are still alive, where can we find them?"

"Inspector, these people are nomadic. They're here one day and somewhere else the next. They might keep to regular haunts for weeks and then, a whim or a new friend might take them to a squat in St. Henri for a month. Try the missions, the shelters. That's all I can say. And I'll ask around. If they show up at my clinic, I'll call you. Find them, Inspector. If they're in danger, find them."

"I intend to," said Vanier. "But who else is looking for them? Any ideas?"

"You mean the prayer group?"

"That seems a reasonable conclusion. Maybe someone is doing some divine intervention of their own."

"No, that couldn't be. It's impossible. The people in the group are all devout Catholics. They're not murderers."

"Why don't we start with some names?"

"Names? It's not a social club, Inspector. If I know anyone who attends, it's because I know them from somewhere else."

"We have to start somewhere. You give us some names, and we talk to them, and they give us some more. Eventually, we should have everyone in the group, and we'll talk to them all."

"Well, I can tell you the ones that I know." He started with Father Drouin and excused himself. "Of course, you know Father Drouin already." He continued with others; a few doctors, two lawyers, a businessman. The mayor of a small town on the West Island was an occasional participant. St. Jacques wrote them down, recognizing a few from occasional mentions on the news or in the newspapers.

"If you think of any others, you'll call me or Sergeant St. Jacques." It wasn't a question, more of a statement.

"Yes, of course, Inspector."

# THE DEAD OF WINTER

## 1 PM

The dining hall of the Old Brewery Mission had been decorated for the holidays with grinning plastic Santas stuck to the walls, and ropes of red and gold tinsel that failed to hide the grim functionality of the room. The room was hot, the air thick with the smell of institutional food, and long mess-hall tables were lined with men and women waiting for a plate to be put in front of them, or slurping down food with the speed of the half-starved. Two cooks stood behind a counter filling plates with a thick stew and a roll of bread. Volunteers moved quickly between the serving counter and the tables.

Vanier and Laurent were sweating in their overcoats. Pools of melting snow were gathering around their boots. Robert Bertrand, the director of the mission, stood beside them surveying the room. "It won't be long now. Serving is what takes the time. They don't linger over the food. Probably ten minutes and you can talk to him."

Every now and then, one of the patrons would look up furtively, trying to decide whether the obvious presence of cops involved them.

As the last plates of stew were placed on the tables, fruit salad was ladled from industrial-sized cans into small bowls, and the volunteers began the circuit again, removing the empty dinner plates and replacing them with the dessert.

"When you've been doing this as long as we have, you get efficient. Three hundred people a day on average, three hours of prep, and it's all over in twenty minutes. Another hour to wash up and we begin the preparation for dinner. We never stop, Inspector!"

"I'm impressed, Mr. Bertrand. It's quite the operation you have here," said Vanier.

"Well, we couldn't do it without help from an army of good people. We exist because of human kindness."

Vanier watched the volunteers move with practiced efficiency. Every plate was served with a quick comment, a smile or a hand on a shoulder; food for the body and food for the soul. As they moved through the room, islands of laughter would erupt from the volunteers and the diners.

"Your people are having fun, Mr. Bertrand," said Vanier.

"Compassion is good for the spirit, Inspector. Our volunteers enjoy themselves. If any of your men are feeling depressed, send them to us and we'll have them fixed up in no time. Perhaps you'd like to try a shift yourself?"

Laurent smiled at the image of Vanier serving fruit salad to the homeless.

"Not me, Mr. Bertrand. But Laurent here might be just the man. He could do with a little exercise in the compassion department."

"Well, gentlemen, anytime either of you want to try something new, you're more than welcome. Just walk in off the street, and we will find something for you to do. I guarantee it will open your hearts. You won't regret it."

"I'll keep that in mind," said Vanier.

Lunch was ending. "Come along gentlemen. Let's go meet Gaëtan."

Gaëtan Paquin's dinner companions had already left, and he was wiping greasy sauce from his lips with a serviette. He eyed them suspiciously as they approached,

"M. Paquin, do you mind if we sit down?" asked Vanier.

"I don't own the table."

Laurent and Vanier sat down opposite Paquin on the long bench.

"I'll leave you to your business then," said Bertrand and walked off towards the kitchen.

Paquin glared at the two men but couldn't hold the eye contact. He looked down at the table, and then back to each of them. His hands were dark with dirt. On a farmer, it would have been testimony to honest work in the fields, but on Paquin it was just dirt. You could have grown vegetables in his fingernails.

"Police. Right?"

"Yes."

"What do you want with me? I haven't done nothing. Think I would be sitting here accepting charity if I had?" he said.

"We're not here for anything that you've done," said Vanier.

Paquin exploded in disconcerting laughter. You couldn't tell if it was amusement or relief. "Ha. What a joke? I haven't done nothing. I've broken every single one of your fucking laws and I'm proud of it. So lock me up. Do me a favour, lock me up."

"We're here about those deaths on Christmas Eve," said Vanier.

His demeanor changed. He was paying attention.

"That wasn't right. I knew two of them. Good people. Just a little down on their luck, that's all. They didn't deserve to be killed."

"You're right. We are trying to find the person who did it," said Vanier.

"So it's true, they were killed? That's the word on the street."

"Yes, it's true. And we have reason to believe that your life may also be in danger. Your name came up in the investigation and we think you may be in danger. We're here to offer you protection for a while, until this gets resolved."

"Me? Who the hell would want to kill me? I'm nobody."

"Just like the others. There wasn't much point in that, either. But they're dead. We want to offer you protection. Just till we find out who did it."

"The police offering me protection?" Again, the off-centre laugh that seemed like it could snap off into delirium at any moment. "You people have hounded me all my life. I've been fucked around by the police for as long as I can remember. It's a joke, you offering me protection." His voice was getting louder.

"I'm sorry for whatever other officers put you through," said Vanier. "But believe me, we're here to help you."

Paquin's mind was racing trying to process so much information.

Life was usually simple, he took decisions on impulse with little thought for consequences. But this was different. "What kind of protection?" he whispered, looking first at Vanier and then to Laurent.

"We've arranged for you to stay in a small men's shelter in the East End. You'll be off the streets for a while. Warm bed at night, good food. Medical help. I understand that you have a condition."

"I get help. I go to Dr. Grenier's clinic when I'm sick. He knows me."

"It's temporary. We're going to resolve this thing soon and then you can do whatever you want. We think you should be off the street for a few days. We can drive you there now if you want."

Paquin wasn't good at decisions. His mind was a jumble of fear and desperation. Shelters had rules and restrictions. The doors are locked at night. Get up now. Shower now. Eat this. Don't drink... don't drink. That was the clincher.

He looked at the officers. "I'm not afraid. I've survived 25 years on the streets." His courage was returning as he talked. "I don't need your fucking protection. I don't need you. Go find your crazy and lock him up. But you're not locking me up in no fucking shelter just because you can't do your job."

"Think about what you're saying. We're not locking you up. We're offering you a chance. Take it, or at least give it a try," said Vanier.

"No way. No fucking way. I can look after myself." He was becoming agitated, looking beyond the officers to the door. "Am I under arrest? Because if not, I'm leaving," he said, but not getting up from the table until they gave him a sign. He knew the rules.

"Here,' said Vanier getting up. "Take my card. If you change your mind, call me. Call me. Anytime."

Paquin took the card, stuffed it absent-mindedly into the pocket of his filthy coat, and stood up. Vanier reached into his pocket and took out two twenties. "If you won't accept our help, take this. Maybe it will help."

"Every little bit helps, Inspector," said Paquin, already planning what to do with 40 dollars as he headed for the door.

## 2:00 PM

As they left the Old Brewery mission, St Jacques called with a possible location for Latulippe. In a few minutes they pulled into a diplomatic parking space outside the ICAO building on University Street. A panhandler was working the cars stopped at the lights, moving up and down the line of cars for as long as the red light lasted, then manoeuvering back to the sidewalk through slow traffic. He was showing a grimacing mouth full of filthy teeth to each driver while waving an extra-large McDonald's paper cup and doing a weird, shuffling dance to music only he heard. His breath formed white clouds in the freezing air, but he seemed impervious to the cold. The light changed to green, and he snaked his way back to the sidewalk. He recognized them as cops immediately.

"Hey, I ain't doing nothing wrong, just exchanging coins for songs."

"Are you Denis Latulippe?" said Vanier.

"What of it?"

"Can we talk?"

He didn't answer, just shook the cup under Vanier's chin. There wasn't much to shake. "Talk ain't cheap," he said.

Laurent got his attention by holding a five dollar bill over the cup.

"We've got a proposition for you," said Vanier. Laurent dropped the bill into the cup.

"What might that be, officers?"

"We think you're in danger. Your name came up in an investigation. Someone threatened to kill you. Do you have any idea who would want to kill you?"

"Kill me? They'd be doing me a favour, and no one done me a favour in a long time. Except for your friend here of course" he said, motioning to Laurent with a yellow-toothed grin, as he pulled the five dollars from the cup and pocketed it. "Who the hell would want to kill Denis? I'm everyone's friend."

He started his shuffling dance again.

"Think about it. You know anyone who would want to put you out of your misery? Maybe for your own good?" said Vanier.

Latulippe was taken aback, but seemed to be giving it serious thought. "Naw. Can't think of anyone. You guys serious?"

"We are. And we think it's serious enough to offer you some shelter. Think of it as a week's holiday in the country. All expenses paid."

Despite his bravado, Latulippe was taking it seriously. His thoughts telegraphed to his face like it was wired directly to the emotional centre of his brain; the worst poker face in the city.

"Wait a minute. Is this anything to do with those people who died on Christmas Eve? Is it about that?"

"Yes," said Vanier. "Your name came up, and we thought it best to make sure that you were out of harm's way. Look, I'm freezing out here, why don't we talk in the car?"

"You're not arresting me?"

"For what, selling songs? We'd have to go after Céline Dion too," said Vanier. "Grab your bags, and we can talk in the car."

Latulippe reached behind a column in the building entrance, grabbed a backpack and a large Holt Renfrew shopping bag, and followed them to the car. The engine started at the first turn of the key, and Vanier put the heat on full blast. He turned to look at Latulippe in the back seat, dwarfed next to Laurent and grinning like a circus clown. He quickly regretted pumping the heat. Sitting with Latulippe in any enclosed space would not have been pleasant, but with the heat going, the air quickly became as thick as the inside of a Port-A-Can on the last day of a NASCAR weekend in August. Laurent cracked his window down and pointed his nose into the cold breeze.

"Seriously," said Vanier, trying to make sense of Latulippe's insane smile. "What would you say to an all-expenses holiday in the Laurentians? A nice house just outside Morin Heights, or we can do a halfway house in the East End. Your choice. Three meals a day, TV, your own room. Just no booze or drugs. You can go outside to smoke. What do you think?"

Latulippe had lost his grin. "I can't think! I need time. Look, I don't understand. Who would want to kill me? Why me? You got a cigarette?"

Vanier raised his hand to indicate no. Latulippe looked at Laurent and got the same response.

"We could buy you a couple of packs on the way if you want," said Laurent.

"Look, I don't think I can dry out that quickly, you know. I need to work up to it. Not saying that I can't go dry – I can. It's just that I need some time, that's all. You know, get into the right frame of mind. I can't do it suddenly. These places of yours. Maybe one of them can change the rules for a few days, give me a chance to work up to it. Time to adjust, you know?"

"They're firm on that one, Denis. No exceptions. No booze, no drugs – they have businesses to run, people who want to get dry. Their clients can smell an unopened bottle of wine at 50 yards, and they won't bend the rules. I already asked."

Vanier knew they were wasting their time. They weren't offering protection, they were just telling him he was a marked man.

"Look, I have to think this over. Maybe I can just disappear for a few days. I know people. I have places to stay. I mean, who is this guy? Why me? Why the others?"

"We don't know. But it won't be long. Listen, give it a try for a day or two. What's the worst that can happen?"

Latulippe didn't answer that one. "No, I'm staying here. I can take care of myself. I can stay quiet."

"Denis, we can't force you to do anything, but this is serious." Vanier saw that he had already lost him. "Tell you what, take a few days to get yourself organized. The offer is open whenever you're ready. Take my card and Sergeant Laurent's. Call either of us any-time and we'll pick you up. And here, take this in the meantime." Vanier handed him two twenties.

Latulippe looked at Laurent, as if willing him to chip in another twenty. Laurent kept his hands in his pockets. He looked at the two business cards in his hand as if reading them.

"What's your name again?" he said, looking at Vanier.

"Detective Inspector Vanier. My number is on the card."

"Well, thanks for the offer, but I gotta leave."

With that, he was out of the car and walking up University Street with his bags. They watched him go.

"So what do we do? We can't have someone follow him around," said Laurent.

"No. And we can't arrest him either. He has his own fucking problems, and they won't let go of him. That's why he's on the street. You think we're the first to offer him help?"

"I suppose not." Laurent transferred into the front seat. "Christ, it's cold out there. Where to now?"

"A surprise I've been planning."

"Great. I love surprises."

## 2.30 PM

Brossard is a small town on the south shore of the St. Lawrence where those who aren't rich, poor or stubborn enough to live downtown can afford to raise a family and still be close enough to commute to the city. Because of the bridge, it's an hour's commute each way, built for the respectable people who work eight-to-four or nine-to-five, the people who keep the castle running but can't sleep within its walls, the FedEx drivers, the sandwich shop owners, the elevator and escalator mechanics who keep everything greased and running, and the bank tellers who haven't been swapped for more machines. In Brossard they raise families in desolate suburban plots where hundred-year-old trees were bulldozed out of the way to lower the cost of putting up the factory-built crap that passes for houses. In the oldest sections, the trees had grown back in orderly rows along the main streets, and with only slightly less order in backyards. In the newer developments, the only nature is trimmed grass and gardens bought from Home Depot. In winter, the landscape is bleak, and the wind blows the snow into great drifts against the only obstacles left: houses, pre-fabricated garden sheds, and above-ground swimming pools.

Detective Sergeants Roberge and Janvier were in a small house, sitting uncomfortably on a small sofa facing Mme. Adèle Paradis, the Grande Dame of the classified advertisement department of the *Journal de Montréal*. She was sitting on a dark blue La-Z-Boy that clashed with everything else in the room, a fat grey cat was asleep in her lap. Two other cats were prowling around, unhappy with the visitors. Mme. Paradis was nursing a hangover and drinking coffee laced with gin in an attempt to pull herself together. She had been asleep when they arrived, and they had waited ten minutes on the doorstep, and another twenty while she made instant java in the kitchen.

"So, what can I do for you? Would you like biscuits? I don't have visitors often."

Sergeant Janvier reached into his bag and pulled out three photocopies. Each was a page from the St. Jude section of the classified ads in the *Journal de Montréal*. On each page, a specific ad had been circled.

"Mme. Paradis, we're interested in the ads that have been circled. We went to the office, but they couldn't tell us much. They confirmed that the ads were all paid for in cash at the counter and there was no address. The people at the office said that if anyone could give us more on who placed the ads, it was you. That's why we're here. Do you remember any of the people who placed the ads?"

Mme. Paradis took the papers with a shaking hand and began to look through them. She was suffering, but doing her best.

"It was the same person. He bought all of them, Pious John. Such a charming man. Always paid cash and didn't want a receipt."

"Pious John?"

"Well, that's what he told me once. When I asked him he said: You can call me Pious John. So that's what I called him."

"You remember what he looks like?"

"Remember? Of course I do. He's handsome, a little strange, but handsome. He has these piercing eyes and such a real smile. You know what I mean? Some people smile and you know they don't mean it. When he smiles, you feel it. I like him. A real gentleman."

"So why do you say strange? You said he was a little strange," asked Janvier.

"I did, didn't I? I suppose it was the way he dressed. He always wore this long black cassock. Like a priest, but not quite. At first I thought he was Orthodox. But then he wouldn't be praying to St. Jude, would he?"

"I suppose not," said Janvier.

"So I asked him straight out. I said, *So, what order are you with?*"

"And?"

"*Not the Church of Rome.* That's what he said. It sounded so strange. *Not the Church of Rome.*"

"Would you recognize him if you saw him again?"

"I couldn't forget his face. Those eyes, they were so expressive. I can picture them now."

The officers watched as she seemed to lose track of the conversation. The little colour in her face drained, and she raised herself out of the La-Z-Boy with an effort, the cat waking up in mid-air and falling onto his paws as though he was used to it.

"Excuse me," she said, rushing past the officers and disappearing again into the kitchen. They listened to her retching and the sound of vomit drop into the sink. By the rattling sound, there were dishes in the sink. She reappeared wiping her mouth with a dishcloth. Her face was as white as the landscape outside the window.

"I'm sorry, but I don't feel well. I'm going to have to lie down."

"Could you come in to see us tomorrow, Mme. Paradis?" asked Roberge.

"I'm supposed to be at work tomorrow. But I haven't been feeling well. So maybe I could call in sick. What time?"

"As early as you can make it."

"So let's say 10.30, shall we? No sense in fighting traffic, is there?"

"10.30 it is, Mme. Paradis. Are you sure you know where we are?"

She squinted at his card again. "Of course. I'll be there at 10.30 and I will ask for either one of you. That's right isn't it?"

"Perfect." The officers got up to leave, and she dropped back into the La-Z-Boy. The cat bounded back into her lap.

"And, Mme. Paradis, perhaps an early night tonight," said Roberge. "We'll need you in top form tomorrow. If you're not feeling well, a good night's sleep might be a good idea."

She promised to be a good girl, and they found their own way out.


## 3.30 PM


Audet was agitated as he looked at the balding civil servant across from him. He was holding himself back with difficulty.

"Tell me again, M. Letarte, you're from where?"

"The Ministère de l'emploi et de la solidarité sociale, you may know it better as the Welfare Services. And, as I said, we have the right to examine all of the books and records relating to the Shelter's receipt of welfare cheques addressed to beneficiaries who have chosen the Shelter as their address to receive benefits. At last count, there were 437 people who received their welfare cheques through the Shelter. So it's really quite simple. I would like to see the records that confirm receipt and distribution of the cheques."

"You got a search warrant?"

"M. Audet, I don't need a search warrant. It says right there in section 83 of the Act," he said, pointing to the photocopy he had given Audet. Then he quoted from memory. "*An Inspector — that's me — can enter any place during office hours to examine and, if found, to remove to be examined at a later time, the books and records of any business or organization that has agreed to receive payments on behalf of beneficiaries under the Act.*"

"Well, I don't have access to these books and records. It's Christmas. We're on skeleton staff."

"Then I would refer you to section 90 of the Act."

Letarte pointed to section 90, which he had also photocopied. Audet stared at the sheet of paper and Letarte began to recite, "*Anyone who fails to produce any books or records in accordance with a request pursuant to section 83 is guilty of an offence.*"

"Wait a second," said Audet. "You don't have a search warrant, and I'm guilty of an offence if I don't give stuff to you? What kind of a country is this?"

"It's the law, Mr. Audet. Now, could you please show me the records relating to welfare cheques?"

"Go fuck yourself," said Audet, rising from the chair. "I don't have to listen to this bullshit. Listen, you want to look at papers, you do what everyone does, OK? You go see a fucking judge and get yourself a search warrant."

Audet got to his feet, moved behind Letarte's chair and pulled him up by the collar until the civil servant was standing on his toes.

"I should toss you out the fucking window, you asshole."

"What are you doing? I protest. This is assault."

"Fuck you."

Holding his collar, Audet frog-marched Letarte out of the office and down the staircase to the front door. Letarte didn't resist. It was all he could do to keep up with Audet and breathe at the same time. Audet pushed open the door with his left hand, and shoved Letarte violently out the door with his right hand, watching him hop, skip and jump down the three steps of the entrance trying to keep his balance before finally losing his footing on a sliver of ice and falling heavily into the snow piled up at the edge of the path.

"Fucking asshole," Audet screamed after him before letting the door close.

Letarte got to his feet slowly and brushed snow off the front of his coat. He was still shaking when he got to the car parked at the corner.

"Why do you upset people like that?" Vanier asked as Letarte climbed into the back. Vanier could see the veins in Letarte's neck pumping blood as he pulled the door closed, pushed the button to lock it, and put his hands between his knees to stop them shaking.

"You didn't tell me he was a violent maniac," he said finally, turning to Vanier. "I could have been killed. I am definitely putting in for overtime on this. Forget any more bloody favours, Inspector Vanier."

Vanier was laughing. "Just imagine what it will be like when we come back, Claude." He turned to the other passenger in the back seat. "So Maître Giroux, can we get the affidavit finished before we get to Outremont?"

"It's all done, Inspector, except for the play-by-play of what went on inside. M. Letarte, did you ask M. Audet for access to the books and records relating to social security cheques?"

"Damn right I did."

Giroux began typing on his laptop.

Laurent had already pulled a U-turn and was heading to the home of Judge Antoinette Cardillo, duty Judge of the Superior Court of Montreal.

"And what was his response?"

"Go fuck yourself."

"Now, Claude, that's no way to talk to Maître Giroux," said Vanier.

"I was answering the question. Audet told me to go fuck myself. Oh yeah, he said that he should have thrown me out the window."

"Great," said Giroux, typing on his portable. "Then what?"

"He said that if I wanted to see the books I should go see a fucking judge and get a warrant."

"His *exact* words?"

"Yes."

"Marvelous."

"Then he grabbed me and dragged me to the door and threw me out."

"Wonderful. Here. Let me read this back to you."

Giroux was drafting and correcting the affidavit while Laurent tried to break speed records. When they pulled up outside Judge Cardillo's house in Outremont, Giroux was printing out the affidavit on a portable printer. Vanier took in the tasteful Christmas lights that festooned the house; tiny white lights strung around the trees nestled in fluffy snow. Giroux grabbed the papers and his shoulder bag and followed Vanier, Laurent and Letarte to the front door. The judge stood in the doorway in a white dressing gown, her blonde hair brushed back. They had called to say they were coming, and Vanier wondered why she wasn't dressed. She waited while they took off their boots and then led them into an office on the ground floor.

"Gentlemen, this better be good, I have 12 people coming to dinner at 7 p.m., and I need to get ready. It's the holiday season, you know."

Vanier watched black-suited catering staff hustling around behind the judge carrying glasses, bowls and cutlery into the dining room. She wouldn't be peeling potatoes tonight.

Giroux presented himself and introduced the two officers and Letarte. Vanier recognized her but didn't say anything. He had appeared as a witness before her about two years before. She hadn't believed him when he said the defendant's statement had been voluntary, and she let the rapist go. Two months later he was picked up again, this time for rape and murder. After a longer trial before a different judge, he was put away for life, without parole eligibility for twenty years. In a fit of anger fuelled by too much whiskey, Vanier had sent Cardillo a copy of the judgment, in a plain envelope, and just in case she had forgotten, he included a copy of her own judgment. It made him feel better.

"We're here to request a search warrant, Madame Justice. Here is the affidavit, and here is the warrant we are asking you to authorize."

She took the papers and began reading the affidavit and the terms of the warrant. She looked up at M. Letarte. "You're the affiant?"

"What?"

"Are you the person who swore the affidavit?"

"Yes, in the car, before Maître Giroux, on the way over here."

"And it's all true?"

"Yes, Madame. It's the truth."

"You've had an interesting afternoon."

"I suppose that you might call it that, yes."

"Why are you conducting these inquiries over the holidays. Why are things so urgent?"

Letarte was lost. He knew that he couldn't say that he was doing it because Vanier asked him, and that he owed Vanier a favour. "I had a call, Madame, suggesting that certain officials at the Holy Land Shelter were defrauding welfare beneficiaries of their allowances. It's my duty to investigate."

"If I could interrupt, Madame," said Vanier.

"I wondered when you might speak up, Inspector," she said, looking at him coldly.

"We consider that the allegations are very important, and if we don't act immediately, important evidence will be lost."

"Inspector Vanier. Didn't I see you on the television yesterday, hiding behind a Press Officer?"

"Well, if you saw me, I couldn't have been hiding very well."

She glared.

"Is this request related in any way to your investigation of the homeless deaths on Christmas Eve? You know that we frown on using pretexts to collect evidence."

"Madame, we have no reason at this time to make any connection between any fraud at the Shelter and the deaths on Christmas Eve. Except, of course, that in both cases, homeless people are being treated very badly."

She got his point. She had more to lose by refusing to authorize the warrant than by granting it. The homeless had become a news item, and she didn't want to be seen assisting in their exploitation.

"Very well, Inspector. Here is your warrant," she said, signing three copies and pushing them across the table. "Go make your search."

The men stood, wanting to be gone.

"Don't stand on formalities. Why don't you just turn and run. You have work to do, I suppose."

"Thank you, Madame Justice," said Giroux.


Vanier was on the phone to his good friend Leroux, a Detective Inspector in the Fraud Squad, before they were in the car. "We're ready to roll. Get the gang down there, and we'll be there in twenty minutes."

They made it in fifteen. Vanier recognized the two unmarked cars and a black van by their occupants, ten officers in all, all of them itching to get out. He got out of the car and gestured to the others to follow. It was fifty minutes since Letarte had been thrown out into the snow, close to a world record for a search warrant. Vanier entered the building and waved the search warrant at the camera with a broad grin before leading six officers and Letarte down the hallway. Giroux tagged along just for the fun of it. Four officers stayed outside to watch the exits. Audet was sitting at his computer and looked up, open-mouthed, as they burst into the room. He started to type quickly, Vanier was already behind him, grabbing a fistful of his hair and pulling him over the chair and away from the keyboard. The chair fell, and Audet hung in mid-air until Vanier released his grip, letting him fall to the floor on his back. Audet knew better than to fight back, storing the anger.

"Fuck," was all he could say.

"I did as you said, M. Audet. I went and got a warrant," said Letarte with newfound courage. Vanier handed a copy of the warrant to Audet.

"Wait. Don't touch anything. I want to call my lawyers. Don't touch anything till I speak to the lawyers." Audet was losing his authority, and he knew it, as he watched officers rooting through the filing cabinets.

"That's not how it works," said Vanier. "Call your lawyers, but we're carrying on. Search warrant, remember? Now, where's M. Nolet?"

"How the fuck do I know? Go find him yourself."

"Why don't we go find him together?" Vanier grabbed Audet and walked him to the door. "We won't be long, gentlemen. Carry on."

"Wait, before he goes," asked Sergeant Filion, the computer geek. "Any passwords I should know about?"

"Fuck you," said Audet. "Want me to spell that for you?"

"Oh, that's OK. I love a challenge."

Vanier pushed Audet out the door in front of him and walked him down the hallway and through the doors leading to the stairwell. It was deserted, and Audet went to climb the staircase.

Vanier pulled him back and swung him against the wall, following with a punch to his gut. Audet doubled over, his knees buckling. Before he could think of reacting, Vanier pulled him up and landed another. Audet went down on his knees. Vanier pulled him up again and delivered a third punch to the gut. Audet fell back down on his knees, gasping for breath.

"OK, that should do it. Now, M. Audet, where is M. Nolet?"

"Dining room. Supervising the scumbags. It's suppertime."

"Right, let's go back to the office and you can sit down."

"I want to call my lawyer."

"You can do that back in the office. Might be safer there."

In the office, boxes were being packed with file folders, and the computer was being disconnected. Everything that was being removed was logged on to a sheet.

"Janvier, could you have someone get M. Nolet. He's in the dining room."

While he was waiting, Vanier began to go through Audet's pockets. "Maître Giroux, does the warrant cover things found on the premises?"

"Yes Inspector, it says, any *other things found on the premises that might provide evidence relating to the receipt of funds from the* Ministère de l'emploi et de la solidarité sociale."

"And is a telephone a thing?" he said, holding up Audet's phone.

"Yeah, that's a thing."

"And what are these?" asked Vanier, holding up two USB sticks that he found on Audet.

"Those things are data sticks. Used to store data," said Filion. "Those are definitely things."

Audet looked defeated. Nolet appeared, looking frightened.

"What's all this about? We're a homeless shelter. What in God's name are you doing?"

"M. Nolet, good to see you again. Just routine work supporting the Ministère de l'emploi et de la solidarité sociale. I believe it's a simple audit of the books. Things got a bit out of hand because of your M. Audet here, but they're under control now. We'll be taking M. Audet off your hands for a while. Seems he assaulted M. Letarte. But you can go on with your work. We should be finished in a few hours, and then we'll be out of here. Oh, by the way, do you have a cell phone?"

"Yes," said Nolet, fishing it out of his pocket. "Why?"

"Seized," said Vanier, pocketing the phone.

Nolet looked from Vanier to Audet, who continued to look at his shoes.

Laurent called for a squad car to take Audet to the nearest station, with instructions to book him for assault. Given the holidays, Vanier hoped he wouldn't get a bail hearing for a couple of days. The seized documents and computers were to be sent to the offices of M. Letarte, with a promise that they would be copied and sent to Leroux's squad. Vanier had given the data sticks to Sergeant Filion and had pocketed Nolet's and Audet's cell phones. He looked at Laurent, "So I can leave you to close up once they've finished."

"Of course, sir."

With that, Vanier shook hands through the crowd of officers, thanked Leroux for the favour, and left.

## 9.30 PM

The office cleaners had finished for the night at Henderson and Associates, and Beaudoin had worked late often enough to know that Henderson never came back to the office after nine o'clock. Even so, he was nervous, and the sweat was staining his shirt. He could feel his heart beating as he sat in front of the computer on Henderson's desk scrolling through files. He decided that the safest and quickest thing to do was to copy everything that was even slightly relevant to the Holy Land Shelter on to the data stick. He could go through it all later. He did a search for all the emails between Vladimir Markov and Henderson, and copied them. He was surprised there were so many. He then turned to Henderson's files on the Shelter. Most of them he recognized as his own memos and draft documents, but he copied them anyway.

While he was scanning through the files, he came across one marked, "Overseas Billings" and copied everything in it. After an hour, he pulled the data stick out of the computer and began shutting down the computer. As he pressed the "Shut Down" command, he heard the electronic ping that announced the front door to the office opening. He pocketed the data stick and picked up the December issue of *Canadian Bar Association Journal* on Henderson's desk. The cover article was on electronic discovery. He almost crashed into Henderson as he left his office, and Henderson's face creased into its habitual broad smile, an unnatural curving of the lips without any sign of joy.

"Pascal. Working late I see. What were you looking for in my office?"

"Just this article on electronic discovery. I knew that we had received it, and it wasn't in the library. I figured it might be sitting on your desk. Don't mind if I borrow it for a while, do you?"

"Not at all, Pascal."

Beaudoin walked quickly back to his office, cradling the data stick in his fist and hoping the computer had shut down.

Henderson scanned his desk for signs that things had been disturbed. Even though the desktop looked like a disorganized litter of files, loose paper and magazines, he knew its contours and could find anything in seconds. It didn't seem to have been disturbed. But when he sat down, he reached under the desk and touched the computer. It was warm to the touch. He picked up the phone and dialed. He let it ring five times before it picked up.

"Vladimir, it's Gordon. I've been thinking. We need to move forward with the transaction."

## 10.30 PM

The small room was lit by two flickering candles that cast their light upwards to a crucifix holding the tortured body of Christ in eternal pain. A figure knelt before the crucifix at a wooden prayer desk, his head bowed into his hands, rosary beads entwined around his thick fingers.

"Dear Lord, I have sought to do only your bidding. With your grace and love, I have done what you have asked of me. I have helped your chosen ones join you in eternal life. I have joined with you in this sacred task. But it is difficult, Lord. I'm weak and need your help. My faith falters, and I need your hand to reach out and touch me. I'm afraid and I need your strength. Restore my soul. Strengthen my conviction. Help me overcome these human frailties and proceed with your work. Lord, I know you have called me. Please understand that I am not rejecting that calling. Just give me the strength that I need.

"You were right. They did not suffer. They left all suffering behind as they joined you in paradise. And they are blessed. How I long for my own time to be with you, to be united with you in your eternal love. As your chosen disciple here on earth, this should be a joyous time for me, but I'm filled with fear and doubt.

"Give me the gift of faith. Give me a sign. Even you, my Lord, even you in your darkest moments asked for help. Remember, in the Garden of Gethsemane, as you waited for the Romans to come to bring you to your death, you asked your Father: *if it is possible, let this cup pass from Me; yet not as I will, but as Thou wilt.* Dear Lord, it was God's will that you drink deeply from that cup of human suffering, that you sacrifice yourself for us. But your Father did not desert you: *and there appeared an angel unto him from heaven, strengthening him*. Lord, you who were once a man. You who walked this earth as a man know how weak I am. I am only a man and I am nothing without you. So I beseech you, my Lord and Saviour, help me to be strong.

"There are more, Lord, and I am testing them to see if they are ready. But there are also obstacles to our mission. There are those who would stop me. If your mission is sacred, how far must I go to protect its fulfillment? I need your guidance."

# EIGHT
## DECEMBER 30

## 11 AM

**Vladimir Markov was sitting alone** in a booth in a nondescript café on Notre Dame staring at the door and talking on his cell phone. Romanenko was sitting at the counter behind him nursing a coffee. The waitress and cook, the only staff in the place, were taking advantage of the holiday quiet and the absence of the owner by drinking surreptitious shots of cognac in the kitchen.

"Yeah, OK. You did great to get the shit out on bail. What do you want me to say? I'm paying you enough that I don't have to say thanks. And, frankly, Audet can rot in prison for all I care. But I want this whole thing closed down, you hear me?" said Markov. Then he listened, keeping his eye on the door.

"Whatever. I don't give a shit about excuses. I just want this problem to go away as fast as possible. Do whatever you have to do. If Audet has to plead guilty, that's his problem. If that's what it takes, he'll plead guilty. Gotta go. Just get it done." Markov clicked the phone off and watched the door as Marcel Audet walked in, all attitude, like he owned the place. He walked over to Markov's booth and eased himself in.

Audet was smiling. "Hey, thanks for the lawyer, Mr. M. He got me out this morning on a promise to keep the peace."

Markov didn't respond. The waitress walked over and opened a notepad, pen in hand.

"Get you something?"

"You have a menu?" asked Audet

"He'll have a coffee. He's not staying," said Markov.

The waitress left and came back with a pot of coffee, a cup and a saucer. She poured the coffee, pulled two creamers out of the pocket of her nylon one-piece, and dropped them on the table.

Markov waited for her to leave and said, "I told you. I wanted things kept quiet."

"Listen, Mr. M. I haven't done anything to mess things up."

"Loan sharking? Money laundering? The way I hear it, you've been running a fucking bank down there."

"So, I helped some people out, that's all. Nothing criminal. I didn't even make much money out of it."

"People connected to me gave you the job. And that means I'm connected to you and your fucking schemes. I got a visit from some fucking cop yesterday afternoon who already made the connection."

"Look, like I said, it's not a big deal. I helped people out, that's all."

"You're in trouble, asshole. And that means I have to waste my time thinking about problems you've created."

"Don't worry. It'll all blow over. It's just that the police are all over the place with these murders. They're jumping on everyone."

"That's what I mean. You think our deal can go through when everyone and their mother are worrying about the fucking homeless? And now the police connect you and me."

"Well, I can see that it creates problems. But what can I do? I'm here to help you, Mr. Markov. You know that."

"First, your private banking scheme is over. Whatever money you took, you give back. And get receipts. Understand?"

"Yes, sir, Mr. Markov." Audet was beginning to sweat.

"Second, who the fuck is the sick bastard killing these people? I want you to find out, and get to him before the police do. If the police find him, this story stays in the papers for the next two years while he goes to trial, and every bloody politician and friend of the poor will be wringing their hands over the plight of the homeless. I don't want the homeless in the newspapers for the next two years. We need to shut him down."

"Well, I suppose I can ask around."

"Listen asshole. You're the one slumming around with these scumbags. Someone must know him. Get rid of this guy, and the press will move on in two weeks. Soon as you deal with him, things will settle down. Not before. You need to do your civic duty with this maniac. Do you understand?"

Audet looked into Markov's eyes and understood perfectly.

"Yes."

Markov looked over his shoulder. Romanenko appeared at the table and dropped his hand heavily on Audet's shoulders.

"So, the chat's over, Mr. Markov?" said Romanenko.

"Yeah, it's over," said Markov.

"And Mr. Audet is leaving?" he said, pulling Audet to a standing position in the booth.

"Yeah, he's leaving."

Audet struggled out of the booth with Romanenko's hand still gripping his shoulder.

"I understand, Mr. Markov. I understand."

"Good, now, get the fuck out of here. And listen. I can't take any more fuck-ups. You're on very thin ice, my friend."

## 11.30 AM

In the still of the empty Cathedral, Fr. Henri Drouin sat on a straight-backed chair in St. Jude's Crypt, his rosary beads swinging almost imperceptibly as he fingered each prayer marker. It was one of his favourite times: after morning services but before the lunchtime show. In the old days people would always be dropping in for quiet prayers, but it hardly ever happened these days. Drouin sensed a presence in the stillness before he heard the shuffling feet. He turned to see a man approaching in a long black winter coat. Snow was still visible on his shoulders and hair, and Drouin smiled gently.

"John, thank you for coming."

The man approached the chair and stood over Drouin.

"I was worried, Father Henri. You sounded concerned."

John was so close that Drouin had to lean back in the chair and tilt his head back to look up at the looming figure.

"I *am* concerned. Did you hear about the deaths on Christmas Eve?"

"I did, Father. It's shocking. But they have gone to their Lord. Isn't that a good thing? Perhaps this answers our prayers. Didn't we pray for their deliverance from pain and suffering?"

"We prayed for these people, John. But not for their death. Murder cannot be God's answer to our prayers. Do you know anything about this?"

"Who are we to question how the Lord answers our prayers? Who are we to question His works?"

"I'm not questioning His works. The Lord didn't kill these people, John. Tell me the truth, do you know anything about this?" His eyes pleaded.

The man smiled.

"No, Henri. I know nothing. I am as shocked as you are. But why do you think it was anything but God's work, calling his servants home after desperate suffering? That's how I would like to remember them. That in their last hours, the Lord took an interest in them and called them to his arms."

"I don't know, John. I just have a bad feeling."

"Father Henri, the police will do what they have to do, and we will see that our friends simply passed on peacefully to a better place. To their reward."

"Perhaps you're right, John."

"I am right, Father. It was inevitable they would die soon. It saddens me that they left, but it's my loss that I mourn, not theirs. They are all much happier now. Remember the struggles of Joe Yeoman. Isn't he better off? And Mary Gallagher, how much more was she going to be forced to endure?"

"Mary Gallagher?" Drouin, blurted, immediately wishing he could take the words back. John said nothing, but both men knew. Drouin tried to rise but John didn't budge, he was still standing over him, and Drouin was forced to remain seated.

The tension was broken when John smiled. "Father, while I am here, could you hear my confession?" He stepped back and allowed Drouin to rise from the chair, the rosary beads still hanging from his hands.

"Of course, John."

They walked together to a confessional box that looked like three wooden phone booths against the wall. The central one was for the priest with a small grille on each side linking into the other two. One penitent would kneel and whisper his confession through the grille, while the other penitent waited for the wooden slat to open the grille when the priest was ready. Drouin hesitated, he didn't want to hear a confession because he knew too much already. He entered the centre box and sat down heavily, taking comfort in the familiar, polished wood smell, leaning forward to pull the door closed. The door stuck, then swung back open, and John entered the priest's box.

He had put on latex gloves. He grabbed Drouin by the neck and pushed his knee into the priest's chest to hold him in place.

"John, what…?"

"I'm sorry, Father."

"John…."

John tightened his grip on Drouin's throat and cut off the words. Using his free hand, he pulled a plastic bottle from the inside pocket of his winter coat and inserted the pointed end between the priest's lips, forcing liquid into his mouth. He let go of the priest's neck and clapped his hand over his mouth and nose. Drouin stared up in terror, his mouth full of liquid and his lungs pleading for air. John withdrew the bottle and put it in his pocket. He reached behind the priest's neck, grabbed a fistful of hair and pulled, forcing Drouin to look up at the wooden ceiling of the box. Drouin's mouth opened slightly, and the liquid flowed down his throat. He gasped like someone drowning, but the hand on his mouth stifled even a cough. Again the bottle, and again his mouth filled with liquid. The knee on his chest was pushing forcefully. In seconds, the liquid had flowed down his throat, and he was drowning again. He couldn't get enough air. Another mouthful, and he looked into John's eyes, pleading. John stared back, and Drouin realized it was hopeless and began to pray in his mind, giving himself up to his creator.

"Father Henri. It's God's work. Even this. You should not have interfered."

Before leaving the box, John checked for a pulse, and then placed the bottle into Drouin's hand, the same hand that was still clutching the rosary beads. He removed an envelope from his inside pocket and placed it on the handrail inside the confessional. He took off the latex gloves, placed them in his pocket and left the box, closing the door behind him. Leaving the Cathedral, he dipped his hand into the holy water in the font by the front door and blessed himself.

## NOON

Vanier was sitting across the table from Mme. Paradis and the sketch artist. Mme. Paradis's eyes were sparkling incongruously from within a tired face and a slouching body. She was enjoying her big day, but her body would have preferred to be lying down somewhere quiet.

"Now, Mme. Paradis, take a good look at the sketch and take your time. Tell me if you think that it's a good image of the man you say placed the ads in the *Journal de Montréal*. The man who signed himself Pious John."

She studied the sketch for a few moments, squinting her eyes.

"That's him. That's him perfectly," she said. "You're very good, M. Beaucage," she said, giving him a practiced smile.

"Thank you Madame, but I am only as good as the witness's memory."

"Are you sure, Madame? Are you confident that this is a good likeness?" asked Vanier.

"Positive," she said, turning back to Beaucage with another smile.

Vanier hated eyewitness identification, and he hated sketched likenesses even more. Eyewitnesses were notoriously unreliable. When six people inside a bank couldn't come up with the same number of men carrying guns, how could you expect them to get the eye colour or even the height correct? But it was easy, and too many cops went along with it. He knew it had put thousands of innocents in jails and helped as many guilty go free. And if eyewitness identification wasn't bad enough, an artist's rendition of what the witness thought they remembered was even worse. A bad sketch, and they were all bad sketches, was a-get-out-of-jail-free card when it didn't look anything like the accused.

Vanier turned to the artist, "M. Beaucage, could you get some 8 ½ by 11 copies, maybe twenty, made up as quickly as possible?"

"Yes, Inspector. There's a machine on the fifth floor that I've used before. I can do it immediately."

Beaucage took his sketch and left Vanier and Mme. Paradis together.

"So, Mme. Paradis, tell me about Pious John."

"What do you mean?"

"Whatever comes to mind."

Mme. Paradis played with her empty coffee cup, but Vanier didn't take the hint. "Well, as I said to the other officers, he was a special sort. He would come in, take a number, and wait for his turn, sitting in that long black cassock like he was just like everyone else. Yet he stood out, like a film star. And when he sat in front of you, I've never seen eyes like that. It wasn't the colour, lots of people have brown eyes, but they looked into you like they knew your soul. I see all kinds of people every day, but he was different. There was deepness about him, a sad look in his eyes, like he knew so much more than the rest of us. And when he talked to you, it was like you were the only person in the world. Like that song from the seventies, "and read each thought aloud."

"*Killing me softly.*"

"What?"

"The song, Roberta Flack, *Killing Me Softly With His Love.*"

"Oh, yes. You're right."

"How long had he been placing ads?"

"I think he started a few months ago. It would be easy to tell because all the forms were signed by Pious John. He always paid cash and never wanted a receipt. And, you know, I never saw him smile. And not that he looked sad, just peaceful. Like he knew there was nothing to be happy about and was OK with that. It's often like that with the St. Judes. But he was different somehow."

"The St. Judes?"

"The people who place ads thanking St. Jude. Usually they're embarrassed, and they want you to understand that they're only doing their duty. With him it was serious. It was like he was proud. As though he was making a statement. I always try to have a laugh, you know, to make the clients feel at ease. But him, he never laughed, but he was always at ease. Like he was keeping score and winning. Confident, he was, that's the word, confident."

"You told the officers that the last time you saw him was December 28, right?"

"Yes. It didn't take long. There was hardly anyone waiting. He placed the ad for the next day."

"And before that?"

"There were only two times. Always the day before the ad appeared."

Vanier looked at the two ads that had been circled on the photocopies. "So that would be December 16 and November 12?"

"Yes. The day before the ads appeared."

Vanier had already sent someone to collect the original requests. Pious John would have signed each one.

"Did he ever tell you anything about himself?"

"Never. He was all business. Polite, patient, but he never told me anything about the story behind the ads. He just wanted the ads placed and to pay."

"You've been a great help to us. After M. Beaucage returns, we'll have you sign off on the likeness, and then have someone drive you home."

"This has been a long day."

"I'm sure it has, Mme. Paradis, thank you. So take the rest of the day off." Vanier got to his feet and left to find Beaucage.


## 2 PM


The chatter in the war room died down as Vanier walked in and moved to the front of the room. The Chief had come through and found warm bodies to run down all possibilities, but it hadn't done any good. Officers had visited 26 businesses that handled potassium cyanide and had come up with nothing. Still, Vanier was happy to have the bodies.

"Ladies and Gentlemen, we're six days out, and we need to make some progress. We have a lunatic out there who thinks he has a direct line to God, and now we have a sketch of the bastard." Vanier held up the image, as Janvier started passing out copies.

"We have a face and a name: Pious John. Likely not his real name." There was a round of subdued laughter. "No last name and no address. Today, we're going to every shelter and drop-in centre in town and every street person we can find. I want others to go back to the companies that store potassium cyanide. Show the sketch around and see if anyone recognizes him. Maybe he worked at one of the companies, maybe he's a customer. I want to find John the Bastard and quickly. He killed five people on Christmas Eve, and he probably started earlier than that. We have a maximum of 24 hours to find him before the sketch goes to the media, and I want him in custody first. We know he's close to the homeless, maybe close to the church as well. Details, that's what's important. Remember, nothing is insignificant. When you're talking to people, listen and think. So let's go find this shit. Laurent and Roberge will coordinate. Any questions?"

There were no questions.

## 4 PM

The squelch of Vanier's wet boots on the stone floor echoed off the walls of the Cathedral as he made his way up a side aisle towards a clot of people milling around the confessional box. He had stayed out of churches for over two decades and was amazed at how deeply familiar it all still seemed. Janvier advanced to meet him.

"It's Father Drouin, Chief. They found him an hour ago. He's dead.

Sitting in the confessional booth. Dr. Segal is looking at the body. There was an envelope, we bagged it but it looks like a suicide note, and a confession."

Segal emerged from the confessional box and caught Vanier's eye. "He's been dead for a few hours. No obvious signs of violence, but I want to do a full autopsy. We'll get the body out of here in a few minutes, and your people can take over. They've already taken photos. And there's this," she said, holding up an empty plastic bottle with a small amount of liquid at the bottom. Looks and smells like orange juice. We'll test it."

"Thank you, Doctor. Any ideas?"

"As I said, no obvious signs of violence, and an envelope that I am told contains a suicide note. Maybe he drank his own Kool-Aid."

"Maybe. When can you do an autopsy?"

"Tomorrow morning, first thing. I'll call with the results."

Vanier sat down on a bench, running his hand through his hair and staring into the open booth where Drouin was slouched. Maybe Drouin was the killer. And maybe it was a suicide. But if it wasn't, it would be a convenient way for the killer to get away, providing he stopped killing. If he were smart, he'd stop and walk away, or wait a year or two before starting again.

Vanier walked over to one of the CS Officers.

"Who has the envelope?"

"It's in the bag, sir."

"Well, get it, and let me see."

The officer came back with the envelope in a zip-lock bag and reached for it with his gloved hand. It was in a Cathedral envelope, complete with the coat of arms of Mother Church over the address. The officer pulled the letter from the envelope and held it up for Vanier to read:

*December 30*

> *What I did, I did in the name on Our Lord and Saviour. What I did, I did to bring peace to poor souls that have known no peace for too long. I crossed the boundary of man's law to do God's work, and I do not regret that. But I realize the consequences. You do not understand, you cannot fathom the joy that comes from being an instrument of His divine mercy.*
>
> *Perhaps if I had been more thoughtful, I could have released more unfortunates from this hell, but I made mistakes. It will not serve the Lord for me to be condemned as a common criminal, for His work to be sullied by my mistakes. So I am ending it here and going to my eternal rest in joy.*

*Henri Drouin*

"Jesus," Vanier mumbled to himself.

Janvier had been reading over Vanier's shoulder. "It sounds convincing."

"It gives us a motive. And it ties in with St. Jude. But it's typed, and where's Pious John?" Drouin doesn't look anything like the sketch."

"So what do you think, sir?"

"I don't know. This is too easy. Let's nail it down. Check the times again. Get the last appearance of Santa on the closed circuit cameras in the Métro and get the time of Drouin's appearance back in the Cathedral. I want to know for certain if he had time to get back here. And if he didn't have time, then he's not our guy, he's another victim and John is covering his tracks. This isn't some end-of-the-road homeless destitute who was on his way out anyway. This wasn't about putting anyone out of their misery."

"Yes, sir."

Janvier opened his cell phone and began making calls.

# THE DEAD OF WINTER

## 7 PM

Twenty officers, armed with the sketch of Pious John, were trolling homeless shelters, drop-in centres, and hiding places under highways and in back alleys. Others were accosting the faithful outside the Cathedral, mixed in with the panhandlers hoping to turn Catholic guilt into coins. The rest were calling on the owners of companies that stored potassium cyanide. Vanier was in the war room pretending to be busy and waiting. He wanted desperately to find Pious John, and all he could do was wait and hope that the sketch wasn't picked up by the media. If it was, they would be inundated with useless calls, and John would disappear.

The phone rang. He recognized Bédard's number and thought of ignoring it again, but answering one in five calls from the boss was a good ratio.

"Yes, sir."

"Inspector Vanier, what the fuck are you doing to me?"

"Sir?"

"Where are you?"

"In the Squad Room, first floor."

"My office. Now."

The phone clicked off, and Vanier took the stairs up.

The Chief was sitting watching the door, probably counting how many seconds it took Vanier to mount the stairs. Vanier took a seat.

"So explain to me, we have a written confession from a suspect, but you still have close to 30 officers scouring the city looking for some guy who placed ads thanking St. Jude? Does that make sense, Luc?"

Vanier tried not to stare at the sweat that had accumulated in the fat jiggling over the Chief Inspector's collar.

"I don't think the priest killed himself, sir. I think he was murdered, like the others. It's premature to name Drouin as the culprit. We don't know that, we'd be guessing. I think we should wait."

"Do you have any idea the pressure that I'm under? And the journalists are ahead of us at every step. What if the suicide note leaks out? What do we do then?"

"We tell the truth." As he said it, he realized how stupid it must sound to Bédard, who dealt in messaging, not truth. If the message happened to be true, that was a bonus.

"The truth?"

"We tell them that we are not certain that the note is genuine."

"Well if it wasn't suicide, it was murder, wasn't it?"

"Yes, sir. But we can't announce it as murder if we don't know. We do what we always do; we tell the press that we are investigating the circumstances."

"Jesus, if the homeless didn't set the city in a panic, a dead priest in a confessional box will. And in the Cathedral, of all places."

"All I'm saying, sir, is that we still don't know what's going on, and we don't want to put ourselves into a position where we have to backtrack. Can't you just stall the press for a few days? At least till we get the results of the autopsy. We don't have to mention the note."

"All right, Sergeant Laflamme is doing a press conference. She's good. I'll tell her not to go any further than confirming the death of a priest. Because of the other deaths, and his work with the homeless, we are investigating it. She may be able to get away with that for a while."

"I think that's best, sir. We'll have something concrete soon."

"All right, get to it, Luc."

Vanier rose to leave.

"And, Luc, and I'm telling you this as a friend, we go back a long time."

"Yes, sir?"

"It wouldn't hurt to make an effort. That suit, it looks like you slept in it, and it looks like you've been wearing that shirt for days. Luc, don't let yourself go, you'll lose the respect of your team."

"Yes, sir." Vanier felt like lashing out. His defenses were strong

190

but sometimes, the occasional grenade managed to make it over the wall and cause damage inside. *Fuck you, you fat bastard* was all he could think of, but he said, "Yes, sir. I'll see what I can do."

"Luc, that's from a friend, not your boss."

Vanier was out the door before he finished. He had forgotten to tell Bédard that he had a sketch of John. If Bédard didn't know there was a sketch, there wouldn't be pressure to release it to the media.

He was watching the clock and waiting for a lead, any lead. Someone must recognize the sketch. The minutes dragged into hours, and he had a pizza delivered. He was on the second slice when Bédard burst into the room.

"Luc, what the fuck are you trying to do? I've just been told that we have a sketch of a suspect. Why didn't you tell me?"

"Chief Inspector, it's one sketch from one witness, and I'm not sure it's reliable – I'm not even sure the witness is reliable. We have officers showing it around at all the likely spots, and if it's good, we should have a name to go with the sketch any moment."

"That's not the point. You didn't tell me you even had a sketch."

"Like I said, sir, I'm not convinced it's reliable. I'm waiting for identification, and we'll have it soon and will pick him up. If he's gone missing we can release the sketch along with a name. You know what a defence lawyer can do with a sketch that's not a good likeness of the suspect. I don't want to make a mistake. This way, if the sketch is any good, we get a name and we can nab him. If the sketch gets out, he disappears."

"Well, it's too late to worry about that. I just got a call from the Mayor's office about the sketch. It's on the *Journal de Montréal's* website. The fucking *Journal de Montréal* publishes the sketch before I even know it exists. Luc, why are you doing this to me? Holding out is bad enough, but someone in your unit has a direct line to that piece of shit newspaper."

"I've checked that, sir, and nobody from this squad is feeding the media," said Vanier, trying to eliminate doubt from his voice. "The witness for the sketch works for the *Journal de Montréal*, and our people have been out all day with the sketch. There must have been hundreds of people who have seen it, and more than a few with copies. He's not even a suspect right now; he's just a loose end. Our suspect is dead."

"Well, your plan to keep this quiet is flushed down the toilet."

"We just have to deal with that. I hope to have something serious any moment now. If the sketch is a dead end, then we'll know quickly enough. We're hitting everyone who might have seen our guy. If nobody recognizes him, then the sketch is probably useless."

"So I tell the Mayor's office that a member of the public leaked it, and we didn't release it because he's only a person of interest, not a suspect."

"That's right. Go on the attack, Chief Inspector: irresponsible action by the *Journal de Montréal* endangering a material witness and jeopardizing a murder investigation. Tell them you can't conduct a rigorous investigation if the media acts irresponsibly, putting the public in danger at the same time. You have enough experience, Chief Inspector, to know that publishing sketches is a last resort. And that's how we were operating, until our investigation was sabotaged by irresponsible journalists." Vanier was beginning to believe himself, and the Chief Inspector was beginning to see an alternative to admitting he wasn't in control.

"I'm sure that you can put it much more convincingly than I could, Chief. It's not a police failure, it's irresponsible journalism aimed at undermining a serious inquiry."

Bédard didn't have an alternative, and there was a grain of truth in what Vanier was saying. There was enough to craft a message around; righteous indignation coupled with a chance to put the boot to the media at the same time. The Mayor might even like it.

"I'll talk to Sergeant Laflamme about this – she's the expert on communications – then we'll pass it by the Mayor. Let's hope that we get some leads from this. Otherwise, it could get very ugly."

"Chief, I am certain we will have a target by tonight. I'll call you as soon as I know."

"Thank you, Luc. Thank you." As the Chief rose to leave, he reached over for a slice of pizza. "Don't mind?"

"Go ahead, take two."

"One's enough," he said, before changing his mind, reaching for a second. "Thanks, Luc."

Vanier watched him leave and went back to his pizza.


And the calls began to arrive. Sr Jacques called from the Cathedral to say she had a name, John Collins, confirmed by two witnesses, but no address. But he fit the description, even down to dressing like a priest. Officers began running John Collins through databases, criminal records, people who had been arrested, suspects. Two officers were working on access to wider databases: passport, army, city and provincial employment, social security, and a host of other sources that collect information on citizens. In the electronic world, everyone is in a database. Just by living you leave traces everywhere. Nobody's anonymous.

The last line of defence for the average citizen was the volume of information being collected and stored. The databases were like haystacks piled up in fields defying anyone to find the needle. But the tools to dig through millions of files in seconds were already in use. In the same way that Google finishes your sentences and has lined up hundreds of thousands of hits before you've pushed enter, software spiders are crawling through stagnant data 24 hours a day, remembering everything and putting it in order, just waiting for the right question.

Vanier used the tools but worried about them. If someone

decided to link all the data – and it wouldn't be difficult - lives would unfold without secrets under watchful eyes. Laboratory rats get used to it and copulate under bright lights in front of cameras.

## 9 PM

Vanier flipped open his phone. "Yeah?"

It was Janvier. "We got an ID, sir, and it sounds like it's good. I'm with Serge Jauron, the owner of the Xeon pesticide plant in St. Lambert; they make private label pesticides for the industry. He says he recognizes the person in the sketch."

"John Collins?"

"That's it. Someone else called it in?"

"St. Jacques got the name about an hour ago. We're trying to get an address."

"Jauron says he's been working at Xeon for years. He drives a forklift."

"He's sure about the identification?"

"Positive. Says it could be a photograph."

"Does he have an address?"

"He said human resources would have an address, but he has twenty people in the house for dinner and doesn't want to go down to the plant tonight."

"Put him on."

Vanier waited for a few seconds.

"Hello?"

"Good evening, Mr. Jauron. I'm Detective Inspector Vanier. I understand that the person in the sketch may be one of your employees."

"Not maybe, Inspector. He is. He's John Collins. He's been with us for six years at least."

194

"Well, we need to speak to him as soon as possible, and I would be grateful if you would accompany Sergeant Janvier to the plant right now and get a home address for us."

"Inspector, I've got twenty people eating dinner here, I can't just up and leave them. I told your men that I can go down first thing in the morning."

"I understand your problem. But you have to understand mine. We believe that Mr. Collins may be able to cast some light on the deaths of several people over the last few days. Tell me, do you keep potassium cyanide at your plant?"

"Yes, of course we do. That's why Sergeant, whatever his name is, and his buddy are here, isn't it?"

"Sergeant Janvier, sir."

"Yes, Sergeant Janvier."

"Potassium cyanide has been used to kill at least five people. It could well be your potassium cyanide, and you need to accompany Sergeant Janvier and his partner to the plant and get an address for Mr. Collins before anyone else is killed. Oh, and by the way, while you're there, it might be useful to check again to see if any potassium cyanide is missing from your facilities. Now, pass me back to the Sergeant while you put on your coat."

Jauron passed the phone to Janvier and went to make his excuses to his guests.

"Yes, sir."

"Call me when you get to the plant, Janvier. Oh, and ask Jauron about any Santa suit. Maybe they had a Christmas party."

"Yes, sir."

## 9.45 PM

It didn't take long for Janvier to call in an address for John Collins. Minutes later, Laurent and Vanier were speeding along St. Antoine, parallel to the Ville-Marie expressway. The address was on rue St. Philippe in St. Henri They turned south off St. Antoine onto du Couvent, then right onto Notre Dame. Two-storey tenements crowded the narrow streets with cars parked haphazardly, fighting for space in piles of snow. They reached the corner of St-Philippe, but couldn't turn into the street; it was blocked by a squad car with its blue and red lights flashing.

"What the fuck?" said Vanier. Then he saw flashing lights from fire trucks, more squad cars, and an ambulance. Firemen were pouring water onto a building that was almost obscured with thick black smoke. Flames were visible through the window and were curling out through the top of the brick walls to lick over the edge of the roof.

They showed badges to the officer standing beside the squad car and began running slowly towards the burning building. Vanier was counting in his head, trying to estimate the street number, but he was sure it would be Collins place that was going up in flames. The fire was at number 149, the last known address of John Collins. It was a converted stableman's house, probably dating from the 18th century. The ground floor stable had become a garage with a "Pas de Stationnement" sign in front of it. The upper floor would be the living quarters. The sidewalk was packed with people watching firemen with hoses making steam and icicles on the building without having any apparent effect on the flames. A city bus sponsored by Sun Youth was running its motor to keep evacuated neighbours warm, as they watched and wondered if their own homes were going to go up in flames. Through the windows they all looked dazed.

Vanier sent Laurent to the bus, "Make sure nobody gets off, and let me know if Collins is there."

Laurent turned and hurried to the bus. Vanier pushed through the crowd and showed his badge to the officers trying to get the sightseers out of the way. A hose led into the front door of number 149, testimony to what it means to fight fires, and Vanier thought about the tough bastards at the end of it. Vanier felt the same fascination as everyone else watching flames pouring out of the upper windows, and it didn't take an expert to see that the building was gone. Even standing across the street, Vanier could feel the heat of the inferno as two men exited in a hurry from the front door, pulling the hose out with them.

There was a flash of light through the small windows in the garage door an instant before the explosion, and Vanier saw the door splintering outwards as a fireball escaped and turned into black smoke. Pieces of the burning door fell into the street, the small flames dying quickly in the snow. What was left of the garage door hung on one hinge, revealing a burning van that quickly disappeared under a wave of water, as firemen trained hoses inside the garage.

The firemen were working in punishing conditions, weighed down by equipment and ice that formed like a protective layer over them, giving them ice-laden eyebrows and silvery, frozen mustaches. The water from the hoses flowed only at the centre of the fire, everywhere else it froze into sheets and thick icicles, adding dangerous weight to the building. If it had been the summer, the whole block would have been destroyed. Now the weather was a friend, of sorts. Vanier could feel the cold taking over his body. The air was heavy with a mix of smoke and moisture, and his coat was soaking it all up. He looked back at the busload of evacuees, and saw Laurent in the aisle bending down to talk with one of them. He started towards the bus, but his path was blocked by an ice-covered giant.

"Police?"

"Yes. I'm Vanier, Major Crime."

"You're early. Your arson guys won't be here till morning."

"I was hoping to interview the occupant," said Vanier.

"It's a bit late now. I'm Captain Leboeuf, and this was deliberate," he said, nodding at the still burning building. "The place stinks of gasoline. And see the van?"

Vanier looked at the garage again, and the van was still burning, still white in parts but mostly black.

"Yes?"

"One of my guys says there's someone in it."

Vanier looked across the street, trying to see into the driver's seat through the smoke filling the inside of the van.

"Who called it in?"

"One of the neighbours, I expect. The call came in close to nine. The caller didn't leave a name, but we'll have his number. It was already too late when we got here. Only thing we can do is try to contain it."

"I'm going to talk to the people on the bus, see if they know anything else. I'll let you know." Instinctively, Vanier reached out to shake Leboeuf's hand, but saw the massive gloves. Leboeuf pulled off his right hand glove and grasped Vanier's hand; like two sides of beef meeting, one hard and frozen, the other hard and warm. Vanier felt as though his hand had been plunged into icy water. Leboeuf smiled but said nothing and moved off towards the house. Vanier walked to the bus.

The driver pushed a button to open the door, and Vanier climbed in and immediately opened his coat hoping to let some of the warmth get to his body. A few people were in dressing gowns over pajamas and wrapped in donated blankets. Two girls were dressed up for an evening out and wearing overcoats; they were getting over the shock by discussing how they might get to meet some of the firemen. An older woman in a fur coat tried to reassure a cat through the wire mesh of a cat carrier. Laurent had already shown the sketch to everyone on the bus.

"Collins isn't here, Chief."

"Seems he's in the van in the garage," said Vanier. "The fire was deliberate, and there's a corpse sitting in the driver's seat. It's probably Collins. What did you get from these people?"

198

"Almost everyone recognized him, but nobody was able to put a name to the face. They all agree that it's the guy who lived in the up-stairs apartment. You know the sort of thing: *Very quiet, kept himself to himself. Nod to him in the street but that's all.* The usual stuff, sir. I'll write it up."

Vanier wasn't surprised. It was easy to live alone in a tight neigh-bourhood. If you hadn't grown up in St-Henri; if people didn't know your parents, and their parents; if you hadn't gone to school with them, they didn't know you, and you were welcome to your isolation. They could live next door to someone for years and know no more about them than they did about life on Mars.

As they were leaving the bus, two Sun Youth volunteers in parkas climbed in to arrange overnight accommodation for the temporarily homeless and give them a change of clothing and maybe some hope. The fire already seemed less fierce. Leboeuf was talking to two firemen.

"How soon to get the body out?" said Vanier.

"We'll let things die down till the morning. Nothing we can do for him anyway. The Coroner said they'll send someone over first thing."

"That's it?"

"Yep. We'll leave a truck and crew here for the night, but it will be morning before anyone can go in."

Vanier turned to walk back to his car. The air was filled with damp smoke that settled on everything, and he was shivering with the cold, feeling like he was walking through a giant wet ashtray. Laurent was standing beside the car looking tired.

"Where to, Chief?"

"Bed. Unless you have a better idea." And then, as an after-thought. "I suppose I should call the Boss. He'll be happy."

# NINE
## DECEMBER 31

8.30 AM

**Everywhere Vanier looked in the Squad Room,** there were pictures of John Collins staring back at him. The *Journal de Montréal* headline under the sketch read, Santa Claus? Other papers were lying on desks, and all had the sketch on the front page. Every TV channel had led with the story. For the press, he was still Pious John, the most famous face in Quebec, and nobody had seemed to pick up the connection with the fire yet. That was a good sign.

The leak of the sketch was probably inevitable, given the number of people it had been shown to. But Vanier still wanted to know who it came from. If the leak came from within, from Fletcher or someone else in the squad, he had a serious problem, but it would have to wait. John Collins's files from human resources at Xeon included a passport-sized photograph that was a dead-on match for the sketch. It also had a next of kin and an address. Visiting the next of kin with news of death is one of a cop's worst jobs, but if you know nothing about the corpse, it's a good place to start.

"Let's go," said Vanier, gesturing to Laurent.

Mme. Collins' apartment was on rue Masson in Rosemont, just south of avenue Jeanne d'Arc. The street was lined with identical two-storey duplexes, each featuring a curved iron staircase leading to the upper apartment. The outdoor staircases feature in Montreal postcards, and tourists think they're quaint, but they were built for cheap, not picturesque. Given Montreal's ferocious winters, it was madness to build curved, metal staircases outside, but they had become ubiquitous features of working-class housing.

The metal steps up to Mme. Collins's apartment were covered in fresh snow that hid two inches of packed ice, and the handrail was encased in ice. Mme. Collins hadn't shoveled the snow from the last storm or the one before, preferring to walk a path through it. The result was treacherous. Laurent, Sherpa-like, led the ascent, with both men clutching the railing as they found footholds.

The door opened a crack on the third ring, and a frail-looking woman peered out from behind a chain.

"Police?" she said.

"Yes, Madame. We would like to talk to you. Can we come in?" said Vanier.

She closed the door to remove the chain and opened it again, turning her back on them, and retreated down the hallway into the mid-morning darkness. They followed, and she was turning on the light as they followed her into the living room. She sat down in the only armchair and gestured with her hand to the sofa, where they sat, their bulk dwarfing the two-seater. Vanier wondered if she had been sitting in the dark before their arrival.

She was all grey and black. Her hair was cut short like a man's and was the kind of grey that says *I don't care*; not a shade you can buy at any hairdresser but a variety of greys that mirrored the gradual decay of age. Her face was colourless, just shadowy lines and folds, and she wore a black woollen skirt with a black cardigan buttoned to her neck.

The furniture was the discount living-room special, popular 30 years ago: a couch, an armchair, two side tables, a floor lamp, and a coffee table, all for one low price. What looked as though it should be made of wood was chipboard and veneer. The walls were bare, and there was no TV or radio. Every flat surface was covered in a film of dust except for the copy of the *Journal de Montréal* on the coffee table with the sketch of John Collins on the cover.

"It's simple. It suits my needs," she said, answering unasked questions.

"Madame, you are Yvette Collins?"

"Yes."

"I am Detective Inspector Vanier and this is Detective Sergeant Laurent."

She peered at them through lifeless eyes.

"We're here about your son, John."

"News?" she said, without enthusiasm.

"I'm afraid it's not good news."

She was holding herself in check but couldn't stop a sudden intake of breath.

"He died last night in a fire." Blunt and to the point. Vanier had done the same thing many times and knew you had to be direct. Get it out up front and don't leave any hope, then deal with whatever happens. There is no typical reaction. Some break down loudly, and others implode silently. Sometimes they argue, as though logic could raise the dead. Mme. Collins blessed herself and looked off in the distance, as though seeking help. Finally she focused on Vanier.

"I always hoped I would see him again."

"When was the last time you saw John?"

"It's been ten years. But I never gave up hope."

"Ten years? Did you have a fight?"

"No."

"So, he disappeared ten years ago and you haven't seen him since then. That's it?" said Vanier.

She said nothing, and both officers let the silence hang in the room until it became palpable, like a fourth person. Finally she spoke, in a whisper that forced them to strain to hear.

"I brought him here as a newborn, and he and I lived together for eighteen years. For ten, he slept with me in the room behind you. Then he slept on the couch you are sitting on. He slept there for eight years. Then he left. That was almost ten years ago, and I haven't seen or heard from him since."

"But you knew where he was?"

"I knew nothing," she continued. "After he left, I searched for him. I had no idea where he might have gone, so I wandered the streets looking for him, hoping I might bump into him. I looked at every face I passed. I never stopped looking, in buses, in passing cars, in stores, on the métro, everywhere. I had a rule, always let the first bus or métro pass by and look at who was on it. If he wasn't on that one, maybe he would be on the second, or would arrive to take it. Once, I was on a bus on Rachel, and I thought I saw him from the window. I got off and ran back to the spot, but he was gone. I went back to the same spot three, four times a week at the same time for months, but I never saw him again. For ten years, Inspector, I've prayed for just one glimpse, one sign that he was even alive. There was nothing. He vanished into thin air. Nothing, until I saw his picture in the newspaper this morning. I never buy a newspaper. If the picture had been inside, I would never have seen it, but it was on the front page. After searching for him for ten years, he was looking at me from a hundred different places, but I still didn't know where he was. And now you tell me he's dead."

"I'm afraid so, Madame."

"You are looking for him because you think he kills people."

Vanier didn't like that she was still using the present tense. She had to realize he was dead. "We want, I'm sorry, we wanted..." He waited for that to sink in. It didn't seem to. "We wanted to talk to him about the deaths of these homeless people."

"And now you can't."

"And now we can't."

"Well, at least I can see his body."

Vanier thought of the pain of looking at the charcoal remains of her son.

"After he left, did you report him missing?"

"The police said there was nothing they could do. He was an adult. He chose to leave. I did what I could."

"I'm sorry, Madame Collins. That was a terrible burden to carry." Vanier meant it.

"How would you know, Inspector?"

Vanier didn't answer. "Did he have any friends?"

She stared at him for a few moments. Laurent shifted uncomfortably.

"Do you think I might have overlooked something in the last ten years?"

"I have to ask, Madame Collins."

"I racked my brains, trying to think of where he might be. Places he might be working, people he might have contacted. I went through every single possibility. Friends? There were none. He didn't have friends. He wasn't an ordinary child. He had an internal life. He was always thinking. We'd sit here at nights in silence, and he'd read his books and wouldn't say a word for hours on end. We never argued. I used to think it was because he was spiritual, holy somehow."

"Perhaps his father? Where is his father?" Vanier was pushing, and he knew it.

"I don't know," she said, her hands grasping into fists.

"Who is his father?"

"I don't know," she repeated.

"So, Madame Collins, just for the record, your son has not been in contact with you recently?"

"Inspector, one day the only person who mattered to me left without saying goodbye and never came back. I've spent ten years searching for him, and in all that time, not one call, no letter, not even a card at Christmas, or Mother's Day, or even my birthday. Do you know what that's like?"

"I can only imagine."

"Imagine all you like. You can never know."

They rose awkwardly to leave.

"Can I see him?"

"The body is badly burned."

"I want to see him."

"I'll have someone contact you."

"Thank you, Inspector."

She walked past them and opened the door to let them out. No goodbyes.


## 11.30 AM


The Squad Room was quiet as Laurent walked in followed by Vanier. Faces looked up, then turned back to the desultory paperwork of closing the investigation: finishing reports and closing circles. There was none of the elation that follows a successful investigation. When you don't have the suspect to deliver to the crowd, there is always the feeling of a job half done. All they had was an explanation and a charred corpse. There was still the question of why, but it was New Year's Eve, and unanswered questions were losing ground to the prospect of forgetting all about it in a New Year's celebration. Those who had been brought in to help were dumping piles of file folders on the desks of anyone who would still be there in January. People were tired and there wasn't anything that wouldn't keep until another day.

Vanier sat down heavily and began tapping out a summary of the meeting with Mme. Collins. Eventually, only he and Laurent remained. Vanier put his hand on Laurent's shoulder.

"Why don't you go home? You can finish that next year."

Laurent leaned back in his chair and exhaled deeply.

"It's never the same when they kill themselves, is it?"

"No. We're supposed to catch them and bring them in. If we don't bring them in, we've failed."

Laurent was standing, putting on his coat. "We didn't fail. We got the right guy. It's just that he was so used to killing that it seemed like a convenient way out. He had maybe an hour left before we got to him."

"And that's all he needed. Happy New Year, Laurent."

"And the same to you, Chief," said Laurent, putting on his coat.

Vanier sat down and started typing again. He was in no hurry to go anywhere. He hardly noticed as it gradually got dark. He was thinking about where he was going to eat supper when the call came in. Another homeless death. He grabbed his coat and headed down to the car.

Even with the siren going and his red dome light flashing, he made slow progress along boulevard René-Lévesque. He pushed forward, trying to intimidate cars out of their lane, but Montreal drivers don't intimidate easily. Eventually, he arrived outside the Forum, the former home of the Montreal Canadiens, once hockey's greatest shrine and now a forlorn multiplex in a lost corner of the city. St Catherine Street was blocked and lit up like a movie set, with the lights from squad cars and snow removal trucks reflecting off the snow banks lining the street.

A uniform removed the barrier, and Vanier drove slowly into the cordoned-off area. He got out of the Volvo and walked towards a group of men who were staring up into the back of an eight-wheel snow removal truck. He followed their gazes to the edge of the dump box where an arm dangled over the side, as though its owner was sleeping peacefully on the snow in the back. A snow blower was parked beside the truck with its motor running, but without the driver. There was a dark fan-shaped stain in front of the blower, and Vanier wondered what it must be like to go through a snow blower and be spat into the back of a truck.

He walked up to the first uniform he saw and pulled out his badge. "Who's in charge here?"

The officer pointed to another uniform standing beside the blower with two city workers, "Sergeant Gamache."

Gamache saw Vanier approach and eyed him suspiciously.

"D.I. Vanier, Major Crimes."

"I wondered if you guys would even show up. We got orders to call you guys with every death on the street, even the accidents and natural causes. So that's what we did."

Vanier looked up at the dangling arm. "Doesn't look like natural causes."

"No, but I don't think anyone threw him in front of the blower either. He probably collapsed in the snow bank during the storm and got covered up. With any luck he was dead before the plow came along; I wouldn't like to think of anyone going through one of those things alive."

"Who noticed?" asked Vanier

"We had a car out working with the crew, and all of a sudden the driver of the blower was screaming. Seems there was an explosion of blood and body parts over his windshield and he lost it. That's him over there."

Gamache pointed to a man sitting in the back of a cruiser.

The door was open and the man sat immobile, staring straight ahead with a blanket around his shoulders, steam rising from a coffee in his hand.

Gamache continued, "So my guy looks up and sees the arm hanging there and stops the work. We're waiting for the Coroner to come and tell us what to do with the truck. Maybe he'll have us get into the back with shovels. Who knows?"

Vanier looked around. Other than the blood and some bits of flesh, there was little to see. He kicked into the snow where the plow had stopped. There was about two foot of loose, grimy snow, freshly ploughed from the street, and below it the older snow was hard as concrete. It hadn't been ploughed from the last storm. It had been dark and snowing since five o'clock, so it was possible that it happened just as Gamache described: the guy collapsed, was covered and disappeared until the plough came along.

Vanier bent to look at the business end of the blower. There was a four-foot hole behind the huge screw, but no screen over it. He turned back to Gamache. "Aren't these things supposed to have screens on them?"

"Yes. It's a city regulation. But when the snow is hard packed it slows down the work, everything gets clogged up. So the driver takes off the screen, and everyone's happy."

"Till something like this happens."

"The screen wouldn't have saved him," said Gamache. "He might have taken a few more turns in the grinder but he would still have gone through."

Just then, an Urgel Bourgie van arrived to pick up the body, causing murmurs of gallows humour; nobody had told them they would need a sieve. Vanier called Dr. Segal for a suggestion, and she arranged to have the truck parked outside the Laboratoire de sciences judiciaires et de médecine légale for the night. Given the temperature, leaving the truck outside the Laboratoire was as good as putting it in a refrigerator. Vanier arranged to have a squad car watch it overnight, and they could figure out what to do in the morning.

## 10.30 PM

From the street, the Blue Angel looked like a dive, the kind most people avoid. It was Vanier's oasis. It was run by Jan and Pavlov, two Polish brothers who came to Montreal on a freighter in 1976 and never left. One of them married the beautiful Gisèle, and all three moved into an apartment over the bar. No one knew for sure which brother was Gisèle's husband. It was a delicate question to ask directly, and you couldn't tell by the way she treated either of them; she had no obvious favourite and was loving and caustic to both in equal measure, complaining to either about the other and praising the absent one to the chagrin of the present. Vanier had long since given up trying to figure it out, putting it down to a simple ménage à trois.

A long mahogany counter dominated one side of the room with wooden stools lined up in front. The wall behind the bar was lined with fridges topped with shelves of back-lit liquor bottles and a 1960s cash register. A single television screen sat on a shelf suspended from the roof. The rest of the room was lined by a Naugahyde-upholstered bench along the length of the back wall and filled with tables and chairs for those wanting a more intimate evening. There was even a postage-stamp dance floor with music from a jukebox that got stuck in 1986, the year the service company went out of business. It worked fine but didn't play anything released after 1986. The walls were decorated with neon beer signs, with their cords descending to electrical sockets. One advertised Dow, a Montreal beer that killed sixteen people in 1966 without denting its popularity. It was twenty years before the brewery finally pulled the plug on it.

People didn't go to the Blue Angel for the atmosphere; they went for the psychic and physical space to drink. No rubbing shoulders in crowds trying to catch the eye of an overworked bartender. No hustlers and preening hunters. When your glass was empty, someone would show up to fill it. If you wanted to talk, you could, and if you didn't, you could sit in silence.

The New Year's Eve trade was brisk, but nobody was rushed. The hockey game was on the TV, and the Canadiens were up 3 to 1 against Pittsburgh, so all was right with the world. Vanier was watching the game and listening to Van Morrison on the jukebox, drinking Jameson with the occasional beer when he got thirsty. He was thinking about Élise and Alex. Élise would be out with friends at some party in Toronto. There would be the inevitable boyfriend that she changed like library books. There would be the promise of a new beginning. On New Year's Eve, everything is possible, even love. And Alex? Vanier wasn't sure. Would he be on duty or celebrating in the comfort of camp?

He felt a hand on his shoulder.

"I thought I would find you here, Inspector."

He turned to see Dr. Anjili Segal standing behind him, not sure how he could have missed her entrance. He broke into a smile. "There's nowhere to hide, is there?"

"Not when you're so predictable, Luc," she said, lifting herself onto the barstool beside him. "It's a hell of an evening to be alone."

"Who said I'm alone?"

She raised an eyebrow as she settled onto the stool beside him, not even bothering to see if some woman was walking back from the Ladies.

"You never change, Luc."

Vanier grinned. "What are you having, Anjili?"

"White wine."

"White wine it is."

Jan had been watching from a discreet distance, waiting to see how the meeting would play out. Now he approached with a broad grin, his arms outstretched as though he could hug her over the bar.

"Dr. Segal. How wonderful to see you again. I am thrilled. Thrilled and prepared!" He reached deep into the fridge on the back wall and pulled out a bottle of white wine. "This is just for you. It has been waiting, what, six months for you come back. Cloudy Bay, a Sauvignon Blanc from New Zealand."

Anjili examined the label and beamed.

"I can't wait to taste it."

Jan made a show of uncorking it, and Anjili made a show of tasting it, swilling it in the glass, admiring its clear pale green-gold colour, smelling the bouquet, and finally tasting a sip, inhaling air through her lips. Her eyes flashed.

"Jan, it's wonderful, I hope you have a case of it back there, but only for me. Luc couldn't appreciate a thing of this much beauty."

"Then Luc is a retard."

"I'll have a Jameson, Jan. That is if you serve retards in here."

"Of course we do," he said, without taking his eyes off Anjili. "We serve almost anyone."

A bottle of Jameson was in his hands as if by magic, and he poured a glass. And then, like all great bartenders, he faded into the background, leaving only goodwill behind.

"So how have you been, Luc?"

"I've had better times, Anjili. But I am glad to see you. And you?"

"I'm on the brink of a new year. What's not to like about that? The past is packed away, and I'm off to the future with a smile. This is a great night. Tomorrow is day one. The key is to make sure that it's not like day 365. And it's all in here, Luc," she said, touching her head with her finger, "and in here," touching her heart.

"Turn the page and everything changes. If only it were that easy."

"It's not that easy, but you have to make the effort to break with the past and embrace the future."

"Yeah."

"Here's to the future, Inspector."

She held her glass up for a toast, and he clinked the whiskey against it.

Gisèle appeared before them, dumping fistfuls of quarters on the bar.

"Do me a favour, Anjili," she said, as though continuing an uninterrupted conversation, "fill that maudit jukebox up with some happy music. It's a time to celebrate, no?"

"Yes."

With the help of Gisèle, she filled the jukebox with happy music, and as the music, the drink, and the company worked on their spirits, they danced. Vanier and Anjili; Vanier and Gisèle; Gisèle with the two Poles, separately and together; and the two Poles with Anjili. Midnight came and went. At two o'clock, they finished with hugs and tears, promises, resolutions, and Polish vodka.

# PART THREE

# TEN
## JANUARY 1

7 AM

**Vanier was surfacing into wakefulness** in the half-light before dawn, and he felt the sleeping presence next to him. He didn't move, replaying the previous night. There were no flashes of regret or shame. He took an exaggerated deep breath and rolled over, pulling himself to her sleeping body. She stirred without opening her eyes, and relaxed again, and he wondered if she was also rewinding the night before committing to the day. They both lay still, and he fell back into sleep. When the sun finally blazed its way into the room, he felt her stir again.

"Well?" he said, the non-committal opener that says *you go first*.

"Well, Inspector. This is not what I expected," she said, rolling into him and making eye contact.

He reached and brushed the hair back from her face. "Me neither. But I feel good, Anjili."

"Careful, Inspector."

"I was just thinking…"

"Don't."

He looked at her and saw that it was her mind that was racing. She was the one doing the thinking.

"I'm starving. How about breakfast in bed?" he asked. "I'll be back in five minutes." He kissed her on the lips and got out of the bed, pulling on a pair of boxers that were lying on the floor. She smiled at him, closed her eyes and lay bathed in the sunlight that was streaming through the window.

Standing up, he knew it would be a tough day. His stomach was churning, his head hurt and his mouth felt furry.

## 10 AM

"Ladies and gentlemen, I will read from a prepared statement and then I will take questions." The journalists were subdued, and Vanier guessed that he wasn't the only one nursing a hangover.

He was getting used to Sergeant Laflamme's press conferences and knew his place was to stand behind her and look dignified, a difficult task on New Year's Day, but not insurmountable. This one had been arranged too quickly, but the Chief had insisted. Vanier would have preferred a positive I.D. of the body first.

Laflamme continued, "During the course of our investigations relating to the murder of several homeless people on the evening of December 24, we identified a suspect, a Mr. John Collins. We believe that Mr. Collins may have been responsible for the deaths of several people, poisoning his victims with liquid laced with potassium cyanide that he stole from his place of employment. Several facts point to his involvement in these murders, and we have reason to believe that the suspect died in a fire at his home on the night of December 30.

We are continuing our investigations to determine whether the suspect acted alone or with others. Now, I will take questions."

"Two part question, Sergeant Laflamme. Did the suspect's stash of potassium cyanide go up in the flames, or is it still missing? And if it did go up in flames, does this pose a health risk for Montrealers?"

Sergeant Laflamme was taken aback and was tempted to look behind her at Vanier for the answer. Vanier was enjoying it.

Recovering, she responded, "There is no evidence that the chemical was kept in the suspect's apartment, and we are continuing our efforts to locate any traces of the chemical that may still be in existence. I must stress that this is still a very active investigation."

"Sergeant, are you certain that the body recovered in the loft is Collins?"

"The body was very badly burned, but we are confident that it was the body of Mr. Collins. The Coroner's office is performing tests to confirm the identity of the body, and we are awaiting those results. Nevertheless, we are confident that this investigation is drawing to a close."

Jennifer Higgins from *The Gazette* yelled, "A question for Inspector Vanier. Inspector Vanier, are you confident that the body is that of Mr. Collins?"

Before he could even think of moving forward to speak into the microphone, Sergeant Laflamme answered, "Inspector Vanier's view is the same as the one I have just given: while we are awaiting a positive identification, we have reached a level of confidence that it is Mr. Collins. Thank you, ladies and gentlemen."

## NOON

There wasn't room to empty the dump truck inside the Laboratoire's building, so they had worked out a protocol. An area of the parking lot had been scraped clean with shovels and covered in two layers of thick painter's plastic. Vanier was there out of curiosity. He wanted to see how they would handle the logistics of emptying a truck full of dirty snow and body parts. Laurent was along for company, and they watched the dump truck back up to the plastic sheets until a man in a white plastic evidence suit raised his arms for it to stop and let its red-streaked load slide on to the plastic mat. Dr. Segal had taken charge of the operation and then moved over towards Vanier. They were both having trouble separating the private and public.

"That's a lot of red snow," said Vanier.

"There must have been a lot of leakage during the night. Don't worry, we'll still have lots to test," she said.

After about a third of the truck's load had emptied onto the floor, the guy in the evidence suit waved the driver to stop. The driver lowered the dumper, and three technicians moved in and began shifting through the pile of bloody, hard-packed snow and street garbage. They worked with shovels, bouncing clumps of snow like prospectors, and it soon became clear they weren't looking for small human nuggets but sizable chunks of flesh. The body parts were separated from the snow and garbage, and they began filling large plastic buckets with flesh and bones, pushing the junk off to the side.

"The snow-blower driver removed the screen," said Vanier, feeling the need to explain the size of the pieces being recovered.

"Nice," said Segal.

The image of the technicians carefully fingering the dirty snow reminded Vanier of TV news footage of bombings in Israel and religious Jews picking through the debris of destroyed lives searching for human flesh so it could be treated with respect and buried properly. The more he watched, the more body parts Vanier recognized; a gloved hand with an arm up to the elbow, part of a leg, still clothed but without a foot, a chunk of the torso, and then the head. The technician brushed snow off the face and cradled the head gently in his hands, turning it face up towards the group of watchers. It had come through the blower cleanly, severed at the neck but otherwise undamaged.

"I've had enough," said Vanier. "Dr. Segal, unless you need me here, I think that I can find something more useful to do. Oh, and by the way, his name is Denis Latulippe."

"You knew him? I'm sorry, Luc."

"He was on the list. Laurent and I tried to convince him to get off the streets for a while."

"We can manage here," she said, putting her hand on his arm. "This is going to take some time. I'll call you as soon as I have something to report."

Light snow was falling again as they crossed the parking lot. Vanier opened the back door and pulled out a snow brush. He handed it to Laurent.

"You do the snow and I'll get it warmed up."

Laurent took the brush and began clearing the snow off the car. It was light and came off without effort. He finished and got into the passenger side, throwing the brush onto the floor in the back.

"So. Denis Latulippe," said Laurent.

"Yeah."

"You think he was killed?"

"We'll know that soon enough. Either that, or I gave him too much money and he went on a bender and blacked out in the snow."

They drove back to headquarters in silence.


6 PM


Two men sat in comfortable armchairs watching flames in a wood stove lick through foot-long logs of maple. An invisible sound system filled the room with a Bach English Suite. The older man was carefully dressed for the country, like he had planned to look relaxed; a thick maroon cardigan over a checkered flannel shirt and brown corduroys, all new. His hair was dyed a youthful dark brown but failed to hide his age. The younger man looked out of place beside him in jeans and T-shirt, with a borrowed sweater draped over his shoulders.

The older man looked at the firelight playing on his companion's face. "John, when was the last time you went to confession?"

"I couldn't say. Years for sure." He didn't break his gaze on the burning logs, but his eyes became distant.

"It's a powerful sacrament, John. It reaches deep into the soul."

"I know. But a good confession takes two people. An understanding listener is essential and they're hard to find. Hearing confessions is routine for most priests, the same sins repeated week after week. They stop listening. I mean really listening."

"Yes, I know what you mean. That's always a danger. We're all human, and human sins tend to be an unimaginative repetition of human frailty. But a good priest learns to listen with his heart. The words aren't important. It's what's behind them. You try to understand and provide comfort and hope, maybe even some guidance. It's a heavy responsibility if it's done properly."

"Standing between God and man is a heavy responsibility."

"You have to destroy your own ego to separate God's message from your own. An old priest once told me you should be a pipeline, not a filter. Sometimes we manage it. Sometimes not. Our egos are strong and you must always ask the question: *is this God's message of love, or is it my opinion of what God's message ought to be*?"

"And how do you tell, Father? How do you know?"

"I don't know, John. You can never know. You must keep testing yourself. One thing I do know is that certainty is a red flag. Only saints and charlatans are ever certain. I am neither, so I always wrestle with doubt."

"Are you certain of that, Father?"

Father Michael Forlini smiled, "Well, I'm certain I'm not a saint. A charlatan? I hope not."

Silence settled as they watched the fire. Outside, snow continued to fall in big flakes covering the woods in a thick blanket, silently covering the tracks of their arrival.

The cottage was simply furnished, but in the storm it had a womb-like quality. Two armchairs and a couch filled the small living space, and an intricately woven Persian carpet lay on dark, polished wooden floorboards. Apart from the murmured conversation and the almost imperceptible harpsichord, the only noise was the occasional burst of the refrigerator motor from the kitchen.

"So, what are we to do?"

The question went unanswered for a long time, both men staring at the flames.

"I have not sinned, Father. I have done God's work."

"So you believe, and if your belief is true, even if you are mistaken in that belief, then it is no sin."

"Do you believe God speaks to you?"

"To me personally?"

"No. I mean that God does speak. To his people, if we have the courage to listen."

"Yes, John. I believe that God does speak to his people, to all of us. The problem is we don't listen. Too often, we hear only what we want to hear."

"God has spoken to me. I believe, with my whole being, that God has spoken to me. I have that certainty that you spoke of. But I am not a saint, or a charlatan. I've struggled for years. I fought against it. I know all the arguments; that it's human vanity, that I am delusional, that I am too unimportant. You cannot imagine how I resisted his voice. And then, one day, I came to the realization that it was wrong to refuse to listen."

"My child, God speaks to us all, but our minds are fragile. We are unreliable."

"That is why I resisted."

"That's good.

"But I didn't give up. I didn't cut him off. I examined what people were asking; good people, people with faith. When there was an answer to a sincere prayer, I became an instrument."

"Ah."

"I can stand before anyone and tell them that I have done only good. All that I have done is to provide answers to the sincere prayers of the faithful. That's all."

"I know, my child. But who would understand?"

"You'll help me, Father?"

"Of course I will help you. I understand your faith. But you must promise me it has stopped. There are serious theological issues we must understand before you do anything else. These acts must stop."

"I know that, Father."

"Was Father Drouin's death an answer to a prayer?"

Again, a long silence.

"He was going to interfere with God's work. What he was going to do would have destroyed everything. It would have harmed the Church and it was against God's wishes. Good Catholics have always done what is necessary to protect Mother Church."

"The Church must be protected. And sometimes that involves very troubling decisions."

"Isn't it our most sacred duty? To protect the Church?"

"Scandal must be avoided. The world is full of evil people, always waiting for any opportunity to destroy us."

"Father, I realize that it has gone too far. But I need help to know what to do, what is right. I need help. I need to understand what I am doing. I need the support of the Church."

"You have our support and you can stay here as long as necessary. I will come and see you, bring all that you need. You must pray and study. Here is the perfect solitude. We need to understand this holy connection of yours. But John, this thing must stop."

## 6 PM

The jarring ring of the cell phone in Vanier's pocket forced a couple of the more aware drinkers to look up from their beers.

"Vanier."

"Inspector, it's Pascal Beaudoin. My daughter, Stephanie, she's disappeared. You've got to do something."

"What?"

"My daughter, Stephanie."

*Oh, Christ*, thought Vanier.

"We're in St. Sauveur. Stephanie came off the hills about an hour ago. One second she's standing next to the ski runs. The next second she's gone."

"I'm on my way. I'll be there in 40 minutes, max," said Vanier. "Wait for me." Vanier folded his cell closed and grabbed his coat. He called the Squad Room on his way to the car and got St. Jacques. She agreed to meet him in the parking lot outside headquarters.

"Tell Janvier to get me the Police Chief in St. Sauveur and patch him into my cell."

"Yes, sir."

She was standing in the parking lot when he arrived. He heavy-footed the gas, and they were back out of the lot and onto the street before she had buckled the belt.

"What's the hurry, boss?"

"The daughter of a friend of mine may have been snatched from the ski hill at St. Sauveur. He just called me. Get on the phone to the SQ and see if you can get me an escort on 15 North. If you can't, just tell them him to make sure they stay away from the car. We're not stopping."

He pushed the car onto the Ville Marie Expressway, accelerating past everything, weaving in and out of lanes like a video game. St. Jacques was clutching the seat with one hand and trying to contact

Central with one-thumb dialing. She looked at the speedometer. He was cruising at 160 km. When they hit 15 North, he gunned the motor and settled into 180 km on the long, straight Autoroute going north to the mountains.

The phone rang; she listened for a few moments and then put the phone on speaker, holding it in front of Vanier. "It's Janvier," she said.

"Yeah?"

"Inspector, I have Captain DuMoulin from the SQ in Ste. Agathe on the line. He's the Director for the area. Go ahead, Captain," said Janvier.

Vanier started: "Captain DuMoulin, Inspector Vanier here, Major Crimes in Montreal. I have a report of a missing child at the ski hill in St. Sauveur. This is a friend of mine. And the child may have been taken. Do you understand me?"

"Yes, Inspector. We're already onto it. I have two men at the chalet checking it out."

"Two? That's all? And I suppose they're walking around together?"

"We're doing our best, Inspector. It's the holidays, you know. The two at the mountain, they've already talked to the parents."

"Captain, I've talked to the father, and the parents didn't see anything. Maybe someone else did. If there were any witnesses, you need to speak to them now. Can we get anybody else out there?"

"For you, Inspector, I'll have two more cars go up. And I'll tell the guys who are there to start asking around. Maybe we can get a description of a car."

"I'll be there in half an hour."

"Excellent, Inspector, I'll be in touch."

Vanier saw the flashing lights in his mirror, an SQ car approaching fast, weaving through traffic and gaining on Vanier.

"Oh, Captain, one more thing before you go."

"Yes, Inspector?"

"One of your guys is coming up behind me. Looks like he wants me to slow down. Can you get him to back off?"

"I'll see what I can do, Inspector, but please drive carefully. What are you driving?"

"Grey Volvo, and I just crossed the Rivière-des-Prairies bridge."

St. Jacques flipped the phone closed and fought with the seatbelt to slip it back in her pocket. The SQ car was directly behind them, playing its siren, the noise barely reaching them. *Christ*, thought Vanier, they'll start shooting soon. In the mirror he saw the SQ drop back for a second and then shift into the middle lane. It sped up again, gaining quickly. As it pulled level, Vanier looked to his right and saw the driver smiling back at him, his right hand pointing forward before he shot ahead and pulled into place in front of Vanier. The SQ escort slowed down to match Vanier's 180 km, clearing the way with flashing lights and a siren. This guy is crazy, Vanier thought.

They continued for twenty minutes, and Vanier's phone rang. He started digging into his jacket pocket to find it.

"Please," said St. Jacques, "Let me. Just concentrate on the driving. You'll get us killed." She reached into his pocket and removed the phone.

"This is Sergeant St. Jacques, Inspector Vanier is busy at the moment. You can speak to me."

She listened for a few moments

"Just a second," she said, taking the phone away from her ear. "Sir, they've found a girl abandoned at the McDonald's at Exit 105, La Porte du Nord. A car is on its way."

"Get the kid's name. What's her name?"

St. Jacques spoke into the phone. "Captain DuMoulin, do we have a name for the child?"

She listened again, then turned to Vanier.

"Sir, they don't have a name yet, but we'll be at the exit in a few minutes at this speed. We should stop there and see."

"OK. We'll stop. But tell DuMoulin that we need a name as soon as possible. Oh, and get onto the SQ to tell Sparky up front that we're getting off at exit 105."

In minutes, the SQ escort indicated he was pulling off, and they followed. Vanier slammed on the brakes in the tight exit ramp leading to a service stop dominated by an Esso Station and a McDonald's. He braked hard in front of the McDonald's and ran in, leaving the driver's door open. There was a knot of people standing around, trying not to gawk too obviously at a distraught girl, maybe eight years old, sitting with an older girl in a McDonald's uniform. They were holding hands. The younger girl's face was red from crying and her cheeks shiny with tears. Vanier squatted down in front of her, an attempt at a smile on his face.

"Stephanie?"

She lit up at the sound of the familiar.

"Are you the daughter of Pascal Beaudoin?"

"Oui, où est Papa?"

"Why don't we get him on the phone, Stephanie."

Vanier dialed.

"Pascal, I have someone who wants to talk to you," he said, handing the phone to the child.

"Papa?"

Vanier stood up, smiling.

St. Jacques approached. "She's the one?"

"Thank God."

Beaudoin arrived fifteen minutes later with his wife and a small boy in tow, walking like a toy soldier in his one-piece snowsuit. In the meantime, Vanier had made friends with Stephanie, both of them drawing pictures on the back of McDonald's placemats and asking each other to guess what they had drawn. Caroline ignored him and grabbed her daughter as though she was still in danger. She pushed her face into the girl's neck and wept with heaving shoulders.

Stephanie looked at Vanier over her mother's head and smiled. He winked at her.

Beaudoin was holding his son's hand. He turned to Vanier, "Somebody took her?"

"It looks that way. We need to get her to a hospital. She needs to be checked out."

"You don't think…?"

"Pascal, I don't think anything. But we have to be sure. We also have to speak to her, find out what she can tell us." Before Beaudoin could object, he added, "We have people who are trained to do these kinds of things. Anyway, let's get her to a hospital and get it over with as soon as possible. The ambulance will take her to St. Jérôme, that's the closest."

"Ambulance, what ambulance?" Beaudoin was beginning to realize that finding his daughter safe wasn't the end of it.

"Pascal, I'm sorry, but that's the procedure. Your wife and Sergeant St. Jacques can go with her. You follow the ambulance, and I'll follow you."

Beaudoin went over to his wife, knowing he wouldn't be able to pry Stephanie from her arms.

"Papa."

"Yes, my love?"

"The man told me to give this to you." She pulled a crumpled pink telephone message slip from her pocket and handed it to him. There was a scrawled message on it: *Hey lawyer man, chill.*

Beaudoin turned to Vanier.

"Can I have it? It's evidence"

Vanier took the pink slip and put it in a plastic sandwich bag he had in his pocket.

Two men from Urgences-santé pulled up a stretcher on wheels, and Stephanie's mother laid her gently onto it. One of the ambulance men covered her with a blanket and pulled the belts close around her. Caroline walked beside the stretcher, holding Stephanie by the hand.

She seemed in a daze as they went to the ambulance, not even looking at Beaudoin.

In the parking lot, Vanier turned to Beaudoin.

"Pascal, this was a warning. This isn't your fight. What's happening at the Shelter shouldn't involve your family. Leave it alone. You can just walk away."

"Inspector, I wish I could. I'll do what I need to do. But we need to talk about how to protect my family."

As Stephanie was raised into the ambulance, Caroline turned to watch the two men, as though seeing them for the first time. She walked over to them and reached down to pick up her son, who was still holding his dad's hand. With the boy in her arms, she looked at Vanier.

"Inspector, I need to protect my children. We're going away for a few weeks. I want the children to be safe. But make no mistake," she said, turning back to face Beaudoin, "I support Pascal in what he is doing. If I could stay with him I would, but my job is to look after the children. Please look after him for me."

She turned and left before Vanier could respond. Pascal looked at Vanier with a bemused expression.

"She's something, isn't she?"

"You're a lucky man, Maître Beaudoin. Let's see what we can do together."

"I'll call you," Beaudoin said as he moved to his car.

"I'll be pissed if you don't," said Vanier.

For a few moments Vanier was happy, but he was already moving past happy into clenched-fist anger. He remembered what Markov had said to him back in Blackrock's office. *Hey, policeman, chill.*

# ELEVEN
## JANUARY 2

## 7 AM

**The kidnapping had changed things.** What had been a minor nuisance, in which Vanier could play at influencing the outcome – but wouldn't lose sleep if he didn't – had now become a street fight. He decided to draw on his deposits of favours owed for past services. His first call was to an old friend in the RCMP. Detective Sergeant Ian Peterson was a drug investigator with the Mounties who had worked undercover for years before slowly moving up the ranks. Years ago Vanier had learned that Peterson was being set up for a frame by Rolf Cracken, a mid-sized dealer with ambition and an oversized grudge against Peterson. It came out in a conversation with an informant who was trying to impress Vanier with his connections and knowledge, and it didn't amount to much at first, only that Cracken was getting ready to stitch up a cop. Vanier could have ignored it as someone else's problem, but he didn't. He spent four days putting it all together and convincing himself Peterson was clean. When he was sure, it was simple enough to deal with. Craken's plan was to dump a brick of cocaine and a couple of thousand dollars in Peterson's apartment, start a small sofa fire to get some smoke going, and call the firemen to put out the fire. They wouldn't be able to ignore the pile of cocaine and cash, and Peterson would be finished in the force.

One morning in July, Peterson let Vanier into the apartment and left for work as usual. Just in case anyone missed him leaving, he stopped as he drove out of the parking garage and got out of the car to check his tires before driving off. Fifteen minutes later, he walked back into the apartment building in a baseball cap and a different coat. Vanier and Peterson waited 40 minutes until the lock in the apartment door was picked and the planter walked in with the drugs and money. Vanier still laughs at the pitiful *I'm fucked* expression on the planter's face when he saw the two cops waiting for him.

In Vanier's world, inter-agency cooperation was officially practiced by bureaucrats on committees who carefully channelled the flow of information backed up by strict rules to prevent any unofficial exchanges. All requests to other forces were supposed to flow through the committees and, because information is currency, the committees became farmers' markets of swaps and promises where none of the farmers trusted each other. Vanier preferred the direct approach, granting and receiving favours with officers he knew, or who were recommended, and always keeping the ledger balanced.

Peterson picked up the phone on the third ring.

"I hope I didn't wake you from your beauty sleep. You, of all people, need it."

"Vanier, you bastard. What the fuck do you want?"

"You recognize me? I'm flattered."

"Don't be. Wait a minute, I've got it. You're calling me to wish me a Happy New Year."

"You guessed. That and something else."

"I might have known, you don't do Happy anything. So what can I do for you?"

"Got a pen?"

"Course I do, I sleep with a fucking pen in my hand. Wait a second."

Vanier heard the phone drop onto a hard surface, some shuffling and cursing, a woman's voice, and then Peterson picked it up again.

"OK, so what is it?"

"Blackrock Investments, a property developer on Chabanel. Vladimir Markov, the President, or something like that, and Ivan Romanenko, the in-house lawyer."

"And?"

"As much background as you can give me. I think they're putting a little too much muscle into the development business, and I want to know if you guys have anything on them. They seem like slime."

"That's it? I thought slimy was a prerequisite for being a property developer. You have anything else?"

"It's just that I had them down as simple businessmen, sleazy as all hell but no more than that. But I may have underestimated them."

"It's urgent, I suppose?"

"You read my mind."

"OK, Luc, I'll see what I can do and get back to you. Now, can I put on my pants?"

"Thanks, Ian."


## 10 AM

Vanier and Laurent spent the morning looking for Marcel Audet. He wasn't at the Holy Land Shelter, and Nolet didn't seem to miss him. Nolet told them that Audet hadn't been seen at the Shelter since before the New Year and hadn't called to say when he would be back. He also said it wasn't unusual for Audet to disappear without telling anyone, sometimes for a week at a time. Then he would show up as though everything was perfectly normal. He wasn't the type to excuse himself.

It took them hours to track down Degrange, the rue St. Denis drug dealer, but they eventually found him in a rooming house near the bus station. He was still in bed when they knocked on his door.

"Who is it?" he asked through the door, protecting the only privacy he had.

"Vanier. Open the door, Louis."

"Inspector. Give me a few minutes and I'll meet you. Why don't you go to the coffee shop in the bus station? I'll meet you there in half an hour."

"Louis, open the fucking door or I'll lean on it." That's all it would have taken, and asking him to open it was a polite formality. The lock clicked, and Degrange's scrawny body stood before them in a dirty white wife-beater T-shirt, black Y-fronts and black socks. He was surprised to see Laurent standing next to Vanier and attempted a smile, showing a mouthful of rotting teeth.

"Can we come in?"

"Inspector, I'm not set up for visitors," he said, backing away from the door as they walked through. He sat down on the edge of the bed and they stood over him. There wasn't room to stand anywhere else. The window was covered by a thick brown blanket that was nailed into place, and the room was dark as a cave. Vanier pulled the chain on a bedside lamp and filled the room with a yellowish glow. It did little to dispel the gloom but illuminated the overflowing ashtray on the table and the empty screw-top wine bottle on the floor next to the bed. The air was close and heavy with the smell of stale tobacco mixed with the disturbingly unpleasant aroma of Degrange. Vanier knew that if he looked around, he would probably find a full jug of last night's urine.

"It isn't much, I know." He tried to regain some humanity. "So,

Inspector, what can I do for you?"

"You didn't call me."

"I was meaning to. But I didn't want to disturb your holidays." He gave Vanier an ingratiating smile.

"So what do you have on Audet?"

"Audet. Yeah, Marcel Audet. I have an address, Inspector. It's here," he said, reaching for his pants on the floor next to the bed. He dragged scraps of paper out of the pocket and handed one to Vanier, who checked it to make sure that it was legible.

"Anything else?"

"No. He's not working with anyone that I know. Maybe he's gone clean. It happens, Inspector."

"You're right. How much?"

"You said fifty."

"And I gave you twenty. So here's thirty. We'll close the door on the way out."

The address was downtown in one of those big anonymous towers that caters to people passing through on their way to somewhere else; twenty identical apartments on each of thirty identical floors. There was no answer when they knocked on the door to his apartment. They tried the neighbouring apartments, and nobody knew anything. The building lobby was as busy as a railway station with strangers passing strangers. The building allowed people to live alone, really alone.

As they were driving back to headquarters, Vanier got a text message to call Peterson when he got a chance. He had a chance half an hour later.

"Ian, it's Luc."

"Luc, where the fuck do you find these people? It's time you started moving in better circles."

Vanier smiled, "Nobody else will have me. Blackrock?"

"Yes, and their wonderful officers Markov and Romanenko."

"So you lads on horses know them?"

"Know them? We'd be galloping up Chabanel on the fucking horses if we could get something on them. Grab a pen, Mr. V."

Vanier began to take notes.

"Markov came to Montreal from St. Petersburg, that's in Russia."

"How do you spell it?"

"Russia or St. Petersburg?"

"Fuck off."

"He came to Canada 12 years ago as an immigrant investor. Basically that's an $800,000 ticket to Canada, but you get to keep the money. You just have to invest it in a Canadian business. We've been watching him ever since. Romanenko came a year later. And let me say for the record, Detective Inspector—"

"In case anyone is listening," said Vanier.

"—for the record, they have never been accused of the slightest wrongdoing. Upstanding citizens, both of them."

"But?"

"Ah, but, that's the thing, there are suspicions. And some would say, though I'm not saying it, that those suspicions are very well founded."

"And what are those unfounded suspicions?"

"That the gentlemen specialize in corruption. No job too small or too large. Let's say that you're a businessman and you want to show your appreciation to someone for giving you some business, or permits. There are a lot of people who would frown on that sort of thing, in fact it's illegal just about everywhere. Well, Blackrock can put together a plan for you, and they take a small commission."

"And then they have the goods on the donor and the crooked politician."

"So you're following me. It's a growth business. Every transaction pays off in money and in influence for the future. The more they do, the more people they have in their pocket. That allows them to pursue their other interests, like property development, much more efficiently."

"Are they are serious players?"

"Luc, they are as serious as it gets. Make no mistake, these are very dangerous people to mess with. They have connections you can't even imagine, and they have muscle they're not afraid to use."

"Muscle?"

"They have three guys on retainer that we know of, all Russian, and we think they have just picked up a local asset, Marcel Audet."

"I know him."

"Thought you might. The three Russians are the same type, very violent. Luc, I advise you to be extremely careful. Do not underestimate these people."

Vanier knew that it was too late for that. "Thanks for the heads up, Ian. I'll keep you posted."

"Please do."

Before Vanier could get lost in paperwork, the phone rang.

"Vanier."

"Good afternoon, Luc, or should I call you Inspector."

"Anjili. Hello will do fine. How are you?"

"I've got news."

"I need good news."

"It's not all good."

"Well, give me the good news first."

"The body in the truck — M. Latulippe — there was no trace of poison. So we're putting it down as natural causes. His blood alcohol level was through the roof. He probably passed out in the snow and that was it. It's likely he was dead before he went into the snow blower."

"That's the good news?"

"Everything's relative, Luc."

"So what's the bad news?"

"The body from the fire is not John Collins. We don't know who it is yet, but it's not Collins."

"Sure?"

"Yes. Mme. Collins was in this morning to identify the body."

"That can't have been pleasant."

"It wasn't. She took one long look at the body and said that it wasn't her son. I was half-expecting her to say that. The body's in awful shape, and any mother would want to deny it's her son. But she insisted. She was very calm. When we were arranging the visit, I had asked her to bring down any medical records she had of him. The blood type is different. She even stopped by her dentist to get John's file, and the teeth are different. The clincher is the broken arm."

"His arm was broken?"

"No, that's the point. She says that he broke his left arm when he was ten, and it didn't set properly. Our victim shows no sign of a healed fracture. Based on all of that, we're certain the fire victim is not John Collins."

"Shit."

"So we have an unidentified corpse, and your suspect is still wandering the streets."

"Anjili, can you fax me a preliminary report?"

"It's on its way, Luc."

"I need to talk to Mme. Collins. When did she leave?" he said, trying to calculate how long it would be before she was back home.

"She's on her way over. She said that she needed to talk to you. She should be there in about half an hour."

"She's coming here?"

"Unless she knows where you live. I only gave her the office address."

"And for that I thank you. Listen, I have to go." Vanier thought for a second of suggesting dinner but let the thought pass; he wasn't sure what time he would be finished.

"Let me know what happens. Luc, you'll find him. I know you will."
Vanier put the phone back in his pocket.

The front desk called twenty minutes later to say that Mme. Collins was asking for him. He told them to put her in the family room. It was still an interview room, but a little softer, with a couch and two armchairs squeezed into the impossibly small space. She was standing up when he arrived. He started to reach his hand out to shake hers but realized that she wasn't offering.

"Please, Mme. Collins, sit down," he gestured to one of the armchairs. She sat stiffly on the armchair and put her bag on the floor, leaning it against her leg.

"I have just come from the Coroner's office. It's good news," she said. "It's not him. It's not my son."

"Dr. Segal called me."

"I thought I had lost him forever."

Vanier watched her carefully, wondering if she would, or even could, be any help in finding him. He doubted it. Mothers couldn't be trusted to turn in their sons. There was always a sub-plot, a faint hope that they could do something to make things turn out right. They would help you just as much as was absolutely necessary, always hoping that along the way they could save him.

"'That doesn't help us find him, and we need to find him. Mme Collins, it's time for you to help us. And we can help you. You couldn't do it on your own but maybe we can do it together." He decided to fight dirty. "Who is the father, Madame Collins?"

The blow was obvious, and she took it like a boxer past his prime.

"What does it matter? It has never mattered."

"If John is alive, and it seems that he is, then someone may be hiding him. And right now, he may be in danger."

"That's rich, Inspector. You don't care about him. You think he's a mass murderer."

"He's a suspect, and I want to talk to him, but this is a messy business. Someone else might think that one way to clean it up is to get rid of him."

She looked at him. He imagined she was calculating, but her eyes gave no clue.

"Mme. Collins, I've seen too many bodies this week, and I want it to stop. If someone is helping him, they are both are in danger. Don't get me wrong, I want your son in custody. I think he's killed several people and could kill more. He needs help. And I need your help."

There are moments when people make decisions and change directions in a heartbeat. The tipping point is unpredictable, but we all have one, when the old arguments finally lose their potency, and we clutch at whatever lifeline is thrown. She slumped forward, and then looked him in the eyes.

"Perhaps you're right. I have not told the story to anyone. It was 30 years ago. If it all happened today, things would be different. I can see that. There would have been counseling, some support. Perhaps it would have helped to talk to someone about it. But life was different back then. I was alone. I have loved three things in my life, Inspector, and each has taken that love and then rejected me. I joined the Church when I was 17 years old to escape my family. It was the only escape. I gave my life to the Church, and then the Church destroyed me. John's father is Monsignor Michael Forlini. Back then, he was just an ambitious young priest following a calling that he thought he had. He's been very successful. I loved him as much as I loved the Church, and I thought he loved me. He didn't. He used me and then rejected me like I was nothing. As soon as our relationship was discovered, I was sacrificed, and he was protected. His sin was to have given in to the temptations of the flesh, an understandable sin that could be forgiven. My sin was the treachery of a woman, the devil's handmaiden. I was left with nothing except my child, and I raised him with no help from his father. Then, 18 years later, he left without saying goodbye. But I still love him. John needs my help and I need him."

She reached for the box of Kleenex on the floor but it was empty. Vanier pulled a Second Cup napkin from his pocket and gave it to her.

"I won't give you the sordid details of how it happened. But, believe me, the holy Monsignor Forlini does not know where John is. He never even acknowledged that he was John's father. He has never had anything to do with either of us. He even arranged to have me banned from the Cathedral. Not officially, of course, but any time that I go in, I am quickly asked to leave. When John first disappeared, I was convinced that his father might have something to do with it. Even though I couldn't enter the Cathedral, I spent months walking around it, hoping to catch sight of John. I would wait outside all the Masses. I watched the doors for hours, more than I care to think of, winter and summer, but I never saw him."

"But that was years ago, Mme. Collins. Have you stopped watching the Cathedral?"

"I came to the conclusion that I was wasting my time, so I stopped."

"If Monsignor Forlini decided to help John, is there any place he might hide him?"

"I have no idea. His life is the Cathedral, and you can't hide someone in the Cathedral."

"I suppose not. Thank you, Mme. Collins, this has been very helpful, and I promise that I will do everything in my power to find your son. Let me have someone drive you home."

"Thank you, Inspector. That would be kind, if it's not too much trouble."

"No trouble. You just sit here and take it easy while I get a ride organized."

"It's been a long day."

"I'm sure it has. I will be in touch."

Vanier arranged for Mme. Collins to get a blue-and-white taxi home. The uniform reported back that she had asked to be dropped off two blocks away. She didn't want the neighbours talking.

## 2 PM

Vanier and Janvier followed a young priest down a carpeted hall-way lined with fading drawings and photographs of the Church's real heroes: not the saints on public display, but the men – and they were all men – who spent their lives in the back corridors and closed rooms nurturing the growth and power of the institution that gave their life importance. The dictators, bureaucrats, fixers and politi-cians of Mother Church. The priest stopped and knocked on one of the closed doors, then waited for some inaudible sign before usher-ing them into the presence of Monsignor Forlini. Walking on the plush ivory-coloured carpet was like walking on sponge. A wall of photographs of the Monsignor with famous people dominated the room. Vanier had seen these walls of self-celebration before, an invi-tation to an ice-breaking conversational opener for any meeting. He declined to break the ice.

The Monsignor was all smiles and offered coffee. They declined, and the young priest left them alone. Vanier placed the sketch of Collins on the dark mahogany desk in front of the Monsignor.

"Do you recognize this man?"

Vanier and Janvier watched closely as he studied the drawing. There was nothing but a calm interest.

"Of course I do. This is the sketch of the suspect in the homeless deaths, isn't it?"

"Yes. Do you recognize him?"

"From the news, and the newspapers, yes. But apart from that, I'm afraid not. Should I?"

"We're told he's your son, John Collins."

If that had an impact on him it didn't show. He looked up and gave a short laugh. "I don't know who you've been talking to, In-spector, but I don't have a son. There was a malicious accusation many years ago but it was totally unfounded. I do not have a son."

There are several kinds of liars. The good ones actually believe they are telling the truth. Others are arrogant enough to think the rest of the world is too stupid to know the difference. Still others work from a rule book only they know, strategizing like poker players, mixing it up: truth, lies, truth that sounds like a falsehood, and invention that sounds like fact. Vanier couldn't make up his mind about the Monsignor, but he didn't have to, just yet.

"Just for the record, sir, I am going to ask you a series of simple questions, and Sergeant Janvier here will record your answers. Will that be OK?"

"Perfectly."

"So, once again, you do not know the person in the photograph."

"Just for the record, Inspector, it is not 'once again.' You did not ask me if I knew this person, you asked if I recognized him. But the answer is the same in both cases. No."

"Does the name John Collins mean anything to you?"

"Of course it does. If I recall the news correctly, Collins is the suspect in these recent deaths. But just in case you fell that I am not being entirely forthright, there is another reason for me to recognize the name John Collins. It's a little delicate, but I can tell you. There is nothing to hide. Many years ago, a certain Yvette Collins, Sister Agnes as she was then, accused me of fathering her son. Absolutely preposterous of course, but she maintained that I had seduced her and caused her to become pregnant. She had a son, and I believe he was called John. She carried on a campaign against me and against the church for several years. I'm sure you understand Inspector, women can be, how shall we say, irrational at times, and the sisterhood seems to attract more than its fair share. It's likely that her sin pushed her over the top, so to speak, and she became convinced that I was the child's father."

"Have you had any contact with John Collins in the last few years?"

"None at all. I wouldn't know him if he were to walk in here."

"So, just for the record, you deny ever having contact with this man, John Collins."

"Correct, Inspector. Now, was there something else?"

"I don't think so. Sergeant Janvier, did you get everything."

"Yes, Chief."

Vanier stood up, "Well, I think that will be all for the moment."

The Monsignor came around the desk, hand out for a shake.

"Well, I don't think that I have been of much help, but anytime you want to talk, feel free to set something up with my secretary. I'll have him show you gentlemen out."

As they walked to the car Vanier looked up at the clear blue sky and nodded at Janvier, "It's a change from the darkness in there."

"Yeah," replied Janvier. "Did you notice the smell?"

"I think it was the absence of women," said Vanier.

## 4.30 PM

The investigation had been shut down prematurely, and it was proving difficult to get the extra people back. Everyone was involved somewhere else. Vanier and St. Jacques were the only ones in the Squad Room. Roberge, Janvier, and Laurent were out interviewing workers from Xeon Pesticides and from the homeless shelters, trying to find anyone who might have been close to John Collins.

Vanier turned to St. Jacques. "Sergeant."

"Yes, sir? Just a second." She was typing at a screen.

"Where did Audet do his time?"

"He got eight years, so he must have been at a Federal facility. I'll check." She started typing searches and pulled up what they had on Audet. It didn't take long. "Donnacona, sir."

"That will do. Give them a call and get his medical records as quickly as you can. Then get them over to Dr. Segal."

"You think Audet might be the guy in the van?"

"Not really. It's a bit of a stretch, but it's worth a try. Nobody's seen him since the day of the fire, and we have an unidentified corpse. Who knows? It's worth a shot."

St. Jacques was on the phone immediately, sweet-talking her way through the bureaucracy of Donnacona penitentiary. Fifteen minutes later she walked over to Vanier's desk. "Denis said that if he could put his hands on it he would fax it to me, otherwise it would have to wait until tomorrow."

"Denis?"

"Yes, Denis. He sounded like a nice guy, not at all like a prison guard."

Sergeant St. Jacques must have made an impression on Donnacona Denis, because a bundle of pages came through the fax 90 minutes later. St. Jacques faxed them on to Dr. Segal and then called Denis to thank him. Vanier heard them on the phone for twenty minutes, and St. Jacques was laughing. He hadn't heard that in a long while.

## 8 PM

Knowledge is power. And in the Church the humble confessional box has always been fertile black soil for harvesting knowledge. Monsignor Michael Forlini knew that, and he loved the sacrament of confession, as long as he was doing the listening. The anonymity of the confessional box was a farce. Its dark boxes separated only by a grille, covered and uncovered for each new penitent, served only to lull the unsuspecting into believing in a protected spiritual conversation with the Almighty. But a priest could identify the most of the penitents by their voices, and was familiar with their weaknesses and unimaginative appetites for the forbidden. But you can build dependence by instilling guilt and then releasing it with divine forgiveness. Priests carry the secrets of the confessional with them, and when they look into the eyes of a sinner leaving Sunday mass with his wife and children, when they greet the wife with a beaming smile and tousle the heads of the children, the sinner knows how much is owed. It isn't blackmail, it's a sacrament. A tool that Jesus gave his priests to help them build and protect the Mother Church, the first and most important goal of every member of the clergy, all the way up to the Papacy.

To influence secular life for good, you need power, and the confessional was the place where power shifted. That's why the decline of the sacrament is seen as such a threat to the Church. While the Protestants might accept that people can confess their sins in a vaguely worded public acknowledgement of weakness, that idea is vigorously resisted by the hard core Catholic clerics. The Church wants to know the sinners and it wants to know the details of their transgressions.

Monsignor Forlini had a sermon that he liked to give to stiffen the spines of believers. Jesus had told His apostles that those whose sins they forgave were forgiven and those whose sins were retained, were retained. This meant that God had given the apostles – and only the apostles – and through them the priests – and only the priests – the divine authority to forgive sin or to refuse to do so. So Jesus Himself had decreed that sin could not be forgiven directly. He put the apostles between the people and Himself, and the priests were the heirs of the apostles. The only way to have your sins forgiven was by confessing them to a priest in the sacrament of confession. And you had to gain forgiveness in this lifetime, because it would be too late after. So the faithful kept confessing their sins.

That was how Monsignor Forlini knew exactly where to go to solve his problem.

He was sitting in Moishe's Steak House, a legend on boulevard St. Laurent, the historic fault line between Montreal's English and French communities that had served Montreal's powerful for over 50 years. Antonio DiPadova, one of Montreal's better known criminal defence lawyers, sat opposite Forlini, nervously scanning the room for clients and potential clients. Being seen dining with a senior member of the Church could be bad for business.

They talked easily of politics and sport, of DiPadova's charitable work, and his substantial donations to the Church. DiPadova was going to Rome in the summer, and an audience had to be arranged and, Monsignor Forlini hinted, a possible Papal acknowledgment of his contribution to the works of Mother Church. Forlini opened at dessert.

"Antonio, I have a problem."

Well fed, and relaxed under the effects of a pound of marbled sirloin and a bottle of a 1998 Barolo that cost as much as the two steaks, DiPadova answered: "And I hope it's something that I can help you with, Monsignor."

"Perhaps you can. But it's somewhat delicate."

"In my experience, between friends it's always better to put everything on the table."

"Perhaps you are right, Antonio. You have been such a good friend. I should put my trust in you." The Monsignor hated being humble but thought it might be effective.

"So, how I can I help?"

"Antonio, there is a child, a child who has reached a dead end and needs a second chance. I can vouch for him, nothing serious, just a second chance."

"And? How can I help?"

"The second chance involves a change of identity. I assume that means a new passport, a driver's licence, social insurance card, the whole thing. A deluxe package if you will. He needs a new life. I am willing to pay whatever it takes."

"Monsignor, I think I can help. Don't worry. My line of work brings me into contact with all kinds of people. I know who can arrange this. But these things aren't cheap. You need to give me details.

You know, since 9/11, this whole identity business has come under close scrutiny. Things are not what they were. Perhaps you could write out some details." DiPadova took out a pen and a scrap of paper, handing it to the Monsignor. "Some simple information, the name that you would like, the height, weight, place of birth. Basic information."

The Monsignor began writing, knowing he was putting himself into the debtor column with every word. DiPadova took the paper when he had finished and read through it quickly.

"Let me see what I can do. I'm sure I can help you."

"Anything that you can do would be appreciated. I really didn't know where to turn. What else do you need? You mentioned the cost."

"You will need to give me ten photographs. Let's wait for the rest. I'll let you know."

"I can imagine that things have become strict, even with passport photographs, I heard you need identification even to have a photograph taken."

"Have your friend go to one of those photo machines and take a bunch of head shots. These people will turn them into passport photographs."

"Your service to the Church will not go unrewarded, Michael."

"It's the least I can do, Monsignor," he said, putting the handwritten note into his pocket.

The delicate business was finished, and Monsignor Forlini ordered brandies and relaxed into the habitual friendly role of the clergy. He asked about DiPadova's family, and about how the children were doing at school. He talked about how difficult it was to love and serve God in the modern world.

DiPadova didn't rush to pick up the cheque. Forlini looked at the leather folder that the waiter had put on the table, and eventually reached for it, already feeling the change in their relationship.

DiPadova had no trouble convincing the Monsignor to accept

a lift back to the Cathedral, and watched the priest relish the soft leather seats of the Mercedes, stroking it unconsciously as the radio played piano jazz through BOSE speakers. As he left the car outside the Cathedral, the Monsignor made eye contact with DiPadova.

"What I asked is very important, Antonio. Your assistance in this will be greatly appreciated. Good night in the grace of God."

DiPadova pulled away, resisting the urge to pump his fist in the air in celebration at something as simple as having Monsignor Forlini in his debt over a new identity. New identities were sold on the streets of Montreal every day. A first class, deluxe package that would withstand scrutiny by U.S. Customs was $10,000 at the most. But to have a future Archbishop, or even a Cardinal, in your pocket for $10,000, well that was *priceless*.

# TWELVE
## JANUARY 3

### 12.30 PM

**John Collins had disappeared** or, more accurately, he had never reappeared. Everyone at Xeon knew him, or thought they did, but each said that he had been closer to someone else. Truth was he was close to no one. He worked among them but was alone. Nobody knew where he lived or what he did outside work. Just about everyone said he was a little strange, but no more than that, not strange enough to be unusual.

It was the same thing with his neighbours. They all recognized him and would nod to him in the street, but that was all. The police had questioned and re-questioned everyone who had attended the Circle of Christ sessions and, again, the face was familiar, but that's where it stopped. They remembered him, but didn't know him and never remembered seeing him with somebody. He was a loner, living within the hive as though he belonged, but passing his life in a universe of one.

Vanier was frustrated. It was like Collins had never existed. And

Vanier didn't know how to find someone who was so disconnected.

His phone rang.

"Anjili, any news?"

"News indeed, Luc. How did you know?"

"About what?"

"About Audet."

"He's the corpse?"

"There's no doubt. The dental records, blood, measurements, height, everything matches. The corpse is Marcel Audet."

"You're certain."

"Luc, we could do a DNA but it seems pointless. In my opinion, there is no doubt it's Audet."

Vanier took a long breath.

"So what does it mean, Luc?"

"I don't have a clue. I need to think."

"Any word on Collins?"

"He's disappeared down a deep hole. That's not so hard if you hardly existed anyway. His own mother couldn't find him and he wasn't even hiding. What chance do we have when he really decides to hide? And how does Audet show up dead in his van?"

"There must be a connection."

"What was Audet up to that he ended up as cinders in the front seat?"

"That's police work, it's what you're good at, Luc."

"People get murdered for a reason. Like the priest."

"Father Drouin?"

"Yes. He probably knew Collins, or knew where to find him. So Collins decided he had to go."

"So perhaps Audet figured it out, too."

"Perhaps. But if Collins killed Audet, he must have had a reason, and Audet must have had a reason for being with Collins. Listen, I have to go. Thanks for this, Anjili."

"Any time."

## 3:00 PM

This time, Vanier had steeled himself against the allure of Ayida and her wonderful coffee. He burst into the offices of Blackrock and walked straight by Ayida, turning right, in the direction that Markov and Romanenko had come from in the earlier meeting. Laurent followed, and then the receptionist, protesting with waving hands and *Non, messieurs, non!* Markov's office was in the northwest corner, with a spectacular view of the mountain. He was on the phone and stopped talking as the two officers walked in.

"Got to go," he said, putting down the phone.

"Officers, we have a receptionist for a reason."

"Won't take long, sir," said Vanier, "Just a few additional questions."

Romanenko entered the room, trying unsuccessfully to get in front of them to protect his client.

"Marcel Audet. Is he an employee of Blackrock?"

"I believe he may be on the payroll; I'd have to check. What's it to you?"

"Let me ask the questions, sir. Is he or is he not an employee?"

"Like I said, I'll check and get back to you," said Markov, regaining his composure.

Laurent made a show of writing down the answers.

"Have you spoken to M. Audet recently?"

Before he could answer, Romanenko broke in, "Officers, this is completely unacceptable. You have no right to barge in here and subject Mr. Markov to questioning. Mr. Markov will cooperate entirely with you, but we will not accept these kinds of tactics."

"So, let's talk," said Vanier.

Markov looked concerned and left it to Romanenko to answer.

"You need to make an appointment and, I should add, indicate what it is that you wish to talk about. Is that clear?" said Romanenko.

"Fine. So can we have an appointment?"

"Certainly", said Markov, breathing easier as he opened a large diary. "How about Tuesday next, at 2.30 p.m?"

"I don't think it will wait until then, sir," said Vanier. "Tell you what, why don't you call me tomorrow morning, after you've read the papers, and we can talk about why Marcel Audet, an employee of Blackrock Investments, was found dead in a car belonging to a certain Mr. Collins, a suspect in the homeless slaying."

Vanier walked out and Laurent followed. Romanenko ran after them, pushed by Laurent, and caught up with Vanier.

"Wait! Let's talk."

"You've had your chance. Here's my card, M. Romanenko, why don't you call and make an appointment?"

# THIRTEEN
## JANUARY 12

6 PM

**Vanier was nursing his third beer** in the Blue Angel, wondering where he should go for supper, when his phone rang. He didn't recognize the number.

"Vanier."

"Inspector Vanier, it's Yvette Collins." He could barely hear her. "The last time we talked, in your office, you asked if the Monsignor had a place he could go to."

"I remember. You said you didn't know."

"There is a place, or at least his mother had a place. It's so long ago, I don't know if he still has it. It was in the Laurentians, in Morin Heights. I'll show you where."

"I'll pick you up in twenty minutes."

It was six o'clock and had been dark for two hours. He called Laurent and arranged to pick him up on the way. Yvette Collins was waiting on the street when they arrived, and she climbed into the back. She caught Vanier's eye in the mirror and said, "Stop in the centre of Morin Heights. I think I'll be able to remember the way from there."

All the traffic was in the opposite direction, skiers heading home after a day on the slopes. Vanier was driving fast, keeping to the outside lane, coming up close behind any cars in the lane and flashing them to move over.

Mme. Collins sat in the back, her silence imposing itself on the rest of the car. Laurent had tried a few phrases at Vanier, but they died away unanswered, and the three of them settled into their thoughts. It took 40 minutes on the highway before the turnoff to Morin Heights, another ten to get through St. Sauveur, and finally they were on a two-lane road through the forest and then on the main street in Morin Heights.

It's still a quiet village, stuck in the 1950s. The main street is dominated by a church with an ancient graveyard that had filled up years before. The Town Hall was next to it, then the Fire Station. A few stores, restaurants and pubs filled the remaining space.

The main street was deserted, and thick, flaky snow fell on the street in a hushed silence. Vanier stopped the car, lowered the windows, and let Mme. Collins look around.

"It's been almost 30 years, Inspector, but things are the same." Her voice trailed off in a whisper. The dome light clicked on as she opened the door and stepped out and started walking slowly away from the car. Laurent was about to follow her out, but Vanier put a hand on his arm. They watched her walk up the main street, huddled against the cold, her black woollen coat pulled tight around her, making her clearly visible in the snow.

She stopped at the crossroads, staring across the street to Marché Vaillancourt. Vanier knew the store from skiing trips with Marianne and the kids, but that was a long time ago. Vaillancourt's was one of those country stores that sold everything from raccoon traps to frozen dinners, and the lights from its windows cast an inviting glow on the snow outside. She stood on the corner for a long time, her head and shoulders gradually turning white under the flakes before she finally looked back and gestured them forward.

They pulled up, and she got in.

"We go down this road," she said, pointing, "for about two miles. Then we turn right."

Vanier watched the odometer and calculated miles to kilometres. At the two-mile mark he slowed almost to a crawl, looking for a turning. There wasn't any. They drove on, and she lowered the window to get a better look. It took three tries from the centre of town before she finally recognized rue du Sommet.

"Follow this street, almost to the top of the mountain," she said.

They followed the meandering road up the mountain while Mme. Collins stared out the open window. Finally she yelped and had them reverse and then turn into an almost invisible entrance. The mailbox had a number, 1365, but no name. The headlights of the Volvo picked up the single, snow-covered track through the trees with the faintest of tire tracks still visible under the falling snow. After two minutes of slow driving, the track opened onto a clearing in front of a dark, two-storey chalet. As they entered the clearing, motion detectors triggered, and they were bathed in light.

"This is the house," she said in a tiny voice. Vanier and Janvier got out, and she made no effort to leave.

Vanier pointed to faint tire tracks that led out of a rectangle formed by snow that had been brushed off a car. Inside the rectangle there was less snow. Whatever footprints had led from the front door to the car had disappeared under the snow.

"Looks like whoever was here has left."

Vanier walked up to the door, pushed the buzzer, and listened to the doorbell ring inside. He rang again and peered through the frosted glass square in the door. Laurent was bending over a cast iron firewood stand at the side of the door. He ran his hand around it and came up with a long string tied to the stand. There was a key at the other end.

"There isn't a cottage in the north that doesn't have an emergency key hidden within six feet of the entrance," he said, grinning, holding up the key for Vanier to see. "I'll go see if Mme. Collins wants to join us."

She didn't, preferring to huddle in the back corner of the rapidly cooling car.

It was comfortably warm inside the chalet. Vanier checked the thermostat, it was set to 58 degrees, the maintenance temperature to stop any freezing, but it would take time before it dropped to that inside. The dishwasher had finished a cycle and was still warm. Two wine glasses stood in the sink. The fire in the wood stove was down to glowing embers, but the stove was still hot to the touch. Whoever had been in the chalet wasn't planning on coming back tonight.

The place was immaculate, sparsely furnished, and clean without any of the personal junk that gives a sense of who lived there; it could have been a suite at the Holiday Inn. Vanier remembered the cottages he had rented years ago in Cape Cod when the kids were young. They all looked like this one, with the bare minimum on display for renters to wreck. But every one of them had a padlocked cupboard where the owners stashed their personal stuff. Maybe there was one here, where Monsignor Forlini locked away his secrets from prying eyes.

Vanier picked up the phone and pressed *69, the last number redial service, and was connected to the Montreal Airport Authority's automated arrivals and departure line.

"The last call was to the airport. Let's go," he said to Laurent while he dropped the phone into its cradle and turned abruptly for the door.

"Get someone at Dorval and ask them about the international

flights tonight; what left and what's still to go? Then get on the phone and organize a search warrant for this place tomorrow morning. I want to know who was staying here."

Back in the car, Mme. Collins seemed to have shrunk even further back into her corner. Her arms were crossed tightly around her chest, and she was shivering. Vanier didn't think it was just the cold. He swiveled to look at her and for the first time he saw life in her eyes. He'd seen the look before; beyond fear, it was closer to dread. Laurent was on the phone trying to organize things, as Vanier did a three-point turn in the driveway.

She caught Vanier's eyes in the mirror. "We used to come here," she said. "This is where it happened."

Vanier returned her gaze and understood. It was a confession. This is where her life ended 30 years ago.

"Don't worry, Mme. Collins, we'll find John. He'll get help."

"I'll never see him again," she said, turning to look out the window. Vanier watched her in the mirror, her face reflecting off the glass of the window. She was weeping. He aimed the car back into the opening in the trees and headed down the track to the road.

"They've started the paperwork for the warrant, sir. We should be good to go, with a full team on site by 11 o'clock tomorrow," said Laurent, and he dialed again.

By the time they got to the highway they had answers on the flights. There had been five international flights since six o'clock: Los Angeles, New York, Frankfurt, London and Paris. Still to go were flights to Rome and Madrid and a late flight to Paris. Laurent had arranged for the RCMP to meet them at the departures level. It was a jurisdictional issue. The RCMP were in charge at the airport, and they needed an RCMP escort. He had also arranged for someone to drive Mme. Collins home.

RCMP Staff Sergeant Carchetti was waiting with a constable by the reserved police parking at the departures level. The constable saluted as the officers got out of the car, and Laurent did his best to return the salute. Vanier reached out his hand. The Constable took charge of Mme. Collins, and Sergeant Carchetti led the two officers into the building. It was 10 p.m., but the terminal was still crowded with holiday traffic with family milling around every passenger.

"We've been trying to find the Collins guy since we got your call but no luck. He's not on any passenger list, and we circulated the artist's sketch to all the security staff. It doesn't look like he's here."

"We're not certain, but we had a pretty good indication that he was on his way here."

"The best we can do now is to go to the gates and see if he shows up," said Sergeant Carchetti. "The Rome flight is leaving right now, we have to hurry."

Vanier and Laurent had to go through security like everyone else, but they jumped the line, causing a stir when they pulled out their guns and left them with the security supervisor. Once through security, Sergeant Carchetti took off running, like he was enjoying the excitement. Vanier surprised himself by keeping up, and then darting ahead once he picked out the gate. It was closed, and he watched the Air Transat plane through the window as it slowly backed away from the terminal building.

Standing behind the gate, a tired looking woman in an Air Transat uniform looked up from her paperwork. "I'm sorry, sir, but it's too late to board. The flight is closed. Can I see your ticket?" She looked disappointed to have to deal with any more passengers and wasn't hiding it.

Vanier looked for a nametag. There wasn't one. "I'm Detective Inspector Vanier, of the Major Crime Squad. I think that you have a suspect on board, and we need to speak to him."

"You think?"

She had a point, thought Vanier.

"Look, is there any way I can speak to the Captain? This is very important."

She looked at the two other officers and realized that she would at least have to make a pretense of being cooperative.

"Well, this is very unusual, but let me see what I can do." She lifted the walkie-talkie and began speaking Italian. She smiled a meaningless customer-service smile at Vanier and handed him the walkie-talkie. "The Chief Steward will talk to you. Press this button to speak, and this one to listen. It helps to say 'Over' when you have finished talking."

After a few static-filled sentences, the Chief Steward passed him to the co-pilot, who passed him on to the Captain. The plane was still moving away.

"Captain, I am Detective Inspector Vanier of the Major Crime Squad in Montreal. We believe you may have a murder suspect on board, a suspect in several murders. We would like to come on board to check."

"Inspector, permit me, but you don't sound very sure? Are you saying that there is a threat to the safety of this aircraft?"

"No, sir. I don't believe there is a threat to the aircraft."

"Do you have a name for this suspect?"

"We've already checked your passenger list and he is not listed. But he may be traveling under an assumed name."

"Inspector. Please. We have 348 people on board, and if we go back to the gate, we miss this time slot, and we may be here all night. Do you have any idea how much that will cost? And even if we just stop to let you come on board, my passengers will be very upset to see police officers walking all over the plane. Inspector, let's clarify this. Once again, is there any threat to the security of this flight? If this suspect of yours is on this flight, are we in any danger?"

"No, sir, you are not."

"In that case, Inspector, I suggest that you contact the officials at immigration at Rome. You have seven hours to alert them to the arrival of your suspect. I promise I will deliver him to Rome. So why don't you fax the details of this person to immigration at Fiumicino Airport, along with your arrest warrant. The authorities can simply refuse him entry, and he will be returned to Montreal."

It sounded reasonable, even to Vanier. "Very well, Captain. Have a good flight."

The walkie-talkie clicked dead and he handed it back to the woman, who rewarded him with a smug grin.

"Inspector," said Carchetti, "we can fax details of the guy to Fiumicino. If he's on the flight they should be able to pick him up. Who knows, maybe you two can get a trip to Rome to pick him up?" Vanier thought about that. There were worse things in life.

They spent the next two hours watching passengers leave for Paris and London. No luck. As they were leaving the secure area, Sergeant Carchetti told him that Mme. Collins was still at the airport. She was waiting for them in the RCMP offices and looked up as soon as they entered. She was resigned, not a glimmer of hope in her eyes.

"We didn't find him, Madame Collins. We'll question Monsignor Forlini in the morning and let you know what we learn."

She said nothing and waited while Sergeant Carchetti helped them put the paperwork together for the Italian immigration people. He faxed it off and promised to have someone call Vanier as soon as they heard back. Mme. Collins followed them to the car and climbed into the back seat without saying a word. Thirty minutes later, they dropped her two blocks from her apartment, just as she had asked. She closed the car door and leaned into the open front window.

"Thank you. Both of you. I know that you're trying to do the right thing and I hope you succeed. He was never a bad boy. But he's had a difficult life."

Then she was gone, climbing the metal staircase.

# FOURTEEN
## JANUARY 13

### 6 AM

**Vanier had been dreaming** of chasing someone past fountains and sculptures through crowded Italian backstreets. No matter how fast he ran, he could never catch up with them. He kept slowing down, distracted by stone warriors and enormous horses pulling chariots. The ringing of his cell phone shook him awake.

"Vanier."

"Inspector, this is Ouellette of the RCMP at Dorval. Sergeant Carchetti asked that someone call you as soon as we had news from Italy."

Vanier swung his legs out of the bed and planted his feet on the floor. "And?"

"We've just heard back from Italian immigration. The passengers from the Montreal flight were given special attention, but there was nobody even remotely matching our guy."

"Shit. Thanks anyway."

"No problem. Hope you find the bastard."

"Don't worry, we will."

Vanier's day didn't get any better. At ten o'clock, the Justice lawyer called to tell him that the request for a warrant to search Monsignor Forlini's chalet had been refused. The judge had decided that the affidavit didn't disclose sufficient grounds to justify the invasion of the privacy of a senior member of the Catholic Church. They had nothing, and he wasn't surprised. Normally, getting a search warrant was as easy as buying a lottery ticket, but getting a warrant to search the house of a priest was a different matter. The judge knew what he was doing; the Church still had clout in Quebec, especially in the legal system. Every September, the new court season was inaugurated by the Red Mass at the Cathedral, and the senior judges and the Church's hierarchy got to wear their best red costumes. You would think the place would be as empty as a Prime Minister's promise, but it was always packed with the top judges and lawyers and those who had helped them move up through the system. After the Mass, there was a lunch with the Archbishop and the Chief Justice as joint guests of honour. If you wanted to go against a member of the Church, you had to choose your battles carefully and get solid support in advance; Vanier had done neither and hit a wall. Now he was sitting across from Chief Inspector Bédard.

"So, you're back to square one. Any suggestions?"

"We don't know for sure that he left the country, sir," said Vanier, "so we keep looking."

"If he decided to lose himself, he could be anywhere on the planet by now."

"I know, sir. But we can't give up."

"I'm not talking about giving up, Luc. I'm talking about using our resources efficiently. If he left the country, he's someone else's problem. I can go through the channels to get a warrant and picture to Interpol. We have a picture, at least?"

"Yes, sir. From a summer picnic at Xeon Pesticides. It's five years old, but it's the best we have."

"Good, I'll have it sent to Interpol, and you can get it circulated in Quebec, to the rest of Canada too. Then we wait, he can't hide forever, can he?"

"No, sir, but he can go on killing people until we find him."

"Luc, unless you can tell me that you have some active leads to follow, I'm going to have to close this down. We can tell the press that we have a suspect and that suspect has left town. Who knows, the papers might pick up on an international manhunt and track him down for us. And even if they don't, as long as the deaths stop, people will move on. Believe me, Luc."

"We do have a good lead, sir. Monseignor Forlini. He's Collins's father."

"That's not a lead. It's the ranting of a deranged woman. We can't go on that."

"What if it's true?"

"I'm not ordering you to drop that line of inquiry. I'm saying that what you have given me so far is nothing. Do you understand me?"

"Yes, sir."

"But if anything comes of it, you let me know."

That was why Bédard had become Chief Inspector and Vanier was still a Detective Inspector. It made sense. Evidence that was good enough to arrest the average Joe wasn't nearly enough for anyone who would fight back. At some point, you had to admit defeat and move on. Vanier had trouble giving up, but he also knew you didn't find people by tracking them down the way they did in *The Fugitive*. You waited for them to make a mistake and get themselves caught. The best you could do was to make sure that their names, aliases, credit card, photos, and anything else you could think of were on as many databases as you could load them into. The average criminal is a criminal wherever he is, and eventually the red light glows on someone's monitor, and they'll place a call to Montreal.

"How long do I have? How long can I keep up the active investigation?"

"Luc, this morning I had a call from the Mayor. He wants this thing shut down as quickly as possible. If we have a good suspect and he's disappeared, he doesn't want the force wasting valuable manpower looking for someone who isn't there."

"Since when did the Mayor run investigations?" He was pushing Bédard, who was walking a fine political line.

If Bédard was angry, he didn't show it. "He doesn't, Luc. But he made his point forcefully, and I have to give it some weight. He also told me he'd had a call from the Archbishop about your visit to Monsignor Forlini. He tells me Monsignor Forlini is very well respected in the Church. Not just in Quebec, in Rome too. Apparently, great things are expected of him. He has friends."

"That's why they want to shut down the investigation, to protect the Monsignor from embarrassment?"

"Luc, the Church has nothing to do with this investigation, apart from their normal interest in making sure you don't bully its priests."

"Fuck the Church. You think I'm bullying Forlini? I'm flattered. No, the church wants this shut down because it's worried about looking bad, not about me bullying one of their holy men. Jesus, one of its own is dead, and the suspect is the bastard son of a nun and a priest. A nun who was hung out to dry when she got pregnant. Maybe that's what caused young John to flip, a regular churchgoer who answers the prayers of the faithful by relieving some innocent poor bastard of his suffering. God's holy messenger, a son of the clergy, operating his killing venture out of the church's head office. And you wonder what interest the church has in closing down this investigation?"

"Luc, give me something solid, and I can help you."

"I have nothing solid, give me a few days to wrap up."

"Take a few days to wrap up. But I want it wrapped up, hear me?"

"Yes, sir."

Vanier rose to leave, and Chief Inspector Bédard reached for his phone.

# FIFTEEN
## JANUARY 19

7 PM

**Pascal Beaudoin could feel the sweat** making his shirt stick to his skin, and he hoped it wouldn't show through his suit jacket. He couldn't remember the last time he had taken a personal stand. The formal jousting over contracts for a client was a different story. As a hired gun, he could do anything. But this was different. He was working for himself, not taking orders, but deciding what he wanted to do, and that made him nervous. He pulled a handkerchief from his pocket and wiped his face dry again.

The night had not been easy. The Governors of the Foundation of the Holy Land Shelter had eaten an early supper at the St. Denis Club, paid for with the Henderson & Associates' credit card, and Pascal had given them the entire story, a full confession of his sins. He didn't expect it to be easy, but he also didn't expect the grilling he received. The Governors were all well into retirement and had left the business world years ago. But they all had histories. In their day, they had all been smart and hard men. Beaudoin's confession had awakened something dormant in each, something close to an instinctive nose for weakness and a dislike of it. Beaudoin felt the heat. The first thing they wanted to know was why the swap was a bad idea. A pile of cash and the promise of a new Shelter were not necessarily bad things. That the people involved might be unsavoury, that was to be expected: they were property developers after all. The Governors were not going to be told how to vote and, anyway, Beaudoin was starting off way behind. He was the one who had taken their proxies with promises he hadn't kept. Why should they believe him now? Beaudoin was grilled on everything he knew and then asked to leave the room, forced to pace the hallway while they came to a decision. He used the time to wonder if he had done the right thing. Unemployment was inevitable, and there was a distinct possibility that the deal would be approved. Then he would be unemployed and a pariah. After 45 minutes he was called back in.

They were sitting solemnly around the large round table nursing brandies. Senator Breslin, the most senior of them, motioned him to take the empty seat.

"Pascal," said the Senator, "my friends have asked that I speak on behalf of all of us. We are all" – he gestured to the group – "troubled by your betrayals. We trusted you, and you let us down. We gave you proxies because we trusted you. There isn't a good way to say this, Pascal, but you lied to us. And that raises the question, why should we trust you now? It's a difficult question, but we concluded that it wasn't the principal question to be answered. We looked at the facts of the proposed transaction. You say it's a setup. You say the Blackrock group can't be trusted. Well, we decided to ignore your advice on that. We looked at the transaction from the position of the Foundation. And we have decided, after considering all of the facts, that the Foundation should reject the deal until sufficient guarantees are forthcoming."

"You're making the right decision, Senator."

"I haven't finished."

"Excuse me."

"After that, Pascal, we considered what to do about you. We have decided, again, after considering all of the facts, that we should consider your role in all of this as an education. You were tested and, at the end of the day, and, seemingly not without some considerable effort on your part, you have emerged as a man of honour. So, we have decided to forgive your betrayals as mistakes and stand beside you."

Beaudoin breathed a sigh of relief and tried to look humble and contrite, knowing at the same time that he had to get these guys moving quickly. Senator Breslin looked around the table. "I believe that accurately reflects our thoughts." His fellow Governors nodded approval.

"Well then, gentlemen," said Breslin, "let's get going. I believe the meeting starts in half an hour. And I believe that Mr. Beaudoin has put on some transportation for us."

The octogenarians started to get to their feet, slowly and with obvious discomfort for some. It was ten minutes before they were outside the hotel, being assisted into the limousines. When they were loaded, and the limousines started to move off, Beaudoin looked at his watch, fifteen minutes to go.

"Don't worry, Pascal."

Beaudoin turned around to face Breslin. "Thank you, Senator."

The Senator was flanked by two other Governors, who were drifting in and out of sleep. Four other followed in a second limousine, all courtesy of the Henderson & Associates credit card, and they were cruising towards the Intercontinental Hotel in Old Montreal carrying a majority.

# THE DEAD OF WINTER

## 8.25 PM

In the Champlain Room of the Intercontinental Hotel, Gordon Henderson and four members of the Foundation were sitting around the table, getting down to business. Vladimir Markov and Ivan Romanenko were watching the proceedings as invited guests. Henderson had brought along a law student as a bag carrier, and she was shuffling papers on her knees. Henderson had been calling Beaudoin's cell phone all day, only to flow straight through to voice mail. Beaudoin was toast, and Henderson felt in control. Two hours earlier, the Board had voted in favour of the deal, and he held seven proxies for the Foundation's 11-vote decision. There was nothing left to do but go through the motions. They would work their way through the agenda, and it would be official, and a healthy part of his retirement would be funded.

As he was getting the papers in order, the double-doors to the Champlain Room burst open, and a mob of about twenty people flooded the room. It was the usual rent-a-crowd radicals who can be counted on to protest any initiative that doesn't come from some cooperative, commune, or other voice of the disenfranchised. They were followed by a cameraman from CBC and a reporter with a microphone. The circus was Beaudoin's insurance policy.

Henderson leaned over to the law student and whispered, "Go get security to come down here immediately. I want these people out of here now." The student ran for the door.

The mob spread out around the room, unfurling banners with various permutations of the same message: "*Save the Holy Land Shelter,*" "*Protect the Homeless,*" "*No Profiteering on the Backs of the Poor.*"

The light attached to the camera went on, and the camera scanned the room, capturing everyone for the TV news. Henderson watched with horror as the reporter approached, pointing a microphone at his face.

"Mr. Henderson, Marianne Désautels, CBC News. Do you have any comments on the protests against the sale of the Holy Land Shelter?"

"No I don't. This is a private meeting. You have no right. Would you please leave the room?" he said, waving his arms as though he was engaged in crowd control. Henderson wasn't used to working in public, and it was taking time to adjust to the new environment. "I said get the fuck out of here. You hear me?" he screamed at the camera.

The only ones leaving were Markov and Romanenko, who got to their feet as soon as the group arrived. They didn't go far, just out of sight of the cameras. Markov called Henderson on his cell phone.

"Look, I can't talk right now," Henderson told him. "Security is on the way. Once the room is cleared, we can get started. Take a few minutes in the bar. I'll call you when we're ready to start."

The cameraman was having a field day, and Henderson knew he looked like an asshole.

"Marianne, Marianne," he said, trying to be heard over the noise, finding his best smile. "I am sorry about that. I thought we were being attacked. Look, if you want some sound bites, I can give you some. Let's start again. OK?"

"Let's go," she said, taking a moment to let the cameraman set up in from of them.

"Mr. Henderson, there has been some objections to the sale of the Holy Land Shelter's land to developers. What do you say to the critics?"

*Fuck them*, he thought. "The Holy Land Shelter is one of Montreal's finest institutions, and its Board of Directors and its Foundation members are committed to Montreal's homeless. Believe me, none of us would do anything that would be against the interests of those that do not have a voice. Tonight, what we are considering is a proposal that will allow the Shelter to continue for decades to come. It's a transaction that will allow the Shelter to build a brand new, state-of-the-art complex. Earlier this evening the Board of Directors recommended approval of Blackrock's offer, and I am sure that the members of the Foundation will do the same thing, because that offer addresses the long-term funding needs of the Shelter and guarantees its future for years to come. I expect the Governors of the Foundation have been rigorous in their examination of the proposal."

"Are you saying it's not a done deal, it needs to be studied?"

"We're saying that if any proposal is approved, it will be because it's in the long term interest of the most vulnerable members of our society. We have a duty to protect those people, and the Foundation takes that duty very seriously."

Two uniformed security guards arrived, and began moving people out of the hall. They went peacefully but not quietly, yelling slogans as they left. Henderson called Markov to tell him he could come back. As he clicked the disconnect button, the doors opened again, and the seven absent Foundation Governors entered, followed by Beaudoin.

Henderson stared in disbelief as they hobbled and limped their way into the room. One of them looked at Henderson, "Is this the place for the meeting of the Holy Land Foundation?"

"Yes," he said, realizing that his proxies had just become worthless scraps of paper.

Beaudoin was beaming. "Hi, boss."

"Don't even bother coming in to get your stuff. We'll send it to you."

The seven members of the Foundation joined the other four around the table.

"If there are no objections, I will act as Chairman," said Senator Breslin.

He looked up and saw Markov and Romanenko enter the room.

Breslin looked up at them, "Excuse me, gentlemen, but I believe that this is a private meeting."

They looked at Henderson, who was seated in a chair, his head hanging down and his chin resting on his chest.

"Mr. Henderson. That applies to you also," said Breslin.

Henderson raised his head and looked at the Governors seated around the table like they owned the place, assuming authority they hadn't exercised in years. He rose slowly in disbelief. Markov and Romanenko had already left. There was nothing to do. Casting one last look at Beaudoin, he pulled the door open and left.

# SIXTEEN
## MARCH 25

Winter doesn't end suddenly in Montreal; it withdraws slowly, in sullen resentment, like Napoleon's army from Moscow. Day after day the temperature struggles to climb above freezing for a few hours around noon and quickly falls back in the late afternoon, leaving tiny rivulets of water to become icy traps for the unwary. The snow that fell weightlessly during innumerable snowstorms is packed tight in stubborn boulders of dirty ice grudgingly giving up their bulk to springtime, revealing the filthy detritus that has accumulated in the cold months: dog shit, torn plastic bags, newspapers, Styrofoam cups, meal trays, pizza boxes, and thousands of cigarette butts. Impatient citizens torment the withdrawing army with picks and shovels, breaking up the rock-hard ice and spreading it to accelerate its disappearance. The cycle of thaw and refreeze continues for weeks until finally the city is liberated, and Montrealers spill out of their winter caverns, and occupy every open space. Terraces and park benches fill up and the streets teem with the survivors of a long siege.

In the Turcot Yard, where the city's snow is piled into dirty grey mountains, the melt is glacier slow and the land only returns to flat in late June. Such is the power of winter that the Stanley Cup is only awarded as the last evidence of winter disappears.

Vanier had watched the slow progression to spring. He had been present when they chipped Mary Gallagher from the river-ice that had held her for months and he had watched as Dr. Segal cut into the long-dead corpse to establish the cause of death. It didn't take long to establish that she died just as the others had.

## 6 PM

The six o'clock Mass was starting, and Vanier was kneeling in a pew at the back of the Cathedral, his head bowed. When he saw Monsignor Forlini take his place in front of the altar, he got up and made for the door, listening to the droning voice over the loud speaker.

*"In the name of the Father, the Son and the Holy Ghost."*

Vanier was outside before the response finished. He knew Forlini would be busy with the faithful for at least an hour. He was in Morin Heights in an hour and a half. This time the lights didn't go on as he drove into the clearing before the chalet; he had pulled the wires out on his last visit. It didn't make much of a difference. The whole area was bathed in the bright moonlight reflecting off the snow that still lay several feet thick. Vanier shut the motor and looked around. He had been inside the chalet three times since January and found nothing, amazed that Monsignor Forlini could leave so little trace of who he was.

With the motor shut off, it was getting cold fast inside the car. Vanier opened the door and stepped out, not sure what he was looking for. He walked the perimeter of the chalet, keeping close to the wall, where the snow hardly reached. He completed a full circle of the chalet, and then struck out through the thick snow towards a large wooden shed about 30 feet from the back door of the chalet. Just like the other times, he was leaving obvious tracks, but he had given up worrying about it. The door to the shed was locked with a shiny padlock from Vaillancourt. Two weeks ago, Vanier had stopped at the store and bought the same kind of lock, but the key that came with it didn't fit the Monsignor's lock. This time he was prepared. He took a crowbar from his overcoat pocket and inserted the business end between the wood and the metal plate, easily forcing the screws out from the old wooden door. He wouldn't be able to replace the plate properly, but he didn't care.

He pulled the door of the shed back and shone a torch around in the blackness. There was nothing but fireplace-sized logs, carefully stacked up against each wall, and a long woodcutter's axe leaning against the wall. He flicked the torch off and pulled the door closed, slipping the screws back into place.

Outside, he looked to the woods beyond the shed. The area around the chalet was clear for about twenty feet, and then the trees formed a dark wall. But he could make out a narrow gap where the trees and underbrush seemed to part, as if it was an entrance into the woods. He struggled through the snow towards the gap in the trees. Up close, he could imagine a path that had been worn over years. He followed it through the trees and came to a clearing about 100 feet from the house, where trees formed a rough circle. Vanier scanned the clearing, trying to imagine what it might look without a blanket of snow. Snow, like water, finds its level, but unlike water it reflects the surface below. There was a Québec artist known for placing buckets and boxes on otherwise flat land in the autumn. When winter came, his random junk would become erotic snowscapes as falling snow accumulated and formed undulating mounds that unmistakably defined naked women lying beneath a white blanket.

He immediately noticed the snow was raised in a smaller circle that looked like it could be a fire pit in the summer. Next to it was what might be a bench where the snow sat high over the ground. Then he saw it, a pronounced ridge in the snow that didn't speak of a campfire clearing in the woods. It was out of place. He moved towards the pile and started to brush the fresh snow aside with his foot. There was crusted ice under the fresh snow, and he kicked at it, digging with the toe and heel of his boot, forcing it to give way. He quickly exposed a piece of blue tarpaulin. He grabbed an edge and pulled, straining to release it from the ice. When it finally gave and lifted he was staring at John Collins, frozen stiff, unburied and waiting for a better life. He was tempted to dig him out of his icy grave and drag the frozen corpse to his car for the drive back to his mother in Montreal. Instead, he turned to leave, pulling his cell phone from his pocket and pushing the on button. He kept walking as he waited for it to find a signal. He pushed Laurent's number as he cleared the woods, but lost the signal.

He retraced his tracks back through the wood, and as he passed the woodshed, he heard a whoosh. He turned his face to the noise just in time to see the baseball bat swinging into it. He ducked instinctively but not quickly enough, taking the blow to his left temple. His knees buckled and his body fell to the floor.

When he regained consciousness, his back was freezing, and snow was melting in his neck. He slowly realized that he was being dragged by his arms through the snow. The snow riding down his back made him vaguely uncomfortable, but he wasn't in pain, and the moon looked beautiful. He kept still, allowing whoever was dragging him to think he was still unconscious as he watched the tops of the passing trees. He could hear heavy breathing, almost grunting, from the person who had a tight grip of his wrists. Eventually, the dragging stopped and his arms dropped, falling with a light thump in the snow. He was wet and freezing and realized that he had to fight back, but lying quietly on his back in the snow seemed so comfortable. He felt the warm blood trickling down over his eye and tried to make a plan. He sensed movement and saw a giant black figure standing over him, arms raised with something like an axe in his hands. The figure started the downward blow and with an effort that seemed to materialize from nowhere, Vanier twisted out of the way of the descending axe. He heard it dig into the snow where his face had been. He had no idea what his second move would be.

It didn't matter. There was a blinding white light, and Vanier looked up to see the axe hanging motionless as the black figure wielding it turned his head to the light.

"Drop it."

Vanier blinked and then someone was holding a gun to the axe-man's head, and the axe was dropped softly to the snow. The last thing Vanier saw before he closed his eyes was the axe-man on his knees in the snow, his head bowed as though in prayer.

Laurent kept his gun trained on Monsignor Forlini and felt for a pulse on Vanier's neck. Vanier opened his eyes and looked at Laurent. He wanted to say something, but he just smiled and decided that he could let go and relax in the snow. He didn't notice how cold he was becoming. He just kept shivering.

# SEVENTEEN
## MARCH 20

2 PM

**Vanier was lying in a bed** in the emergency room of the hospital in St. Jérôme, in stable condition. He was still in the emergency ward because there wasn't a bed available anywhere else. Laurent and St. Jacques were standing by his bed. There were no seats for visitors, the result of a hospital policy designed to discourage concerned relatives from getting too comfortable and cluttering up the emergency room. It didn't work, people still milled around sick relatives and friends, but it did make for a lot of disgruntled visitors.

"So, how are you feeling, Boss?" said St. Jacques.

"There's a lot to be said for drugs." Vanier turned to Laurent, "I owe you, my friend. How did you know?"

"Mme. Collins called me. She had been wandering around outside the Cathedral and saw you leave. The Monsignor left right after you. Apparently he excused himself after the Mass started and took off for Morin Heights. She thought you might need help."

"How right she was. That was a little too close. And how is the Monsignor."

"Cooperative. In his own way."

"Why don't you see for yourself?" said St. Jacques, pulling her laptop from her bag. "We have him on tape." She plugged in the computer and waited for it to start.

"Have you spoken to Mme. Collins?"

"I called her this morning with the news," said Laurent. "She didn't seem surprised that John was dead. *I knew*, was all she said."

St. Jacques put the computer on the bed with the screen facing Vanier and pushed some buttons. A video began to play, and Vanier recognized the inside of Interview Room 6 and the view from the camera mounted high up on the wall. The image was of the Monsignor and Laurent sitting at the table.

"This is all my fault," said the Monsignor.

"That's a good start," said Vanier.

On the screen, Laurent asked, "Why don't you tell me what's on your mind."

"I did what I had to do to defend the Church. But I failed. It's such a sordid story."

"I have all the time in the world, Monsignor."

"Don't call me that. I have no right to the title. I have disgraced myself and the Church."

"Well let's start somewhere. How long have you known John?"

"I have always known him. He was my son. I refused to acknowledge it. When he first showed up, I didn't know how to react. He was my son, and I had spent my life denying it. I couldn't jeopardize my position. I refused to see him in the Cathedral, but I met him from time to time in various places. He's my son, you can understand that. He persisted, and I found him a job at Xeon and tried to help him along. I forced Henri Drouin to act as a go-between. Henri and

I were at seminary together, he trusted me.

"When he needed money, I would give it to Drouin to deliver. The arrangement was satisfactory. I could avoid direct contact with John, but I could help him from time to time. Father Drouin got John involved with the homeless, and he seemed to take to it. He was good with those people and seemed to find some fulfillment. I thought the boy was trying to be a good Catholic, but over the years he became more disturbed. He started wearing a cassock, never to the Church, he didn't go that far. It's as though he knew there were limits. But Drouin would report back to me that he was wandering around the city in a black cassock like a priest. I should have seen then that he was just mocking me.

"Things really started to fall apart in October. He was behaving very erratically, and then that awful man Audet showed up. Apparently he had noticed John's relationship with Father Drouin. He was a predator looking for opportunity. He broke into John's apartment and found letters between the Archbishop and that woman, John's mother. He took them and came to see me. Imagine, that man in my office in the Cathedral. He wanted money, and I gave him some, but he refused to give me the papers. He showed up twice in November and again just before Christmas.

"When people started dying – and I have to tell you I don't believe that Christmas Eve was the start of it – I didn't know for certain that John was involved, but I was suspicious. During one of our meetings, John started talking about the power of prayer. Now, I believe in the power of prayer, but he sounded like one of those American evangelical preachers, *ask and you will receive*, literally and immediately. He was attending Drouin's Circle of Christ and was excited about prayers and having them answered. Father Drouin told him about a family that was facing eviction because they fell behind on their rent. The wife had filled in a card asking for a thousand dollars, and John slipped a thousand dollars under the door of the family's apartment. It could have been his own money, or perhaps he stole it, I don't know. But it worked. They weren't evicted and the father found work. John was elated. It was pitiful. He acted as though he had found his mission, his mission to be God's little helper on earth. He started attending the Circle more frequently, always consulting the cards. And I think he started making prayers come true.

"Everything changed when his picture was published. That's when he killed Audet. He went home and found Audet in his apartment. It was the day the sketch was shown on the evening news. John said that Audet attacked him, but he killed Audet instead. He called me, asking for help, and I drove him to the chalet. I couldn't understand the Audet thing, because Audet had never been interested in John. I'm the one he was blackmailing. But I have to admit that I was relieved that Audet was gone.

"John stayed at the chalet for a while, and I arranged for new documents. I got him a passport, a driver's licence, and a new credit card. I had arranged for him to be cared for in one of the Church's establishments in Rome; very private, very secure, and he would be looked after until he got better, or forever. I had the flight booked, and everything looked like it was going as planned. We decided to finish the bottle of wine before we left, barely a glass each.

"But it wasn't over. While he was bringing the suitcases out to the car, I switched our glasses. I don't know why. Some other time I might have seen God's hand in that, God working a miracle to serve his loyal servant. We sat at the table, saying nothing, and we clinked the glasses in a toast and drank the wine.

"He realized almost immediately that he had the wrong glass. He ran to the sink, trying to make himself vomit with a spoon, a little came out but it was too late. He sank down to the floor and was having trouble breathing. It didn't take long, two, maybe three minutes, and then it was over. I didn't move for a very long time. I just stared at his body lying on the floor. I had to do something, and I just thought, that was it, the end. His death and Audet's death were the end of it. Life would be normal again. Eventually, I dragged his body outside and down into the woods. I covered it with a tarpaulin and left him there. It was supposed to be temporary until I could think of a more permanent solution. It was snowing hard, and I knew the tarpaulin would be quickly covered in snow. I walked back to the chalet and watched the snow cover the tracks into the wood, and then I drove back to the Cathedral. I still have his suitcase in my apartment there, I haven't touched it.

"Three days later, I went back. I planned to put him in the trunk and drive him somewhere far away. I couldn't bury him, because the ground was frozen, and I was in a panic because I knew that you had tried to get a warrant to search the chalet. But I couldn't move him. He was frozen solid and stuck to the ground, locked in the ice that had melted under him and then frozen again. I tried to chip away the ice, but it was too much, he wouldn't budge. I had no choice. I replaced the tarpaulin and covered it with snow. Can you imagine what I was going through? Every day, every minute, it's all I thought about, and I couldn't do anything about it.

"I began to imagine that someone had been to the chalet. I saw small signs, probably nothing, but in my state I built it up. Then, as I was saying Mass last night, I saw your Inspector Vanier in the congregation as I walked in, and a moment later he was gone. He was the one. I knew it. He was the one who had been to the chalet. Who else? I excused myself from Mass and drove up as fast as I could. And I was right. There were tire marks in the driveway, so I parked the car further up and walked to the chalet. From a distance, I saw a light in the woodshed and then it went out. I didn't know where he was until I saw him hurrying back from the woods. By that time, I had the axe. It was obvious he had found John, and so I acted."

"You tried to kill Inspector Vanier?" said Laurent.

"I tried to stop him reporting what he had found. I wasn't

thinking about how to stop him. But yes, I was going to kill him."

"Let's stop it there, shall we," said Vanier. "I've had enough."

St. Jacques stopped the video. "There isn't much else, anyway. Laurent takes him through the story again, and it pretty much matches the first time."

The curtain surrounding the bed parted, and Dr. Segal came in with a huge bunch of red and yellow tulips. They looked almost magical in an emergency room in St. Jérôme, a sign that winter was ending.

"Dr. Segal, what a treat. My friends here were just leaving. They have work to do."

St. Jacques smiled at Segal and grabbed Laurent by the arm. "We'll see about getting you transferred to Montreal, sir." The two officers left the patient with his visitor.

"They're beautiful," he said, nodding at the tulips. "They're lying when they say that food is the fastest way to a man's heart."

"I know. I have a saw that's much quicker."

He laughed, but it hurt.

She leaned over and kissed him, a kiss of relief, and of hope.

# ACKNOWLEDGEMENTS

The mistakes are all mine, and that's how it should be, but I owe a huge debt of gratitude to so many people for their help and encouragement along the way. Special thanks to the wonderful ladies of NDG, Shannon, Ayana and Karin, who have been reading and commenting on my work for years. I have learned a lot from great teachers like Ann Charney, Trevor Ferguson, Peter Dubé and Nadine Doolittle who gave me insights, tips, critiques and invaluable encouragement. To the poets, Rolf and Claire, and to the insightful Sarah who encouraged me to drink champagne more often, many thanks. To Alexia, Albert and Brandon, for their support and wise comments, and to Deborah and Julia for their help with the manuscript. To my brother Jim, whose wisdom and unflagging support has been a source of strength. All of you have helped me more than you can realise. Lori Schubert and Julia Kater at the Quebec Writers' Federation deserve thanks for their untiring work in providing a welcoming community for aspiring writers. I want to give a special thanks to Linda Leith for having the faith and courage to publish this book. Finally, and most of all, to Jess, whose constant and unwavering love, support and encouragement kept me believing in myself. It was always more than I deserved, and just what I needed.

My heartfelt thanks, to all of you.

Peter Kirby